I DON'T FEEL ANYTHING. NOTHING.

Allie walked until she found herself next to the girl's bathroom. She sank down and sat on the filthy floor, hugging herself. *Don't feel anything. Don't. Nothing—*

"Why?" she whimpered. "Why, Seal? Why did you set me up?"

Grow up, the cold voice inside her answered. *You don't need her. You don't need any of them. You're better than them. Stronger. Unique.*

Alone. Like an Ice Queen. Like Ginger.

"Yeah," she muttered. Ginger Josslyn, the coldest Ice Queen, sneering, sarcastic…Ginger, who probably never darkened the doors of a church in her life, who was cruel and cold and strong…

Ginger wouldn't stand by and let herself get humiliated or insulted. Ginger wouldn't be the good little girl, like Nikki.

Ginger would get *back* at them.

Boom.

She looked up, frowning. She had barely heard it—a deep, muffled sound. And other sounds, barely audible—water. Water swishing.

There. It was coming from a battered metal door a few feet away.

Hmm. Allie walked up to the door. *Interesting.*

SUMMER OF MY DISSENT
John Paul 2 High Book Three

Also from Chesterton Press:

<u>The Fairy Tale Novels</u>
Fairy tales retold by Regina Doman
www.fairytalenovels.com

The Shadow of the Bear
Black as Night
Waking Rose
The Midnight Dancers
Alex O'Donnell & the 40 CyberThieves

<u>The John Paul 2 High Series</u>
by Christian M. Frank
www.johnpaul2high.com

Book One: Catholic, Reluctantly
Book Two: Trespasses Against Us
Book Three: Summer of My Dissent

Look for more upcoming titles at
ChestertonPress.com

Christian M. Frank

SUMMER OF MY DISSENT

John Paul 2 High
Book Three

CHESTERTON PRESS
FRONT ROYAL, VIRGINIA

To Katie.
All the best ideas were
yours.
(There, I've said it.)

Cover design by Regina Doman. Photo from Spiering Photography.
Interior images from iStockphoto.com, Regina Doman, and Spiering
Photography.

Chesterton Press
P.O. Box 949
Front Royal, VA 22630
www.chestertonpress.com

Summary: After her best friend is murdered, Allie Weaver falls into
depression, heightened by conflicts with the new students joining her
small high school. An invitation from an old friend leads her to find
healing at a Protestant evangelical church and question her Catholic
faith.

ISBN: 978-0-9827677-4-0

Printed in the United States of America

www.johnpaul2high.com

CHAPTERS

CHAPTERS

And then Gogol said, with the absolute simplicity of a child--
"I wish to know why I was hurt so much."

—G.K. Chesterton,
The Man Who Was Thursday

IT'S ALL A LIE...EVEN JESUS.

She swayed a little as she knelt, feeling weak and sick.

No. Jesus isn't fake. Maybe I am, but He's not.

"Jesus..." she whimpered, and then said the word again, and again. "Jesus...Jesus...Jesus..."

She heard footsteps, and then a voice. "Allie? What are you doing?" Celia asked. She sounded scared.

Allie stood up. "I'm done with all this Catholic stuff," she said flatly. "Here."

She pulled the rosary and tossed it to Celia.

Celia caught it, looking startled. "What's that?"

"Your rosary," Allie said. "Yeah, the same one that you gave me the first day at John Paul 2 High. I kept it all this time, but I guess I don't need it any more. Since I was a fake friend. Actually, I'm tired of faking it. Faking being a Catholic."

She yanked off the chain around her neck. "And here. Take this. George's Mary medal. Tell him no offense, but I guess I don't need it either. Since I haven't really changed."

Celia's eyes were round with shock as she took the medal. She had stopped talking, as though it were slowly dawning on her what was happening.

"Okay, so now this is real," Allie said brutally. "I'm really leaving the Catholic Church. You're done with me. Just like you said. No more faking it. I won't be bothering you anymore. You can walk out of here free. Free from me. Congratulations, Celia. You're done. And so am I."

1

Allie turned around and, spotting something lying on the bench, grabbed it and shoved it into Celia's hands. "And take this too. It's a bible. Try reading it sometime."

She turned away and strode to her car, but not before she saw, with a savage pleasure, Celia's face crumple in horror. She knew exactly how Celia would feel later. And she was happy.

"Allie, wait, please, stop, I shouldn't have said—" Celia's voice was faint.

"Goodbye, Celia."

ONE MONTH EARLIER...

1

HUNTER

CRACK!

The girl's eyes snapped open and stared unseeing at the ceiling.

She was still asleep.

She was still watching Nikki's mouth open in surprise, the cherry red stain spreading on her blue ruffled dress.

CRACK!

She sat upright in bed, tense, rigid, her mouth open, caught halfway between a scream and a gasp.

She blinked. She glanced over at the clock on her bedside table. 2:30 a.m.

With a groan she threw off the covers, and stumbled over to her bureau. She switched on the lamp, and a pale, frightened face stared out from the mirror, framed by a mane of wild blond hair.

"Just dreaming again, stupid," she muttered. Her voice was thick and groggy from sleep, even though her heart was still racing. "Just a stupid dream."

She pulled her hair back and tied it. *It wasn't your fault. Remember that. No matter what she says.*

The face looked a little less frightened. But there was a haunted look in the blue eyes, and behind it was darkness. No sound besides the crickets cheeping in the warm summer night. She was alone.

No. Don't think that. She glanced down at the bureau and saw a rosary made of silver chain and glass beads gleaming dimly in the darkness. Celia's rosary. Celia had given it to her on the day they had met eight months ago. Her first day at John Paul 2 High.

And you'll see Celia tomorrow morning, she reminded herself. *Along with everyone else. So cheer up. Be like Celia. What would she do if she was in your shoes?*

Well, that was an *easy* question. She scooped up the rosary, walked back to her bed and sat down.

"Hail Mary, full of grace..."

But the words coming out of her mouth seemed dry and dead. She hardly ever said the rosary alone. It felt awkward. Fake. Her heart wasn't in it, and her mind kept wandering. It wandered back to that first day at John Paul 2 High. Everything had been different then. She had been normal—just another kid at Sparrow Hills. She had a boyfriend: Tyler Getz. She had a best friend: Nikki Miller. Now Nikki was dead, and Tyler was in the hospital.

Back then she had only a vague idea of what a rosary was. She hadn't even *known* any Catholics. Now she knew six—she went to school with them. Until recently, she had dated one of them.

George... Unconsciously her hand moved to her neck, where a small silver medal hung from a chain.

It's a Miraculous Medal... The Blessed Mother promised special graces to anyone who wears it.

She shook her head. 'Special graces' were nice, but she'd rather have George's help, and his advice. He'd understand what she was trying to do; and even though they weren't dating anymore, she still missed his friendship. *Got to email him again. He didn't answer my last one.*

"Holy Mary, mother of God, pray for our sinners...wait." She frowned. Was it *our sinners* or *us sinners*? She could never remember. *Our sinners* didn't really make much sense, but it sounded better...*oh, what's was the point?*

She tossed the rosary down, walked up to the window and glared out in the darkness. She couldn't waste time on this.

He was still out there.

She could just make out the shape of a police car parked in the street outside. There was always a police car outside her house, every night, with two cops inside, awake, guns at the ready.

Because *he* was still out there.

She gritted her teeth. *Eight weeks and he's still out there.*

She reached under her bed and pulled out a battered, slightly bulging binder with a purple cover. She held it firmly—the Velcro binding was old and unreliable—and walked out of her bedroom, across the hallway and into the study.

She sat down in front of a shiny new laptop computer—a recent present from her mom. As the laptop powered on, she glanced down at the binder and grinned.

There was a cartoony picture of a unicorn with a goofy smile on the cover. There were words written with a marker over the unicorn's head:

Rufus the Unicorn!!

And underneath was a message in thin, childish, scraggly handwriting:

Happy 10th birthday Allie! Don't you just LOVE unicorns? I do!
love, Nikki

She chuckled. *Still the worst birthday present ever.* She hadn't used this binder since grade school, but now she had taken 'Rufus the Unicorn' out of retirement—to remind her why she was doing this.

She flipped open the binder, revealing pages of hand-drawn diagrams, photographs, pictures torn from gun magazines, and pages and pages filled top to bottom with her own firm, neat handwriting.

"All right, Rufus," she whispered. "Let's get to work. Let's find this guy."

Over her snow-white veil with olive cinct
  Appeared a lady under a green mantle,
  Vested in colour of the living flame.

The boy followed the words with one thin, brown finger,
mouthing them wordlessly, his brow furrowed in concentration.
He shifted in the hard wooden chair and leaned a bit closer to the
desk lamp.

And my own spirit, that already now
So long a time had been, that in her presence
Trembling with awe it had not stood abashed...

"Oh, come on," he mumbled. "That's so cheesy."

"Brian! Phil!"

A blonde woman in a flowered skirt bustled into the room. "It's
eight o'clock! Rise and—"

"I'm up, mom," the boy said quietly.

"Oh!" his mom looked taken aback for a moment; then she
shrugged and went over to the bunk bed on the other side of the
bedroom. "Phil, wake up now, breakfast's ready!"

His brother's voice came from beneath a pile of blankets:
"Leemee alone!"

His mom drew up the shades. Brian's eyes squeezed shut in the
harsh morning light. A groan came from the top bunk.

"You should have woken him," his mom said briskly. "How
long have you been up, anyway?"

"Since six," Brian said. "I've been reading the—"

"Well come on down to breakfast. You and Melissa have to be
at John Paul 2 in an hour."

"What?" Brian looked up. "Why?"

"For the meeting, of course!" His mom rolled her eyes. "Mr.
Costain asked all the students to a meeting this morning. I told you
last night; don't you remember? Honestly, Brian, sometimes your
head's in the clouds..."

7

Brian sighed, put a bookmark on his page and snapped the book closed. "Mom," he said, getting up, "I have a question about—"

But his mom was already gone. A moment later, he heard her voice further down the hallway. "Melissa! Judy! Up!"

Shaking his head, Brian walked across the bedroom and stripped the sheets off his nine-year old brother. "Come *on*, Phil."

Allie leaned close to the bathroom counter as she put the finishing touches on her makeup. *Too pale. Too thin. Not enough sleep. I look like I'm falling apart...*

Well, aren't you?

The blue eyes looked questioningly back at her.

"I'm not," she told them sternly. "I just didn't get enough sleep."

Yeah, because you spent two hours looking at different rifle barrels on the internet. And taking notes. Why do you keep doing this? You think you can find something the cops can't? Or the FBI? Maybe you are falling apart.

Maybe; but she'd make sure she *looked* normal, at least. She glanced over her outfit one more time: white tank top, blue gym shorts, white sneakers. Normal summer outfit. She hitched a bright smile onto her face. *There. Normal.* She skipped down the stairs. *At least I still have my looks.*

Her mom was already in the kitchen, dressed in her business suit and having breakfast. Allie walked over to the coffeemaker and poured herself a cup. "Hey mom, don't leave without me. I need a ride—"

"I *know*, Allie," her mom said grumpily. "You're going to John Paul 2 High, right?"

"Yeah, Celia and I have our meeting there. Everyone's coming."

Her mom frowned as she sipped her coffee. "I still don't like you going outside the house when they still haven't caught that psycho."

Allie rolled her eyes. "Oh, come *on*, mom! You really think he's gonna pop up and kill me at school over summer vacation?"

Her mom shook her head. "Maybe you should go stay with your father until this is over. I'm sure he wouldn't mind."

"Yeah, because he'd probably be away on sales trips the whole time," Allie retorted. "Leaving me with Tracey. No way. I'm not spending the summer in Maryland. My friends are here. Besides, Celia has this project she really wants my help on…"

"But you haven't hung out with any of your friends for months—not even Nikki—"

Her mom stopped suddenly and turned pale at the look at Allie's face.

"All the friends I have *left* are at John Paul 2 high," Allie said coldly. "You sent me there, remember?"

Her mom pursed her lips. "I'm sorry," she said quietly. "That was a little insensitive—"

"We're going to be late." Allie glanced at her phone. "You gonna drive me or not?"

Her stepfather Larry walked into the kitchen. "Diane, have you seen my red tie…" He noticed Allie. "Hey kiddo. Get some breakfast?"

"I'm not hungry," she muttered.

"And we have to go anyway." Her mom slammed down her coffee. "Come on, Allie."

B rian!"

Brian looked up from the open book. "Sorry," he said distractedly. "What was that?"

His father's broad, brown face crinkled in a wry grin. "I asked," he said, "if you were still working through Dante. It appears that you are."

His mom shook her head as she plopped a plate of eggs and toast in front of Brian. "That's really advanced, Brian. College-level stuff. You probably won't understand all of it."

"Nobody's *making* him read it, dear." His father put down his *National Review*. "So do you like it?"

"Like it or not, you got to put that book down and eat," his mom said, walking back to the kitchen with a load of dishes.

"Seriously, Brian," she said, returning to the porch a moment later. "Everyone else is done."

Brian glanced down the long oak table. The plates of all his siblings (Melissa, Judy, Lucy, Phil, Faustina and baby Gus) were empty. Melissa and Judy were chattering together, Lucy was collecting the plates, Phil was looking over a picture book, and two-year-old Faustina was poking one-year old Gus in the stomach and squealing with laughter. Gus was wailing in protest.

"Judy, help your sister clean up," his mom said briskly. "You too, Phil...and put that book away in the *bookcase*. Melissa, stop Faustina from torturing Gus."

Amid the chorus of protests, whines and laughter that followed, Brian scooted his chair nearer to his father, the thick book in his hand. "Dad, I can't figure this part out," he said. "Right here, in Canto 30."

His dad leaned over the book. "Ah, yes. This is when Beatrice comes down from Paradise and Virgil departs, right?"

"Dad," Melissa said petulantly as she grabbed Faustina (who was now shaking Gus's high chair violently and shrieking with laugher), "What *are* you guys talking about? Who's Dante?"

"Mind your own business," Brian said testily.

"Brian," his dad said warningly. "Patience." He leaned back, his large frame creaking in his chair. "Brian's reading a long poem called the *Divine Comedy*, written by a man called Dante Alighieri who lived in the Middle Ages."

Melissa gave Brian an exasperated look. "He's reading *that*? For fun?"

"Ah, but wait till you hear what it's about," his dad said. "Dante goes on this long journey. First he goes through Hell—"

"Dad said bad word!" Faustina squealed, pointing.

Chuckling, their dad went on. "And then he goes through Purgatory. And then he goes through Heaven."

Melissa blinked. "Hm. That's...weird."

"Yes, but I have a question about *this* part," Brian said, grabbing at the book. "Why does this happen?"

"What happens?" Melissa grabbed at the book too.

Calmly, their dad pulled it away from both of them and examined it. "Okay," he said in deep, measured tones. "You see, Melissa, Dante needs a guide wherever he goes. So when he goes through Hell and Purgatory, he's guided by a man called Virgil—"

"Who's he?"

"Virgil was another great poet who lived in Roman times. He was sort of Dante's boyhood hero."

"Yes, and he's really brave and really smart," Brian added. "Dante couldn't get anywhere without him. That's why I don't understand what—"

"Let me finish, Brian." His dad arched an eyebrow. "So Virgil guides Dante all through Hell and then through Purgatory. But when the time comes for Dante to visit Heaven, Virgil disappears, and this beautiful lady called Beatrice appears to guide him instead."

"Oh..." Melissa smiled wistfully. "Beatrice. That's a pretty name. So this angel called Beatrice comes to bring this Dante guy to heaven?"

"She's *not* an angel!" Brian said. "That's what's so cheesy!" He glanced at his dad. "Can I tell this part?"

His father shrugged and waved a hand.

"Beatrice was a real person," Brian said. "In real life, I mean. She was this girl Dante had a crush on. When he was a teenager."

"I wouldn't call it just a crush," his dad said. "After all, she did inspire some of the finest love poetry ever written. And in this book, Beatrice is his guide into Heaven."

"No way!" Melissa's eyes shone with delight. "That's so beautiful."

"No, it's cheesy!" Brian snorted. "He should have chosen someone cool like St. Michael the archangel, not some girl! I don't get it!"

"Well, Brian," his dad said. "Most people think that Virgil represents human reason, and Beatrice represents God's love. It's a—"

"Of course Mr. Spock doesn't *get it*." Melissa rolled her eyes. "Mr. Spock doesn't understand *girls*."

"Don't call me that!" Brian snapped.

"Girls do not compute," Melissa said in a stiff monotone. "Do not compute...not logical...error..." Her eyes rolled back, and she collapsed in her chair, her tongue hanging out. "Not...logical..." she whimpered, and then grinned.

The table burst into laughter. Brian scowled. "Well, *you're* a girl, so you don't even *use* logic," he snapped.

"Okay, lesson's over." Their dad closed the book. "Now, Brian, for your homework riddle..."

Brian sighed. This was how their dad always taught them: he would give them a question and withhold the answer. They had to figure it out on their own.

"Yes?" Brian said. "What's my riddle?"

"You've already asked it. Why did Dante idealize Beatrice? Think about it. Dante chose Virgil—a famous poet—as a symbol for human reason. But he chose Beatrice—'some girl' as you put it—as a symbol for God's love. Why?"

"Easy. Dante was nuts."

His dad chuckled. "Well, he *was* nuts for Beatrice. After all—" He grabbed their mom around the waist as she came back onto the patio, and ran a hand through her long blond hair. "I got *my* guide to heaven right here."

"Ack! Stop it, Dennis!" Their mom swatted his brown, balding head with a dish towel, as Brian and Melissa exchanged looks of revulsion. "Come on, you have a client meeting in a few minutes, and I got to drive these two to the school. Brian, *eat*."

"Hey, Dad," Melissa said. "If mom's your guide to heaven, what are we? Guides through...purgatory?"

His father's ruffled Melissa's hair. "No, you *are* purgatory. Go help your mom clean up."

Mom," Allie said, "Slow down! Just because you're ticked off at me—"

"Ticked off? I'm not ticked off," her mother said, making a right turn so hard that the wheels screeched. "I just don't want to be late for work."

Allie rolled her eyes and glanced out the car window. They had just turned onto Sojourner road, and Sparrow Hills High School loomed up on their right. She shuddered and turned away. *I can't even look at the place now.*

"Oh, *come on!* What's this?"

They had come to a stop behind a long line of cars. "There's *never* traffic here!" her mom snapped. "I'm gonna be late!"

They both sat in silence as the car inched forward. Then her mom snapped her fingers. "I almost forgot. Somebody called for you last night. "Ginger. Do you know a Ginger?"

"Ginger? Wait a second. Ginger *Josslyn?*"

"That's right. So, do you know her?"

"Well…sort of," Allie said, puzzled. Ginger and her friend Madison Williams were the head Ice Queens. That's what everyone called the clique of girls who were the oldest, the prettiest, and the coolest in Sparrow Hills. And Ginger was the oldest and prettiest—and the scariest.

"She left her number." Her mom handed her a slip of paper.

Allie glanced down at the scribbled name and number. Why would Ginger Josslyn call *her?* Ginger was two years older than Allie—she must have already graduated. Allie didn't know her as well as she knew Madison.

Ginger had known *Allie*, of course; Allie had made sure of that. She had worked so hard her freshman year to get close to the Queens, and she had gotten Nikki in too. Allie felt a faint stirring of pride at the thought. Only the best hung out with the Ice Queens: Tyler the wrestling captain, Brad Powell the quarterback, Simone and Tara the cheerleading captains…and Allie and Nikki, freshmen. It had seemed so exciting. Now it seemed so stupid. The Allie from that time seemed like a different person…someone younger.

"Finally!" The car picked up speed, passing by some dump trucks.

"Construction," her mom muttered, as if it were a dirty word.

Allie shrugged and looked across the road. On the other side, there was a field with a few black and white cows grazing. One of them looked up at her with a perturbed expression. Allie broke into a smile, remembering. *So that's where J.P. got his cow.* Suddenly she couldn't wait to see them all again, even J.P. She chuckled. *I must really be desperate.*

But there was one person that she *had* to see: George. George knew about guns. She'd been asking him for help for a while, but he had been reluctant. She hadn't even heard from him in the last week; he hadn't returned her calls or emails…

They pulled into the parking lot of JP2 High. "Well, here you go," her mom said, bringing the car to a stop. "When will this thing be over?"

"Um…" Allie opened the door and stepped out. "I'm not really sure."

"Fine. Just call me." Her mother drove off quickly, leaving the parking lot just as another car—a battered green Volvo—pulled into it. *Looks like Celia and her dad are here.*

"Hi Allie!" Celia Costain waved at her excitedly from the front seat as the Volvo pulled into a parking space.

A few moments later Celia was running up to Allie, her dark curly hair bouncing on her shoulders. As usual, she was smiling. "You all ready for the meeting?"

Allie stifled a yawn. "As ready as I'll ever be."

"Great! So did you print out that stuff?"

Allie blinked. "What?"

"Hello Miss Weaver," Mr. Costain walked up to the two girls. "How are you?"

"Um…fine," Allie said, glancing from Celia to Celia's dad with a feeling of unease. Not that there was anything disconcerting about

Mr. Costain, except that she wasn't used to seeing the John Paul 2 High principal in jeans and a t-shirt.

"I'm really happy that you and Celia came up with this idea," Mr. Costain said with a friendly smile. "Celia, I'll be in the school office if you need anything."

Celia watched her father walk into the school, and then turned back to Allie, her smile fading. "So you didn't print out the information sheet I emailed you yesterday? And the map I drew? We need it for the meeting, but our printer's broken."

"Oh…no," Allie said, blushing. "Sorry. I forgot."

"You forgot?" Celia looked hurt. "I was really counting on you to print them out. I wanted to hand out copies to everyone."

"Um…sorry." Allie felt a twinge of guilt. "Well, maybe your dad can print it out right now. Isn't there a printer in the school office?"

Celia brightened. "Good idea! Come on, let's ask him." She turned to go. "And on the way you can tell me what you're gonna say in your speech."

Allie froze. "My what?"

Celia turned around, frowning. "Your speech," she repeated. "You know, that you're going to give the school. We're each going to give a little talk about why we're doing the work camp. Remember?"

Suddenly, Allie *did* remember Celia mentioning this in one of her emails—but she hadn't thought Celia was serious. "I don't have a speech!" she said, panic-stricken. "I can't give a speech, Seal! I don't want to be the center of attention!"

"Okay, okay!" Celia said quickly. "Don't worry, you don't need to make a speech. I can do it on my own." She sighed.

"Look, Seal," Allie said in a pleading voice. "I totally support you. I think this idea of yours—"

"You mean *our* idea." Celia's brow wrinkled.

"Right!" Allie corrected hastily. "I think *our* idea is great. But I'm still going through a lot right now…"

"Of course." Celia smiled sadly. "You're still grieving. I guess I shouldn't have…"

She trailed off, but Allie could guess what she was thinking. *That she shouldn't have counted on me.*

"Well… I'm going to go inside," Celia said after an awkward silence. She walked away, her shoulders drooping. Allie watched her go—then she leaned against the bike post and crossed her arms.

She felt ashamed, but angry too. Ashamed for letting Celia down, and angry at Celia for pretending to be okay with it…and then more shame for being angry with Celia, and then more anger because this whole work camp thing *was* Celia's idea.

It had all started a couple weeks after the funeral. She'd been talking to Celia about Nikki and about how lonely she was now that it was summer…and then all of a sudden Celia had this idea…sure, it had all seemed like a lot of fun at the time, but Allie had just been starved for company.

But soon all Celia seemed to care about was this work camp thing. It had become Celia's little project. She had been sending Allie emails every day, going over ideas, plans, requests…and Allie hadn't been able to keep up. She had been too busy with the other thing. The only thing that mattered: catching the shooter.

She sighed. *I wish I could tell Celia what I'm really doing.* But that was ridiculous. Celia wouldn't approve. She would say it was too dangerous, and risky, and make a million other excuses because people like Celia weren't cut out for this stuff. Good people. Nice people. *Soft* people.

People like Nikki. Nikki and Celia had a lot in common, actually. Nikki had often made Allie feel both ashamed and angry— because Nikki was so…freaking…*nice.* Such a pushover. She would let Ginger and Madison walk all over her…

Ginger… Allie glanced down at the slip of paper her mom had given her. *I wonder what she wants.* She searched her memory, wondering if she had done anything to get on Ginger's bad side.

She had seen Ginger reduce another girl to tears once...the memory wasn't pleasant.

Nikki had *hated* Ginger. Nikki had hated that whole crowd, though she still hung out with them for Allie's sake. Nikki didn't need to; she was naturally popular. Smart, funny, cheerful and cool. Good family (*her* parents weren't divorced), well-off...and she was good, like Celia. Kind to people...

And then a thousand other memories of Nikki flooded into her mind. Places they'd been together, late night talks, scheming about boys, sharing dreams, laughing about stupid stuff...

Grief and sadness came then, like a wave of dark water, strong and savage. It hit her so hard that she almost staggered. She hugged herself with both hands clutching her side, her empty stomach churning.

Stop it. Stop it. STOP IT!! With a supreme effort of will, she regained control. *Got to stay steady.* She straightened, smoothed her hair, and tried in vain to smile.

But she couldn't. *Great.* This was what she had been afraid of: freaking people out.

2

FREAK

"Hey Brian," his mom said, "Can you and Melissa get a ride back with the Costains? I have to meet someone for lunch, and I don't know if I'll get back in time."

"I guess so." Brian glanced out the passenger side window as the family van barreled down the highway. "But I don't know about *her*." He shot Melissa an annoyed look.

"Now, Brian..."

"Why is she coming, anyway? She's not a *student* like me."

Melissa reached over the passenger seat and rubbed his curly black hair. "Oh, is Mr. Spock annoyed?"

"Quit it!" He knocked her hand away.

"Mr. Spock *is* annoyed!" Melissa grinned. "Mr. Spock is confused by sister. Mr. Spock does not understand girls...even though his *best friend* is a girl..."

Judy and Lucy erupted into giggles. "Melissa! Stop teasing your brother!" his mom said, but Brian could see that she, too, was fighting back a smile.

"Oh, very funny," Brian mumbled, staring out the window as they turned onto an exit and left the highway. "You're just hilarious."

Melissa didn't know what it felt like to be treated like a freak. Even at John Paul 2 High people thought he was weird, and at Sparrow Hills...

He shook his head. He had wrestled at Sparrow Hills last fall, and although it had ended well, there had been some rough times.

18

Really rough. No one knew how bad it had been except George (because he had been there) and Liz.

Liz Simonelli—short, athletic, with dirty blond hair and a dry sense of humor—was in the same grade as he, and they had started hanging out a lot last semester. At first it was just to play tennis; but he found Liz was just fun to be around. She seemed to really *get* him, and it was ridiculously easy to talk with her, unlike most girls. Most girls were like his sisters: giggly and annoying. Or like...

"Hey!" Melissa called out. "Allie's here!"

Brian looked up just as the big white van pulled into the school parking lot. There was Allie Weaver...his eyes widened.

He was used to seeing Allie in the school uniform—white blouse, black skirt—*not* in a skimpy tank top and short shorts...his eyes were drawn down to her smooth tanned legs like a tractor beam...

"She looks so sad," his mom said quietly.

Brian glanced up at Allie's pale face and felt a twinge of embarrassment.

"You two should be kind to her," his mom said. "Ask her how she's doing."

"Um...sure, mom," Brian muttered. He doubted that Allie would want to talk to *him*. Allie was the kind of girl he avoided: stuck-up and worldly. She may be Catholic *now*, but she still acted like she was attending Sparrow Hills Public High School up the road. He scowled. *Why do girls dress like that anyway?*

The van rumbled to a stop, and Brian and Melissa hopped out. Brian started for the front doors, but Melissa ran straight up to Allie. "Hey Allie!" she said. "How's it going?"

"Oh hi, Melissa. Hey, Brian!"

Brian took a deep breath and turned around. *Okay...just avert your eyes.*

"Hello," he said politely, keeping his eyes firmly on a spot just above Allie's shoulder. "How are you?"

"I'm fine," she said in a surprised voice, and looked over her shoulder. "What are you looking at?"

"Looking at?" He shook his head. "Nothing." *I'm trying to, anyway.*

"Um...okay. So how old are you now, Melissa?"

"Thirteen." Melissa grinned happily. "I'm the second oldest. I can't wait to come here! I've always wanted to go to a *real* school, you know?"

"A *real* school?" Allie sounded amused. "So I guess you don't like homeschooling...what do you think of that, Brian?"

Brian was looking at a new car that had just turned into the parking lot. *I wonder who that is.*

"Brian?"

He shifted his gaze down to his own feet. "What?" he said in what he hoped was a casual voice.

"Um...hello??" To his horror, she leaned over, trying to catch his eyes. "I'm up here!"

He saw her grinning and waving at him—and then he was looking straight down—

He felt his face grow red—then, with a snort of frustration, he walked away.

Allie's mouth dropped open. She watched Brian vanish into the school doors; then she turned to Melissa. "What's wrong with your brother?"

Melissa looked just as startled. "I don't know! I'll go talk to him." She ran away.

Allie leaned back against the bike rack, shaken. It wasn't just that Brian had walked away; it was the look on his face. He had looked at her like she was *dirt* or something. She didn't know Brian that well, but he had always been nice to her. What had she done to deserve that look?

Just then she heard two new, unfamiliar voices.

"Are you sure this is the place?"

"Of *course* it is, Mary! Look! It's a school!"

Two girls walked up to her, dressed in light pastel dresses that swept down past their knees. One had dark, shoulder-length hair and looked rather nervous; the other had long, willowy blond hair and a cheerful, open face. They looked like girls out of some old-fashioned storybook.

The blond girl's eyes lit on Allie. "And there's a student! You go look in the school, and I'll introduce myself to her!"

"Hi!" She ran up to Allie. "What's your name? And are you a student?"

"Yeah," Allie said with a bemused smile. "I'm Allie Weaver. Are you here for the meeting?"

"That's right!" The blond-haired girl said cheerfully. "I'm Jacinta Summers! My sister Mary and I are going to be students here too! So..." she added curiously. "What's this school like, anyway?"

"Um...well..." Allie was still taking in the news that there would be *more students*. She smiled. "Let me tell you..."

Brian leaned against the wall just inside the school front doors, glaring at the floor. *Why do girls dress like that?* he thought again. *Don't they realize—?*

"Hey!" The front door banged open and Melissa ran in. "What's your problem?"

"You wouldn't understand," Brian said testily.

"Why were you so rude to Allie? Was it something she said, or—"

"It wasn't what she said. It was—oh, never mind!" He threw up his arms. "You're just a kid! You don't understand *anything!*"

Melissa scowled. "Now you're being rude to *me*. Look, Mom told us to be nice to her! Her friend was murdered, remember?"

"Of course I remember! I was there!"

"Excuse me."

They both looked up. A girl stood in the doorway; a girl in a pink dress, with long brown hair, and big brown eyes.

"I couldn't help overhearing," she said in a soft, breathy voice. "Did you say somebody was...murdered?"

"Yes," Brian said automatically, staring at her. "That girl outside, Allie Weaver—her friend was murdered a few weeks ago."

"Oh!" the girl put a hand to her mouth. "That's terrible! How?"

"At Sparrow Hills. In the school shooting."

"She was *there?*" The girl looked shocked. "Oh, that's so sad! I better let Jacinta know!" She turned to go.

"Wait!" Brian blurted out.

The girl turned around. "Yes?"

"Um...I didn't catch your name," he stammered.

The girl smiled slightly...and instantly Brian noticed two things happen. One was that he felt a little dizzy. The other was that Melissa was grinning broadly.

"Mary." The girl strode forward. "Mary Summers." She held out her hand.

Brian took it. It was very soft...soft and warm.

"Well, it's nice to meet you, Mary," he said. "I'm Melissa, and this is my sister Brian."

Mary broke into a grin, Melissa snickered, and Brian suddenly wanted the earth to open up and swallow him. "No! I mean, *I'm* Brian, and—"

"And *I'm* Melissa!" Melissa skipped forward. "We're here for the meeting!"

"Yes," Brian said woodenly. "There's a meeting. It's starting in a few minutes. My name's *Brian*," he said again. For some reason it seemed very important to make this clear. "Brian Burke. And this is—"

"Your sister Melissa." The girl looked amused. "Got it. Well, I better tell Jacinta. Bye, Melissa. Bye, Brian."

She made a little wave at him, and then she was gone. Brian watched the front door slowly close. "Wow," he said blankly. "What was her name again?"

"I think it was *Beatrice*."

"Yes..." Brian said vaguely. Then, noticing Melissa's smirk, he added, "Huh? I...I don't know what you're talking about."

"Sure you don't...*Dante*."

So there were only *seven* students here last year?"

"Yeah." Allie nodded. "It freaked me out too."

"I'm not freaked out!" Jacinta said eagerly. "That's so cool! You must be so close!"

"Well...sort of..."

22

A few more cars drove into the parking lot, and people were getting out. There was J.P., and Liz, and...

She felt a rush of happiness as she saw the tall, well-built boy, his light brown hair cropped short, dismounting from his bike.

"Excuse me," she said to Jacinta. "My boyfrie—I mean, my friend just got here."

She turned around and almost collided with Celia who had hurried out of the building at the same time. "Whoops! Sorry Seal!"

"Um...no problem," Celia said, giving Allie a funny look.

Uh oh. Did she hear me almost call George my boyfriend? That would be...awkward... "Come on," Allie said to her. "George is here."

Celia brightened immediately. "Really?" The two of them ran up to George just as he finished locking up his bike at the bike rack.

"George!" Celia hugged George. "You're here! I didn't expect that!"

"Of course he's here!" Allie said jokingly, punching George in the arm. "Thanks for answering my emails, jerk!"

"Oh, hi Allie," George said with a startled laugh. "You've been emailing me? Sorry! I couldn't really answer in the woods, could I?"

Allie gave him a baffled look. "Woods?"

"He's been on retreat, Allie." Celia beamed at George. "You got back last night, huh?"

"Yep. A week in the woods with no cell phone or internet." George grinned. "Fr. Borgia organized it. It was so cool!"

"Awesome! Tell me all about it! And then you got to go inside and tell my dad!"

The two of them started chatting, apparently forgetting that Allie was even there. Allie watched them, feeling miffed. *That's the problem with hanging out with George and Celia,* she thought grumpily. *They've known each other forever, they're so close...you always feel like an outsider.* Then another depressing thought occurred to her. *Who am I kidding? I'm an outsider with everyone here. Everyone else here is more Catholic than me.*

"Oh, Allie..." Celia glanced at her. "I got to tell you something else."

She stepped closer and lowered her voice. "Be careful that you, er, make a good impression on people."

"What do you mean?"

Celia paused, and her eyes flitted up and down, looking Allie over. "You see, there's some new students coming to the meeting, and I want them to have...a good first impression of the school."

"You mean the Summers?" Allie said, confused. "They're right over there." She pointed to Mary and Jacinta.

"Oh! Why didn't you tell me?" Celia glanced at Jacinta, who was talking with her sister Mary in whispers. Suddenly Jacinta gasped and looked at Allie, horrified. Allie heaved a sigh. *Guess those two just heard all about me. I bet they'll be too weirded out to talk to me.*

"Hey! Welcome to John Paul 2 High!" Celia ran up to the new girls. Allie turned around. *Well, at least I can talk to George now.*

But George was gone. She looked around, but he was nowhere to be found. He must have gone inside already to talk to Mr. Costain about this retreat—the retreat he hadn't bothered to tell *her* about.

Well, what do you expect? a cold voice said inside her. *You two split up, remember?*

But he's still my friend.

Sure he is. Like any guy just wants to be 'friends.' Maybe with a girl like Celia. Not with you.

She shook her head. *Why are you thinking these things? Just talk to somebody else.* She looked around, and saw J.P. and Liz talking near Mr. Costain's Volvo.

"Hey guys!" She walked up to them. "How's your summer going?"

J.P.'s eyes bulged in his thin, freckled face. He looked her up and down for a few seconds, and then blurted out, "Omigosh! I'm gonna go to hell!" He sprinted away.

Allie stared at his retreating figure. *That's weird. Even for J.P.*

Liz rolled her eyes. "Nice going, Allie."

"What? What did *I* do?" she said irritably.

"Wasn't it obvious? He was checking you out. Then he felt guilty about it."

"Why?" Allie rolled her eyes. "Never stopped him before. Anyway, there's lots of girls here for J.P. to gawk at, so—"

"Um, Allie...you kind of stick out."

"What? How?"

"Your clothes. Look around."

Allie glanced around and suddenly realized that Liz had a point. All the other girls there wore jeans or long skirts. Liz herself was wearing overalls and a t-shirt, her dirty blond hair pulled back in a ponytail.

Allie glanced down at her tank top and shorts. "Oh," she mumbled. *So that's why Brian wouldn't look at me. And Celia—that's what she meant by a 'good impression.' Will I never fit in here?*

"Yeah, that's it." Liz shook her head. "You just had to wear short shorts, didn't you?"

Allie scowled. "*You're* preaching to *me* about modesty?" She knew how Liz dressed when her strait-laced mom wasn't looking.

Liz shrugged. "All I'm saying is that you should try to blend in more. Stop with the attention-seeking. It'll come back to bite you."

"I'm *not* attention seeking!" Allie retorted. "And anyway, weren't you the one who was all over Rich Rogers last year, bragging about hickeys? How'd *that* work out?"

Liz's eyes narrowed. "Whatever. I was just trying to help." She walked away.

Allie leaned against the Costains' car and glared down at the asphalt. No one wanted to talk with her; Brian, because he hated how she dressed, J.P. because he *loved* how she dressed...Celia was too busy, and George didn't seem to care about her anymore. And now Liz was mad at her too. *I give up.*

She stayed there, wrapped in her own thoughts. The next time she looked up, she was alone. Everybody, apparently, had gone inside. No one had noticed her.

"Hello, Miss Weaver."

She looked up. There was James Kosalinski, the oldest and weirdest kid at John Paul 2 High. He wore exactly the same clothes she had always seen him in: a white shirt, black tie and black pants—the John Paul 2 High uniform. He stood next to his big black car, his hand on the open door, and his large grey eyes were fixed on her in a strange, glassy stare. James always stared at her like this. It creeped her out.

Well, Creepy Boy's better than nobody, I guess. "Um, hi James," she said warily. "How's your summer going?"

"Awful," James said. "I have something for you."

"Really?" she said listlessly. "What?"

James reached into his car and pulled out...roses. A bouquet of red roses, wrapped in white paper. He held it out to her. "Here."

Allie gaped at him for a moment before taking the roses with an astonished laugh. "Omigosh! Thank you! These are *beautiful*, James! Why did you—hang on." She looked up suspiciously. "Why are you giving me these?"

"They're not for you. They're for your friend." He pointed to a small card attached to the bouquet. "See?"

Allie glanced down at the card. There was a message in black, elegant handwriting:

In Memoriam: Nicole Miller
Requiescat in Pace

"You could plant them at her grave," James said stiffly. "I hope that I picked the correct kind—I'm not sure what kind of flowers Nicole would have liked."

"Nikki," she whispered, gazing down at the flowers. "Her name was Nikki."

"Oh, of course." James nodded sagely. "I don't usually hold with nicknames when speaking of the dead, but of course you were close to her, and some allowances must be made. But *I* wouldn't presume that air of informality—argh!"

He made a sort of strangled cry as Allie hugged him, her arms barely reaching around his waist. "Thank you," she whispered. "Thank you so—"

And suddenly she realized what she was doing.

She pulled away, her face reddening, wondering what James would say.

But James looked, for once, at a loss for words, his mouth open in astonishment, his large face even paler than usual. "There's…" he took a deep breath. "There's no need," he said sternly, "to collapse into feminine hysteria."

Allie giggled. For the moment, she forgot how much she disliked James. She just felt incredibly grateful. Finally somebody understood, if only a little.

"Nikki loved roses," she said, running a hand over the flowers tenderly. "They were her favorite flower. How did you know?"

James didn't answer. He just watched her, an intense, focused look in his eyes.

Then, to her surprise, he made a formal, old-fashioned bow. "I'm glad I could help, Miss Weaver," he said quietly.

Allie blinked. She didn't know how to respond. James shouldn't have been nice to her. She didn't deserve that, not after how she'd treated him. A painful memory popped up in her mind: James in the woods, his face pale and shocked as she yelled at him, calling him FAT and *CREEP* and *LOSER*…

But who's the loser now? Who's the outsider?

She stared back into James' grey eyes, and suddenly she realized why James' looks had always creeped her out. When other boys looked (and they *all* did) they never looked into her eyes. They looked everywhere else. James looked into her eyes, and it freaked her out. It made her feel shy, somehow—like he could see inside her. Deep inside. Like he could read her as easily as one of his vampire books, and he already knew everything about her…

Because he's an outsider. A freak. Just like you.

That's why he understands. He knows how to be strong. He is *strong.* She glanced at James, and for the first time noticed how tall he was, how bulky—and it wasn't all fat, either. He wasn't *that* bad looking. There was something…*cool* about how he didn't care what anyone thought. How he always stood alone. It was kind of…*glamorous*, really…

What am I thinking? That's crazy.

She turned away, flushing. *What's* wrong *with you? This is* James! *Get a grip!*

She took a deep breath. "All right," she whispered. "Well...thank you, James. And thank you for the flowers. It was so sweet. Just what I...um...needed..." She bit her lip. *Stop talking! You're gonna say something stupid that'll make him think...*

James frowned. "Is something wrong?"

"No! It's just that...well, you're the first guy to ever give me flowers."

"No. I'm not."

"Huh?"

James rolled his eyes. "They're not for you, remember? They're for Nicole's grave. So technically, I *haven't* given you flowers. Why would I?"

Allie blinked. For a second she was furious with him—and then she laughed. "Of course!" she said playfully. "Why would you? Come on, let's go inside."

But after he lumbered inside the front door, she darted back out to drop the roses on the bench. After all, James was still a little weird. And she didn't want to field any awkward questions if anyone saw her with the flowers. Especially George.

3

THE PROPOSAL

> Christ has no body but yours
> No hands, no feet on earth l
> Yours are the eyes with which
> Compassion on this world,
> Yours are the feet with which
> Yours are the hands, with whi
> Yours are the hands, yours ar
> Yours are the eyes you are, l

Liz threw herself into a chair next to Brian. "Hey, Burke," she grunted.

"Hey," he grunted back. He stared at the gym floor, lost in his own thoughts, the sounds of conversation washing over him.

After a few moments he glanced at Liz. She looked up at the same time, and for a moment they stared at each other.

"What's eating *you?*" they both said.

Brian grinned. Liz chuckled. "You first," Brian said.

"Oh, nothing." Liz fiddled with a few strands of her hair. "Just ran into Allie, and she got under my skin."

Brian grimaced. "She got under my skin too. In a matter of speaking."

"What do you mean?"

"Well, um…" Brian hesitated. "It was more like *her* skin, you know…"

"Oooooh…" Liz gave him a sidelong glance. "Well, that proves it."

"Proves what?"

"You *are* a guy. Sometimes I forget."

"Why?"

"Well, you never checked *me* out. Not even at the dance when I wore that cute black dress—"

Brian frowned. Liz had worn that dress for Rich. That loser. "Well, I didn't check Allie out either," he said. "I avoided *that* temptation by looking somewhere else."

29

Liz rolled her eyes. "Sometimes I worry about you, Burke. You're such a goody two shoes. When are you gonna learn how to act normal?"

"I don't want to act 'normal' if that means disrespecting women! Isn't that what girls want? Respect?"

Liz snorted. "Like you know anything about girls." She yawned. "Sometimes I wish you *would* check me out instead of being so *perfect*."

"Um...no thanks." Brian chuckled. "I don't want to get maced!"

Liz's brow wrinkled. "Um. Right."

"So why *did* you date that guy Rich anyway?"

"Let's talk about something else." Liz bent down to tie her shoe. "So you really didn't like that little black dress?"

"No. It was too little."

"But that's what made it cute!"

Brian hesitated. Although he would never admit it to Liz, that dress had made him uncomfortable—especially since Liz was the one in it.

"It was a temptation," he said firmly.

"Oh, thanks," Liz said testily, sitting up again. "Is that all you see girls as, Burke? A temptation? Is that how you see me?"

"Of course not!" Brian protested. "You're my friend! As long as you're dressed decently—like you are now."

Liz looked down at her overalls. "Right now I'm dressed like a boy."

"Exactly," Brian nodded. "No temptation."

All right, people," said Mr. Costain. "Settle down; we need to get started. As you know—"

A pencil fell down from the ceiling and clattered on the cafeteria floor. Brian grinned to himself.

Mr. Costain glanced up quizzically, and then looked back to them, his grey eyes twinkling behind half-glasses. Not only was Mr. Costain the principal and founder of John Paul 2 High: he was also the English, History and Theology teacher. Plus, he was also one of the best teachers Brian had ever had, besides his own dad.

"As you know," he continued. "We're here to discuss an idea that Celia and Allie had. It's strictly voluntary but I'll let them explain it."

Celia stood up, looking a bit nervous. "I guess it's better if I'm the one who explains it," she said with a glance at Allie, who was looking at her nails with a preoccupied expression, "Well, first off, some of you might have already noticed that we have some guests here: Mary and Jacinta Summers!"

Jacinta waved happily. Mary looked a little embarrassed.

"They're coming to school here in the fall," Celia continued, looking a bit more cheerful now. "Along with twelve others, so far! So we're gonna have a lot of new students; the school's gonna be three times as big—"

"Aw, not *math*," J.P. said. "I can't do math! It's still summertime."

Celia let out a giggle and went on. "So there's a lot of changes on the horizon, and well, we thought that it would be a bit easier on everyone if we all spent time together over the summer. You know, because some of us might get...lonely."

Again she glanced in Allie's direction. Now Allie looked annoyed.

"And finally, the school needs work," Celia went on. "So we—me and Allie—thought we could solved all these problems at once. The problem of getting to know the new students. The problem of keeping in touch over the summer. And the problem of the school needing construction."

"Construction?" said a deep derisive voice from the back of the room. Brian hadn't realized that James was even at the meeting. "You want *these* people—" he gestured with one fat hand in J.P's general direction, "—to do construction?"

"Well, yeah," Celia said. "Think about how much money we could save if we fixed up the school ourselves! And if the new students come, we can get to know them! It's a win-win-win situation!" She looked at them eagerly. "Right?"

Brian shifted uncomfortably in his seat. Fixing up an old building wasn't exactly his idea of the perfect summer, even if it *would* help the school.

"What do you think?" he whispered to Liz. "Sounds a bit crazy to me."

Liz nodded in agreement. "Mr. Costain—" She raised her hand. "Do you really think this is a good idea?" She jabbed a finger at the ceiling lights, half of which were flickering. "This school needs serious help. I mean, electrical work, stuff like that."

"And plumbing and new drywall," Mr. Costain said gravely. "Yes."

Liz shook her head in frustration. "And you still want to have us *kids* do this? Have you talked to my dad?" Liz's dad was in construction.

"We did, and guess what?" Celia said. "Your dad's going to help us! He's going to oversee the whole thing, Liz, and he said he could teach us a little—like shop class. It'll be fun!"

"That's odd," James said dryly. "I didn't read the fine print, but I don't remember my parents paying for *that* on the curriculum. Unqualified students working with live wires and sewage leaks. It does sound like *so* much fun—"

"You know, James," George said loudly. "I don't think anyone asked what *you* thought."

"At least I *have* thoughts, Georgie," James retorted.

"All right, that's enough," Mr. Costain said sharply. James and George shared a mutual hatred, as everyone knew. "Celia, you were saying?"

Celia gave George and James a worried look. "Um...I was also thinking that we could make a tradition of this." She recovered her happy expression. "Every summer we could clean the school, or maybe help out some other needy families who need construction work done. And finally, we wouldn't have to do a fundraiser this year!" She beamed at them. "So...what do you think?"

No one replied. After a few seconds, James raised a long hand. "Excuse me," he said coolly. "Is this the only reason for this meeting? To draft us into a work force?"

Celia hesitated. "Well..." she said. "No, not *exactly*—"

"Will we be compensated?"

"Huh?"

"*Paid*," James said impatiently. "Will I be *paid* for the work? I'm trying to save up for college, and—"

"Of course you won't be paid!" George snapped. "It's a volunteer thing! That's what volunteer means! Look it up in the dictionary!"

"I wasn't talking to *you*," James shot back. "And I know what volunteer means. It means that I'm going to be spending time here that I could better spend elsewhere." He looked back to Celia. "Isn't that right? Doesn't that sum up your whole scheme?"

"Um...James?" Allie raised her hand hesitantly. "It's my scheme too," she said in a small, nervous voice.

James looked taken aback. "That's what Miss Costain said," he admitted, frowning at Allie. "So maybe *you* can convince me of the merits of this plan."

"Leave her alone, James," George broke in with a scowl. "Why did you even *come* to the meeting if you didn't want to—"

"I'm glad he came!" Allie burst out. Then she hesitated, red-faced as everyone, James included, looked at her in astonishment.

That isn't like Allie at all, Brian thought. She was usually more cool and tough, not shy and blushing—and she hated James as much as George did. She was *never* nice to him.

"I'm glad you *all* came," Allie continued timidly. "I mean...we're all friends, right? Couldn't we spend the summer together?"

"Yeah, exactly!" Celia beamed at Allie, and Allie gave her a small smile in return. "Let's work together for a change, James. Like Allie said, we're all friends here."

"This isn't about friendship," James said gruffly. "And I don't think *all* of us are friends." He gave George an ugly look, and stood up. "Sorry to leave so abruptly," he said in a distinctly un-sorry voice. "But I have a date with the library. I'll see you in the fall." He walked out of the gym.

Celia looked a bit shaken as she watched him go. After a second she turned to the others, took a deep breath, and said, "Um...so what do the rest of you think?"

"I'm in," George said angrily. "I think it's a great idea." He glared at the rest of them as if he was daring them to disagree.

"Thanks, George," Celia smiled warmly. "Anybody else?"

Mr. Costain cleared his throat. "I think you should all know," he said, "since Mr. Kosalinski seemed confused on this point, that this is strictly voluntary. However..." He sighed. "It *will* help out the school if you commit to this. Think about it, please. Pray about it. Maybe this would help." He picked up a sheaf of papers and started handing them out. "It's a poem by St. Theresa of Avila."

Brian looked down at his copy of the poem. This was typical of Mr. Costain; he liked to use quotations from famous people to make a point. There was even a "Great Wall of Quotes" in his classroom. The gym grew quiet as everyone read the poem.

Christ has no body but yours,
No hands, no feet on earth but yours,
Yours are the eyes with which he looks with
Compassion on this world,
Yours are the feet with which he walks to do good,
Yours are the hands, with which he blesses all the world.
Yours are the hands, yours are the feet,
Yours are the eyes, you are his body.
Christ has no body now but yours,
No hands, no feet on earth but yours,
Yours are the eyes with which he looks with
compassion on this world.
Christ has no body now on earth but yours.

Brian glanced up, feeling a bit disgruntled. It was a beautiful poem, of course...but what it *really* meant was that they had to spend the summer in this dusty old building.

"I think it sounds fun," Mary's sister Jacinta spoke up. "I mean, we're new here, but I think Mary and I would be glad to do it." Brian glanced quickly at Mary, in time to see her nodding. Suddenly the prospect of spending time in the school building seemed more appealing. A little. He blinked and looked away.

"All right," said Mr. Costain. "Let's take a vote. All in favor of Celia's idea?"

Slowly, every hand rose.

"All right!" Mr. Costain said. "We'll start a week from today. Now, let's go over some things..."

"Dude! Dude!" J.P. whispered to Brian.

"What?"

"I can't believe it!" J.P. looked dazed. "I just *voted to go to school and work!*"

Brian shrugged. That *was* weird. But then again, James had a way of turning the whole class against him.

Hey, Allie!" Celia ran up to Allie as the meeting broke up. "Wasn't that great? They all agreed! Even the Summers! And I'm—"

"Hold on a sec, Seal." Allie had just noticed George heading for the double doors. "I got to talk to George about something. I'll call you later, okay? George!"

She ran after George and caught him just outside the school office. "Can I talk to you?"

He turned around with an apprehensive look. "Oh, hey, Allie. Look, I'm sorry I didn't tell you about the retreat—"

"I don't care about that." Allie waved a hand impatiently. "Look, we need to talk. In private."

"Oh. Okay." Looking only slightly less troubled, George followed her to a quiet corner of the hallway near the school office.

"Here." Allie pulled out the paper from her purse, unfolded it and handed it to him. "Check these out."

George glanced down at the paper, perplexed. "Um...what's this for?"

"George, you were closer to the window!" Allie said eagerly. "And you know more about guns! Look—" She snatched the paper back from George and glanced at it again. It showed photographs of ten different rifles. "We know that he used a .45 caliber, but we still don't know what kind. You got a better look at the shooter than me, and I thought you...could..."

She faltered. George was shaking his head slowly. "I can't tell, Allie. The cops asked me the same thing, and the FBI too, and I couldn't tell them either. You know that."

"Well...I thought maybe you remembered something else...oh, come on, George, just *look* at it!" she said furiously, holding the paper out to him.

He didn't take it. "Allie, no. I can't do this. And neither should you."

"Do what?"

"Try to do things yourself. That's what I did, and I screwed everything up. Just leave this to the cops."

"The cops can't find him!"

"And I can't either!" George shook his head. "Look, I'm no good at this stuff. You should talk to somebody smart, like Brian."

"Brian's not my friend! *You* are!"

"Look, Allie." George took a deep breath. "When I was on retreat, I prayed a lot about what had happened. I kept thinking about it...about how much it was my fault."

"Your fault?" Allie said impatiently. "Come on, George, it wasn't *your* fault! If anything, it was..."

She looked down at her shoes, her heart in her throat.

"Allie," George said hesitantly. "Look, um...I think you should pray more. That's what you really need."

"I need to *find* him, George! And I need your help!"

"That's what I'm trying to do. This week, I really felt God's love. That's what helped me get through."

"Love, huh?" Allie snapped. "Guess that love doesn't extend to James, huh?"

"James?" George scowled. "Why bring *him* up?"

"I...uh...never mind!" Allie gritted her teeth. "Look, are you gonna help me find this guy or not?"

George hesitated. "I can't help you, Allie. Not with this."

"Fine." Allie turned, picked up James' bouquet of roses from the bench, and started away.

"Hang on!"

Allie spun around. "What?" she snapped

"Those flowers. Where'd they come from?"

"What do you care?"

"Where'd they *come* from, Allie?" George said forcefully. "Did someone send them to you, or—"

"I got them myself, okay?" Allie said, improvising quickly. She had no intention of letting George know the truth. "They're for Nikki's grave. See?" She took off the card and handed it to him.

George perused it for a moment, and then gave it back with a frown. "Okay. Sorry. Look, I never told you this, but—"

"I gotta go." Allie walked away, her face hot with anger. *How could I have been so stupid? What does George care? He didn't know Nikki. Probably never even went to her grave. It doesn't matter to him that she's dead and her killer's still out there. He's more worried about 'not making a mistake'. He doesn't really care.*

"Fine," she muttered. "I don't need him."

4

HATE

"Oh, come on!"
Allie leaned in closer
to the laptop screen
and read the email
again.

Dear Ms. Weaver,

I'm sorry to inform
you that I cannot
give you any details
of the investigation,
since much of it is
confidential. I am
emailing you a copy of the official press release (see attachment)
but I believe you have that already.

I understand your desire to assist us, but the thing you should be
concerned with now is staying <u>safe</u>. The evidence suggests that
the suspect's actions were connected to you, and as long as he
remains at large your personal safety may be in jeopardy. Stay
indoors whenever possible, avoid being alone in public areas and
traveling at night, and inform us of any suspicious activity—ANY
activity.

Sincerely,
Gerald Hichborn
SHPD

"That's it, huh?" she whispered furiously. "Just stay home while
you guys *don't* find him? Be a good little girl like Celia? Or Nikki?"

She glanced down at the purple binder. Rufus the Unicorn
seemed to look at her reproachfully.

"Sorry," she muttered.

It had been a week since the meeting, and she had made zero
progress. But she wouldn't stop. She *couldn't* stop. If she did, *he*
would have won. She would just be another victim, broken,
traumatized, defeated. Like the girls at Nikki's funeral, blank eyes

staring out of pale, tear-streaked faces. Or like George, gushing about 'love' and giving up because he was too scared of making a mistake. Heck, she might even end up like Brandon Brock.

The news had broken a few days ago. They found Brock's body in some woods near his house, a pistol by his side and a bullet in his head.

Suicide. The police confirmed it and his family said they had seen it coming. Brock had been traumatized by the shooting, his family told the papers. After all, Tyler Getz had been shot — Brock was one of Tyler's best friends. They had known each other since grade school — just like her and Nikki.

Maybe Brock had known how it felt to see your best friend struck down, and wonder why you couldn't stop it...to feel like it was your fault...

She glanced out the study window. It was pitch black outside. It felt pitch black inside, too. Like there was a black hole inside her, gaping like a mouth to swallow her...

"Stop it," she hissed. "Work."

She double-clicked on the file attached to Officer Hichborn's email: the police report, full of all the evidence. Dry. Clinical. Facts. She knew them already, but it didn't hurt to go over them again. Her eyes jumped to the middle paragraph.

```
15 shots were fired total ... first shot
occurred approximately 21:45 ... Victim, Tyler
Getz (age 17) was wounded in lower abdomen ...
```

Tyler was still in the hospital. She hadn't visited him.

```
... victim, Robert Henderson (age 18) was
wounded in left shoulder by bullet fragment.
```

Bobby Henderson was another wrestler, a senior. He and Ginger had dated a bit last year. *Hmmm. Still haven't called Ginger back.*

```
Victim Ariadne Pirolli (age 16) was wounded in
right arm (ricochet) ...
```

Ariadne was in her class, a friend of Nikki's...Now she went back to the top of the report and read the first paragraph, which she had automatically skipped, and forced herself to read it.

> Unknown suspect fired rifle from skylight into the school gymnasium ... First victim, **Nicole Miller** (age 16) was shot through heart and killed instantly.

The first shot was the most accurate, of course—Nikki had been a sitting duck, standing by the drink table and chatting with Ariadne. He had probably taken his time; probably felt a thrill of excitement as he aimed and fired and seen her go down...

Her fists clenched.

He had fired another shot at Nikki, just to make sure she was dead. That's the one Ariadne had caught...not that he had cared...

"I hate him," she muttered, her insides on fire. "I hate him so much."

She wanted to keep hating him. That's what George didn't understand. Love wouldn't help her—love might destroy her. It was *hate* she needed now. It was hate that kept her going, pumping through her like fuel—that hot, coursing feeling, that desire to catch him, and *hurt* him, and make *him* suffer. Make *him* squirm: *that's* what she wanted. She wanted it more than anything; the desire for revenge filled her up, keeping her from feeling anything else.

And that was good. Because if she stopped hating him, she'd remember how much she had loved Nikki. And how much she hated herself.

Are you going to go to the dance, Nikki?

Eh, nah...No one's asked me.

You have to go! I won't have any fun if you're not there!

"No," she mumbled. "Don't think about that." She turned back to the police report.

> Conflicting reports from witnesses on the perpetrator's movements ... figure seen climbing off roof with rifle ... car leaving SH

40

```
parking lot at high speed at approximately
21:55, make unknown ... other witnesses
reported seeing perpetrator in the woods
outside school.
```

"Seal and Liz," Allie muttered. They had seen the guy in the woods right after. They had heard him laugh — that low, nasty laugh: *heh heh heh*. That proved (at least to her) that he was the hacksaw guy who had tried to get at George in the Sparrow Hills wrestling gym, back in the fall...but that story had a happy ending. They had chased him away. No one had gotten hurt *that* day. All the bad guys lost: first the hacksaw guy, then the poltergeist.

The Poltergeist... Allie smiled slightly, remembering how J.P. had rigged the school with bells and lights and stuff, trying to catch a mysterious person who was breaking windows at JP2 High. Well, it had worked—they had all seen the thin, dark figure running away after J.P.'s alarms went off, jumping into a car and peeling out of the parking lot...

"Wait a sec." Allie glanced back at the police report.

```
car leaving SH parking lot at approximately
21:55, model and make unknown ...
```

Her brow furrowed. *That's odd.*

She hadn't noticed that part about the car. After all, it wasn't the *shooter* in the car. *He* had gone to the woods.

But who *was* in that car? Whoever it was had left right after the shooting...peeling out of the parking lot and driving away at high speed. He had escaped, just like the poltergeist had...

Could the shooter and the poltergeist...be working together?

If she hadn't been so desperate for *something*, she would have dismissed the thought as a coincidence. But wasn't it kind of funny that on that day back in the fall, they had run into both the shooter *and* the poltergeist on the same day?

Even funnier that on *that* day, the hacksaw guy—who could be the shooter—had escaped on foot, and the poltergeist had escaped by car. And the exact same thing had happened on the night of the dance.

41

She closed her eyes and tried to think, but her thoughts were sluggish and fuzzy. Here was another puzzle, and the purple binder was already full of them. She wasn't any closer to finding Nikki's murderer...she hadn't solved *anything!*

You should talk to somebody smart, like Brian.

Hmmm. Maybe George had a point. Brian was definitely smart, and calm, and level-headed. Plus, he was friends with J.P.; maybe he had more information about the poltergeist.

I should just talk to J.P. then. That would be easy. J.P. was like most guys: they *loved* to talk to her, as long as they got a chance to stare at her legs or her chest or something.

Brian hadn't, though. Brian had looked grossed out. Why?

Maybe I'm overreacting. Maybe he just...didn't like what I was wearing. Maybe I got to find what he likes.

He's still a guy. I can get him to talk to me.

As she closed down her email, she spotted an email from Celia with the headline, "Our First Day Tomorrow!"

Yeah, Seal, I haven't forgotten. She groaned to herself, and didn't bother to read the email. *I'll be there, don't worry. I need to talk to Brian and J.P.*

She headed back to her bedroom. *Got to plan my outfit. Find the right approach. What do black geeks like?*

5

NEW CROWD

"Oh, Brii-aaaan!" Melissa sang, walking up to the school doors. "My oh my, I wonder who will be here today!"

"Shh," Brian muttered.

"Liz will be here...so will J.P...and Allie and Celia and George..."

"Melissa, be quiet!"

"But that doesn't get you excited, does it? There's only

one girl that gets Mr. Spock excited, and that girl's name is—"

Brian made a grab at his younger sister. She dodged him nimbly and ran into the school, laughing hysterically.

"Great," Brian muttered, walking up to the front doors. "Just great." Over the last week Melissa had become *fixated* on Mary Summers. He could tell. She didn't talk about it, of course, but he just *knew* she was reveling in his humiliation, going over every detail...

He stopped. Wait. That wasn't Melissa. That was him.

He glanced up at the school doors, his stomach squirming uncomfortably. Mary Summers was in there. And he didn't want to see her. No...he *did*. He did and he didn't. He gritted his teeth. *This doesn't make any sense!*

"I gotta talk to Liz," he muttered. "Maybe she'll know what to do."

He walked up to the door, his jaw set.

The door banged open, narrowly missing his face.

"Watch it, Burke!" A burly man with olive skin and cropped grey hair emerged from the front door, carrying one end of a rusted metal school desk.

43

"Mr. Simonelli? What——?"

"Get out of the way!" the man grunted in a gravelly voice, and backed down the stairs. The rest of the desk came into view, held by another burly man with short black hair and tattoo-covered arms.

The tattooed man's face crinkled into a smile. "Yo Brian! What's up?"

Brian grinned. "Hey Hank." Hank was Mr. Simonelli's right-hand man; Brian had met him a couple times at Liz's house.

"Let's save the small talk for later." Mr. Simonelli said. With a heave, they threw the desk on the grass lawn in front of the school.

"Whew," Mr. Simonelli grunted. "They made 'em out of iron in those days. How ya doing, Brian?" he said, extending one beefy hand.

Brian shook it. "Nice to see you again, sir."

"Sir!" Mr. Simonelli chuckled. "You crack me up, kid! Hank, you better get over to the Dunhill site. Make sure you tell them——"

"——that the walnut cabinets won't be in till Monday." Hank chuckled. "I heard you the first three times." He walked off to a battered red van with the words SIMONELLI BROS. CONSTRUCTION stenciled on the side.

"Is Liz here?" Brian said. "I need to talk to her."

"Inside." Mr. Simonelli jerked a thumb to the door. "Third door on the left. J.P. and Joey are there too."

"Thanks!" Brian headed for the door.

"Vince, have you seen my keys?" Hank yelled.

"What, did you lose them again?"

Brian walked through the door. He was in the second wing of the school, where most of the construction was taking place. Tables, chairs and desks were piled against the lockers. Part of the plan for the summer was to renovate the rooms here and make them usable.

BANG! Brian's heart jumped in his chest as the hallway shook. *BANG! BANG! BANG!*

"Uh oh." Brian spun around to see Mr. Simonelli grinning at him. "Looks like they got started."

Allie dug around in her purse. "Darn it!"

"What's wrong?" her mom said as the car pulled to a stop at a red light.

"I forgot my lipstick."

"You sure? That purse is so big—I don't know *what* you keep in there..."

Allie hesitated. "Just this and that," she said evasively. "Do you have any lipstick?"

"In my purse." Her mom gave her a worried glance. "Allie, are you feeling okay?"

"Super-duper," Allie said, retrieving the lipstick and pulling down the visor mirror. If she was quick, she could finish before the light turned green.

The truth was, she didn't feel too good. She felt weak and tired. Plus her skin was dry and itchy, and she had broken a nail that morning.

But that didn't matter. She looked *good.* She had finally lost the last of her baby fat and her cheekbones were real well defined. It made her look older. Less cute and more glamorous. *At least I got my looks.*

The car started moving. "Did you eat breakfast?" her mom said.

Allie shrugged. "I wasn't hungry." It was true. She hadn't felt hungry in a long time.

"Honey, you got to eat." The car turned left onto Sojourner road.

Allie's throat tightened a bit. *Not this again.*

"And you got to sleep," her mom added. "Were you up late again last night?"

"You shouldn't have gone down this way," Allie snapped. "There's still construction."

As her mom swore and made a U-turn, Allie looked down at her outfit: a cream-colored off-the-shoulder peasant blouse, loose, tan pedal pushers, and leather sandals. She especially loved the blouse: it was both old-fashioned and bold, especially with the way her blonde hair hung loose around her bare shoulders. Brian was old fashioned. Maybe he'd like that.

"What's the occasion, anyway?" her mom said irritably. "Why the nice clothes, the lipstick?"

Allie shrugged. "Just wanted to look good."

"It looks a little *too* good for construction work."

"Construction work?" Allie blinked. "Oh. Right. I forgot." She had gotten so involved in this outfit that she had almost forgotten about *why* she was going to JP2 High. She just loved looking good. It made her *feel* good.

"You *forgot?*" Her mom shook her head. "You've been acting real strange lately. It's worrying me."

"What's 'strange' about caring about your looks?" Allie retorted. She glanced scornfully at her mom's rumpled brown pantsuit. "You should try it sometime."

Her mom pursed her lips, and drove a little faster. Allie turned away, feeling grimly satisfied. *That shut her up.*

"Ginger Josslyn called for you again yesterday, after dinner while you were in the shower," her mom said. "Just in case you care."

"I don't." Allie tossed her head. "But thanks for telling me."

They pulled into the JP2 High parking lot. "Hmm," her mom said. "More crowded than usual." The little parking lot was full of minivans and station wagons. Allie grinned. She liked crowds.

As she walked through the front doors, the first thing she noticed was the noise: voices talking, yelling, laughing. Footsteps echoing up and down the halls.

The second thing she noticed was a little boy, because he ran into her.

"OOF!" She staggered a little. The little boy stared up at her with wide blue eyes. He looked about five.

"Hi there!" Allie knelt down with a smile. "What's your name?"

To her dismay, his face screwed up and he starting screaming wildly, clutching his head.

"Michael!!" A short, heavyset woman walked up and scooped up the toddler. She had grey-streaked brown hair, tied up in a bun.

"I'm so sorry!" Allie said hastily. "He just ran into me when I walked in…"

"That's okay." The woman bounced the toddler in her arms, looking Allie up and down. "Can I help you?" she said in a stiff, cold voice.

"What?"

"Are you lost? Looking for directions?"

Allie giggled. "Um, no. I'm here for the work camp. I go to school here."

"You *do?*" The woman's eyes narrowed. "Really?"

"Hi, Allie!" A tall blonde woman in a long skirt walked up to them, also carrying a toddler—only hers had brown skin and curly black hair.

"Hi, Mrs. Burke!" Allie said, grateful for the distraction. "Hey, Gus!"

The little black boy gurgled happily and reached for her. "He remembers you!" Mrs. Burke laughed. "Allie, this is my friend Rosemary Summers. I think you've already met her two daughters."

Mrs. Summers gave her a curt nod. "Nice to meet you, Allison. Sue, I was thinking about your proposal for Project Rachel. I don't know if it will...quiet, Michael!" The toddler had started wailing.

"So how are you doing, honey?" Mrs. Burke said to Allie, ignoring her friend. "You lost some weight."

Allie looked up at Mrs. Burke's concerned face. "I'm fine," she said lightly.

"Really?"

"Yeah, really," Allie said, smiling back at her.

Sure you are, a cold voice said inside her. *Liar.*

"Okay," Mrs. Burke gave her a strange, sad smile. "Well, you should head for the gym. That's where the other girls are."

"What about the boys?"

"Just go to the gym, Celia's there, she'll explain everything."

"Thanks!" Allie said, and walked away quickly, dodging a few children on the way. She didn't like the look Mrs. Summers was giving her.

Once she got to the gym, she was immediately greeted by Celia, dressed in jeans and a paint-spattered t-shirt that said GET HOLY OR DIE TRYING. "Hi, Allie!" She waved a paint brush at her. "Are you ready to help get this show on the..."

Celia trailed off. She looked Allie up and down, frowning. "Are those your *painting* clothes?"

"Um, no." Allie rolled her eyes and laughed. "I'm such an idiot; I didn't realize we were painting *today*."

"Didn't you get my email?" Celia's frown deepened. "I listed all the job assignments and told you what to bring..."

"Really?" Allie said, abashed.

"And I wanted you to bring your MP3 player too...I was thinking it would be great to have some music..."

"Sorry," Allie said sincerely. "Really, Seal, I'm sorry. I just don't know where my head was..." She glanced around and suddenly noticed something. All of the people working in the gym were girls.

She frowned. "Where are all the boys?"

"In the second wing with George and Mr. Simonelli." Celia gave her a funny look. "Why?"

Allie shrugged. "Maybe I should work there instead. I mean, with my clothes..."

"I'm pretty sure there's nothing non-messy to do over there," Celia shook her head. "They're knocking down walls and moving furniture. Look, I have a few smocks I brought from the house. Maybe that will save your clothes. Unless you want to help me out with organizing some of the other people..."

"Nah, I'll paint," Allie said, glancing around. She wasn't in the mood to meet new people just now anyhow. What she needed to do was talk to Brian. *Maybe at lunch. Yeah. I can catch him alone then.*

Five minutes later Allie was facing the gym wall, roller in hand, wearing a dirty grey smock and holding a paint tray.

She glanced around at the other girls. Only one of them had a smock like her: a pretty girl with long curly black hair and a sour expression, as if she were too cool to be there. Allie recognized her: Miranda, Celia's younger sister.

Miranda threw down her roller in disgust. "Celia! Come *here!*"

Celia walked over, looking uncharacteristically annoyed. "What now?"

"I can't paint here! The wall's all flakey!"

Celia examined the wall. "That's because you started in the wrong place. Josephine and Mary Rose haven't cleaned this part yet. I told you to start over there, remember?"

"Don't blame *me* for this! You didn't plan it right! You're messing the whole thing up, like you always do!"

Ouch. Allie winced, half expecting Celia to crumple up or burst into tears or something.

But Celia didn't bat an eye. "At least I *try* to help out instead of just complaining all the time," she replied.

"And another thing," Miranda said. "I got paint all over my nails!"

"Oooh," Celia said dryly.

"Do you know how much money I spent—"

"Don't you mean *Dad* spent?"

"Actually, I paid for these nails myself!" Miranda replied hotly. "And now they're ruined!"

"Well you should have thought about that before you volunteered to paint," Celia said impatiently. "It's too late now. This is oil-based. You're going to have to use paint thinner."

"Paint thinner?!"

Celia glanced at Allie and rolled her eyes. Then she walked away, shaking her head. Allie chuckled. It was nice to see Celia stand up for herself for a change.

She heard an answering chuckle, and noticed Jacinta Summers grinning at her. She and her sister Mary were painting a few feet away, both in old t-shirts and long skirts, their hair up in bandannas. Jacinta nodded to Miranda. She looked down at her nails, pulled a horror-struck look, and pretended to faint.

Allie giggled. Jacinta giggled too—and then stopped. She looked nervous, and turned away. Allie's smile faded. *She's still treating me like I got two heads.*

"What's so funny?"

A girl walked up to her: a slight, small Hispanic girl, wearing an overlarge shirt and baggy pants. "You laughed," she repeated. "What's so funny?"

"Oh...nothing," Allie said, blinking. "Um...I'm Allie."

The girl pushed back her stringy black hair to reveal a thin brown face with large brown eyes. "I'm Isabel," she said. "Isabel Reyes. I'm an artist."

"Oh...really?"

"That's right." The girl nodded rapidly, suddenly excited. "Do you know any other artists? Painters?"

"Um...I don't think so. Why?"

"Well...I was just thinking. About this room." The girl turned slowly around, her eyes bright with excitement. "We could do so much more than just *paint* it! We could put portraits of the twelve apostles, six on each side—" She spun around so quick that her hair flared out and pointed to the front wall. "And over *there*, a big portrait of John Paul the Great, our patron!" She turned back to Allie. "What do you think?" she said eagerly.

"Um..." Allie hesitated. "Have you asked Celia about this?"

The girl's face fell. "Yeah," she said. "She said she thinks it's too much for one artist to do. That's why I need to find other artists. You know any?"

"Still no." Allie grinned. "But I'll keep my eyes open, okay?"

"Thanks!" Isabel turned to go. Then she stopped, and turned back to Allie, looking thoughtful. "I think I like you, Allie."

"You do? Thanks!" Allie said warmly.

"But I wouldn't have worn that blouse. It's not modest."

She said it in such a bland, matter-of-fact way that Allie was speechless.

"See you later." Isabel walked away.

Allie turned back to the wall, feeling disgruntled. *Oh-kaay. Weirdo.*

Die, wall!" J.P. screamed, slamming the sledgehammer into the classroom wall. "Die!"

"J.P.!" Brian said, aghast. "What are you doing?"

Mr. Simonelli chuckled. "He's supposed to do that. Well, not the 'die, wall, die' part, but you get the idea." He pointed at the back wall, half of which was already gone, exposing some faded gray studs and wiring. A short, stocky boy was prying away more drywall with a crowbar.

"Hey Joey!" Mr. Simonelli said. "I got you some help!"

Joey Simonelli looked up. He had the same broad friendly face as his father and the same dirty blond hair as his older sister. "Hey Brian!" he said, grinning. "So you got roped into this too?"

Brian grinned and walked over to take a closer look at the wall. There was insulation behind the studs; not the normal pink kind, but some sort of faded gray material that looked like shredded paper.

"Mr. Simonelli?" Brian pointed to the strange insulation. "What's that?"

Mr. Simonelli laughed grimly. "Newspaper." He pulled some out and handed it to Brian. "See? That's how some builders used to insulate when they wanted to cut costs. It's really dangerous, and totally illegal these days."

Brian glanced down at the faded newsprint. One of the pieces had a date on it: *Aug. 7, 1958.* "Wow," he said. "This is incredible."

Mr. Simonelli scowled. "What's incredible is that this place hasn't burned down yet. One spark, and this whole room would go up in flames in a few minutes. We gotta check all the wiring; that's why I asked Hank to come."

"Hey!" a familiar voice said, accompanied by a familiar punch in the arm. He turned to see a grinning Liz in paint-stained overalls, her hair flecked with dust and bits of debris. "About time, jerk! We've been here since six!"

"Yeah, we have," Mr. Simonelli said gruffly. "And you've been busy *not* working the whole time." He ruffled Liz's hair, sending out clouds of dust. "Hey kiddo, you seen Hank's keys?"

"What, did he lose them *again?* He had them last night!"

"Yeah, well, why don't you go ask around? Somebody must have seen them. Take Brian with you. He needs to get some sledgehammers from Hank; and give him this." He handed Brian the ancient piece of newspaper. "He'll get a kick out of it."

Allie frowned down at her paint tray. Celia hadn't put much paint in it, and she was already almost out.

"Hey," she said, carrying her pan over to Jacinta. "Can I borrow some paint?"

51

Jacinta gave her a nervous look, but nodded. "Sure."

Allie tried to pick up Jacinta's tray, but it was heavier than she expected; her arms trembled a little.

"Here, let me help," Jacinta knelt down beside her, and together they re-filled Allie's tray and carried it back to her station.

"Thanks." Allie wiped her brow. She felt a little dizzy. *Maybe it's these paint fumes.*

"No problem. Uh, Allie…" Jacinta hesitated. "I heard about your friend. I'm so sorry."

"No no, it's fine!" Allie said quickly. "No big deal. Hey, I don't think I've met your sister yet—"

"You *haven't?*" Jacinta spun around and yelled, "Mary! Come meet Allie!"

Mary walked over, looking at Allie curiously.

"Hi!" Allie said as Mary made a cautious wave in her direction. "So, what do you guys think of this place?"

Mary opened her mouth, but Jacinta beat her to it. "We love it!" she said brightly.

"Mom's a little worried, though," Mary said, her brow creasing slightly.

"Mom *always* worries." Jacinta waved a hand dismissively. "But *I'm* thrilled. Maybe Mom will keep us here!"

"*Keep* you here?" Allie said.

"Yeah. We've been to a lot of different schools. We were at Vernon Academy last year—"

"Really?" Allie said. "You mean that really preppy—" she caught herself. "—er, that school in the city?"

"That's the one! And it was *super* preppy!"

Mary frowned. "I liked Vernon."

"—And before that we were at this experimental school, the Harper School for Girls—"

"That place was weird," Mary interjected.

"And before that we were home schooled…although Mom didn't like that too much." Jacinta looked around. "But I like this one best of all."

"Why?" Allie laughed. "It's so small!"

"That's *why* I like it!" Jacinta said. "It's so cozy! Only seven students...you guys must be such good friends! Nobody left out; no cliques..." She twirled around, and her pink, paint-flecked skirt flared out prettily. "It feels like home!"

Allie smiled. *Celia's gonna love this girl.* But then she thought about James. And herself. "Yeah, well, not everyone fits in," she said quietly. "There's a few weirdoes here."

"I know!" Jacinta waved at herself. "Like me! So who are the other weirdoes? I want to know who my best friends will be!"

Allie giggled. "Well, there's James, but he's not here...and Brian, I guess."

"Ooh!" Jacinta turned around to Mary. "Brian! Didn't you meet him before?"

"Yes." Mary gave Allie a sharp look. "But I didn't think he was weird."

"Oh...well..." *Oops.* "He's okay, I guess," Allie said hastily. Actually, I was hoping to talk to him...if you see him, can you let him know?"

"Mary likes Brian," Jacinta said brightly.

"I do not!" Mary said, looking nervous. "And keep your voice down! If Mom hears—"

Allie gave Mary a curious look. "What's the big deal?"

"Well," Mary hesitated. "Mom's very concerned about our education. She wants to make sure we get the very best Catholic education. And that we make friends with kids who are really strong Catholics."

"Oh," Allie said. *She's one of* those *moms.*

"Mary!" Almost as if she had heard her name, Mrs. Summers walked up to them, holding a set of keys. "We found these in the kitchen," she said briskly. "Could you give them to that contractor, Mr. Monelli? Maybe they belong to him or one of his men."

"Um...sure, mom," Mary said, taking the keys and walking away. Mrs. Summers lingered a moment longer, glancing at Allie.

"Jacinta," she said shortly. "Stop fooling and get back to work."

Allie scowled as Mrs. Summers walked away. *I guess I don't make the cut.*

So," Brian said to Liz as they walked down the hall. "Are you working with your dad now or something?"

"Yep." Liz looked pleased with herself. "Didn't I tell you? I'm officially part of his crew."

"Really?"

"Yep. Dad said he finally trusts me to not accidentally kill myself." She beamed. "This is, like, the best summer ever. Last night I was in the girls' bathroom cutting two-by-fours. It rocked!"

Brian grinned, wondering if any girl except Liz got excited about cutting two-by-fours. But that's why he was friends with her: because she didn't act like a girl. *Speaking of which...* "I need your advice on something."

"Shoot."

"Well..." he hesitated. "There's this...girl that I want to avoid today."

"Who? One of the newbies?"

"Yes."

"Was it Miranda? Because if she's giving you a hard time, I swear I'll kick her—hey! You!"

Liz sprinted away. Further down the hall, a girl in a blue bandanna was about to enter the girls' bathroom. A girl with long brown hair... *Oh, crap.*

"Don't go in there!" Liz ran up and slapped Mary Summer's hand off from the doorknob.

"Why not?" Mary snapped.

"It's under construction! Don't you see the sign?"

"What sign?"

Liz glanced at the door. "What the heck," she muttered. "I put an out-of-order sign there last night. Anyway," she turned back to Mary. "You got to use the boys' bathroom. It's on the other side of the school."

"The *boys'* bathroom?"

"Just knock before you go in!" Liz pointed firmly. "Now go. Get out of here."

Mary glared at Liz. "Okay, *okay.* I'm going...oh! Hello, Brian!"

"Hello," he croaked.

"Can you do me a favor?" Mary said, turning away from Liz as though she wasn't there. She held out a set of keys. "I need to give these to Mr. Monelli. Do you know who he—hey!"

Liz snatched the keys from her hand. "I'll take those," she snapped. "And it's *Si*monelli."

Mary scowled. "How do you know?"

"Because I know my own last name. Now go on, newbie." She made shooing motions with her hands. "Beat it."

Mary looked affronted. "Fine. Oh, Brian, by the way—Allie Weaver wanted to talk to you."

"To *me?*" Brian said blankly. "Why?"

"She didn't say," Mary replied. Giving Liz a nasty look, she walked away.

"Man!" Liz turned back to Brian with a grin. "These newbies are everywhere! We got to keep them in line, or they'll take over the—"

"How could you be so rude?" Brian hissed.

Liz's grin faded. "Rude?"

"Don't you see how offended she was? Why couldn't you just let her use the bathroom?"

"My tools are in there! I don't want her messing with them! Anyway, the power's off in this wing."

"Why didn't you just *tell* her that?"

"What do you care? You don't even know—" Comprehension dawned on Liz's face. She looked at Mary's retreating figure, then back to Brian. "Is *that* the girl you're scared of?"

"I'm not scared of her!" he retorted. "I'm just..." he gaped at her for a moment, then threw up his hands. "And then *you* go and offend her, and I'm with *you*, and she's gonna think—"

"Burke." Liz put a hand on his shoulder. "Take a breath."

He glared at the floor, his face hot.

"Feel better?"

"Yes," he muttered. "Sorry."

"No problem. You still want my advice?"

He nodded mutely.

"Okay. Forget about that girl. You and her—it would never work out."

Brian looked up. He opened his mouth, intending to tell Liz that the idea was silly...irrelevant...that he didn't intend to date anyone in high school...that even if he *did*, his parents would never let him...but all that came out of his mouth was: "Why?"

"Because you're...well, you're beneath her."

"What?" Brian said in a shocked voice. "Why? Because I'm black?"

Liz rolled her eyes. "Don't be stupid, Burke. You're no good at it."

"Huh?"

"You being black has nothing to do with it. *That* chick—" she pointed back down the hallway. "—is an Eight. And *you*—" she poked his chest. "—are a *Three.*"

Brian stared at her, baffled—but suspecting that he was being insulted. "A Three?" he repeated.

"Yep. A Three. Out of ten."

Brian scowled. "Great. Thank you so much."

"Don't get all huffy! I'm just telling you the truth!"

"Hmmph. So I'm a three. What number are *you?*"

"I don't *have* a number, Burke." Liz grinned. "I'm a wild card. A blank slate. I can be anything I want."

"Huh?"

"Here, I'll show you. Let's go see Hank."

6

HERO

"Hey. Mind if I paint here?"

Allie looked up. Miranda Costain stood in front of her. Without waiting for a reply the younger girl plopped down her tray and started painting.

It was striking how different Miranda was from her sister. Celia was nice-looking in a farm girl sort of way...but Miranda was just *gorgeous*. Pale, almost translucent skin, steely blue eyes, arched, thin eyebrows...it was hard to believe she was only fourteen.

"So," Miranda said. "Are you still friends with *Celia?*" She said it like being Celia's friend was an unforgivable sin.

"Of course I am." Allie frowned. "Why?"

Miranda smirked. She lifted the paint roller lazily, took a few more strokes, and then glanced at Allie again. "By the way, nice outfit."

Allie glanced down at her smock. "Very funny."

"No, I saw you before Celia put you in that smock. Where did you get that blouse? Maybe I can borrow it." She sighed. "But what am I thinking? I can't wear it. It would break one of Dad's *rules*."

"Rules? Your dad's got rules on what you wear?"

"My dad's got rules for *everything*. Fashion, dating, friends..."

Allie frowned. "That doesn't sound like Mr. Cos—I mean, your dad."

"Try living with him!"

"Celia doesn't seem to mind."

"That's because Celia *likes* the rules," Miranda snapped. "She *loves* being the good little girl. That's why she's never asked George out, even though she's in love with him." She gave Allie a shrewd look. "But you already knew that."

"I knew she *liked* George—"

"She *loves* George," Miranda said. "When you were dating him, she was *so* messed up. That's why I was surprised you two were still friends."

"Well, we are," Allie said defensively. "We got beyond that."

"Anyway, how do you get away with dressing like that?" Miranda said. "Doesn't your dad make a stink?"

"I don't see my dad that often," Allie muttered. "My parents are divorced, remember?"

"Hmmph. You're lucky."

"No," Allie said coldly. "I'm not."

Miranda seemed to know she had crossed a line. "Sorry," she said. "All I meant was...you've *lived* a little, you know? Not like Celia." She lifted the edges of her smock and made a mock curtsy. "Everyone's *so* good, and *so* holy, and *so* boring here! But you and me: we're different. They'll never understand us."

"Hmmph." Allie turned back to the wall. *She's right, you know,* a cold voice inside her said. *None of them understand. Did you really think they would? You're still alone.*

She was getting dizzy again. *It must be the fumes again...stupid fumes.*

Hank's such a dope." Liz twirled her dad's keys on one finger. "He lost his keys last week too." She stopped right before the doorway and turned around. "Listen. Whatever I do out there, just roll with it, okay?"

"Okay. Wait, what?"

But Liz had already stepped outside. Bemused, Brian followed.

They saw Hank digging through the back of the red van, looking annoyed. He looked up as they approached. "Hey! Did you find my keys?"

"Hi Hank!" Liz sang out. "Got 'em right here!" Skipping forward, she took his hand and placed the keys in it then giggled—giggled! "You left them inside, you goofball!"

Brian stopped short, his mouth agape in astonishment.

Hank, on the other hand, looked simply embarrassed. "Er...thanks, Liz," he said. "I thought I left them at home..."

"Ooh, really?" Liz cocked her head to one side and smiled idiotically. "Where do you live?"

"Um...hey, Brian!" Hank said, turning to him. "You need something?"

"Er...yes," Brian said, still staring at Liz. "A couple sledgehammers. And Mr. Simonelli wanted you to see this." He handed him the newspaper. "It was in the walls."

"In the *walls?*" Hank looked at the ancient newspaper clipping with alarm. "Wow...that's messed up. Hang on a sec." He disappeared into the van.

Brian turned to Liz. "What are you doing?" he hissed.

"Brian," Liz said through her teeth, still smiling that vacant smile, "Why don't you just *roll with it?*"

Hank emerged from the back of the van, holding two short sledge hammers in one beefy hand. "Here you go."

"Ooh, Hank!" Liz burbled. "You're so strong!"

"Um...right," Hank said, handing Brian the hammers. "You know what? Bring this in too." He gave Brian a red fire extinguisher. "Just in case."

"All right!" Liz chirped. "See ya, Hank!"

As the red van rumbled out of the parking lot, Liz pumped the air. "Ha! Told ya! It worked!"

"*What* worked?" Brian said, exasperated. "Liz, will you *please* explain what's—"

"All right, all right. Stop hyperventilating, Burke." With a grin, Liz took one of the hammers from Brian. "I've been conducting this...experiment. I wanted to see if I could get Hank to believe I had a crush on him."

Brian stared at her.

"So I've been acting like a ditz around him for almost a month now. At first I acted all shy and blushing. Then I turned on the charm—acting all bubbly and always saying how *strong* he was, and how much I *loved* tattoos. The poor guy was so embarrassed!"

Brian kept staring at her.

"And I wasn't sure it would work, y'know? Hank's been working for my dad forever. He's known me since I was *ten*. Could I really fool him? Well, I did! Ha!" Liz pumped the air again. "Isn't that—"

"Liz," Brian said faintly. "That is sick!"

"No," Liz said loftily. "It's *acting*."

"But *why?*"

"It was a challenge!" Liz said, grinning. "I wanted to see if I could do it!"

Brian shook his head. "You...you're *unbelievable*, Liz!"

"Thank you!" Liz bowed with a flourish. "Thank you!"

Hey, Allie? Miranda?" Celia was at one of the double doors of the gym, two paint cans in her hands. "Can you give me a hand?"

"Sorry, Celia!" Miranda smirked. "Too busy painting!"

Allie gave her a look of distaste, and ran to hold the door open for Celia.

"Thanks," Celia propped open the door with one of the paint cans. "How's the painting going?" She handed Allie the other can.

"Okay, I—ahgh!" Allie let out a gasp and nearly dropped the can.

"Allie! Are you okay?"

"Sure." Allie tried to smile. "No problem."

She turned, took a few steps...and suddenly her knees buckled and she fell to the floor. The lid of the can popped off, spilling white paint all over her.

"No, you're not okay!" Celia said. "What's wrong? You don't look so good!"

"Gee, thanks, Seal," Allie muttered. She stood up with an effort as the other girls in the group came running across the gym towards her. Her head was spinning, and her empty stomach was heaving. Then she looked down and saw the paint splattered all over her. Oil-based paint.

She cursed, causing scandalized gasps from several of the girls. "Um, Allie," Celia said. "Maybe you better calm down." She glanced nervously at the moms who were coming towards them.

"Fine, I'll go to the bathroom," Allie said under her breath as she grabbed her purse from the pile by the door. "I know I don't *make the cut*."

"Celia! What happened?" Mrs. Summers was asking.

"Just a spilled paint can," Celia said in a loud, cheerful voice. "I'll clean it up right away..." She gave Allie a meaningful look, and Allie slipped through the doors into the hallway.

She pulled the smock off and more paint splattered on her hair and bare shoulders. It was as she feared—her clothes were ruined. She must look ridiculous.

With another curse, she threw her purse. It slid into a corner and burst open. The purple binder fell out, scattering her notes, papers and drawings on the floor.

Great! She looked around anxiously. *If anyone sees this...*She had brought the binder into school to take notes, after talking to Brian and J.P....

But her hands were covered in paint. She needed to wash them before she could pick up her papers. She staggered off to the girls' bathroom.

It took her a while to get there; her head was still spinning. She opened the bathroom door and flipped the light switch.

A cacophony of noise filled the air: whirring, grinding sounds. At the same time, a blinding, blazing light shone in her eyes.

Allie staggered back and almost fell. Catching herself, she found the light switch and turned it off.

Instantly the lights and sound ceased. She stood in the hallway, breathing hard, too astonished to move.

Then she heard it. A muffled shouting, footsteps, and then a voice yelling. "Fire! Fire! Everybody get out!"

Dude, I am *still* so pumped about this!" Liz said as she and Brian re-entered the school. "I can't believe I pulled it off!"

"Yes," Brian said stiffly. "Congratulations. Good for you."

"Oh, stop being so huffy, Burke. I'm just fooling around!"

"You're manipulating people!"

"It's just a prank, Burke! A prank! You never gave me a hard time about pranks before!"

"This is different."

"Why? I'm not *hurting* Hank! You're just mad because I proved that I can be any number I want."

"No," he retorted. "You can't just change how you look by *acting*."

"Sure you can! And besides, it's not just about looks. It's about attitude, and the right clothes...I could get *you* to like me if I wanted. I guarantee it."

"Yes, well, don't, okay?" Brian muttered. He didn't really believe Liz, but he had to admit she excelled at...*acting*. He didn't like it, but she was good at it. "You know," he said irritably. "This is exactly what bothers me about girls—"

"Hang on a sec." Liz frowned. "You smell that?"

Brian sniffed. "Yes. It smells like..."

Liz's eyes widened. "What the..."

"Fire!" George and J.P. burst out of a doorway, looking terrified. "There's a fire!" George shouted. "Everybody out of the building! Go tell the others!"

As J.P. and Liz sprinted down the hallway, George pounded up to Brian and grabbed his arm. "Come on, let's go! One of the power lines started sparking, and I think...the newspaper in the walls..."

Brian's heart caught in his chest. He looked down the hallway and saw smoke curling out of the classroom doorway. Then he looked down at the fire extinguisher in his hands.

Instantly everything became clear in his mind. He tore free from George's grasp and rushed into the classroom.

He blinked, coughed and staggered back. The room was full of smoke—he couldn't see a thing. *Come on, think.* He took a deep breath, dropped to his hands and knees, and started crawling inside, dragging the extinguisher.

"Brian!" George's hand grasped his ankle. "You idiot! Get out of—ow!"

Brian kicked savagely, and George's hand was gone. *There's no time.*

There was a red flicker on the other end of the room. He crawled rapidly towards it, trying not to think about what Mr. Simonelli had said: *One spark, and this whole room would go up in flames in a few minutes.*

He reached the wall. A section of it was aflame, belching out clouds of black smoke, and it was growing larger.

He pulled the pin on the extinguisher, stood up, pointed the rubber hose at the flames, and pressed the trigger.

Whoosh. Instantly the wall was covered in white foam, drowning the red flicker. A clean, sharp chemical smell filled the room. Smoke swirled around him and he coughed, but kept spraying methodically until the last of the flames vanished. Then he turned and made his way back out into the hallway.

"Brian!" Mr. Simonelli ran up to him, followed by George. "Are you nuts?" Mr. Simonelli said. "That fire—"

"It's out." Brian said, coughing. "The fire's out."

Allie ran down the hallway, surrounded by other teenagers, parents, and little kids. She passed through the front doors. A crowd had already gathered outside.

She trudged a little away from the crowd, her heart pounding. She felt a little better after the fresh air, and she was already thinking hard about what had just happened. She had flipped the switch, and then...*did I do this? Will they find out?*

Find out...the binder! Rufus! Her stomach clenched in panic. Nikki's binder was still inside. She glanced at the school, and the smoke rising from one of the windows. *I can't lose it!*

She turned and ran around the side of the school. *I can get in through the gym door.*

She entered the deserted gym, sprinted across it and into the hallway. It smelled of smoke, but otherwise everything was quiet.

And there was her binder and papers near the girls' bathroom. Breathing a sigh of relief, she knelt down and started gathering them up.

"Hey!" Footsteps rang down the hallway, and Liz ran up to her. "What are you doing here?"

"Nothing," Allie muttered, shoving the papers into the binder. "Just grabbing my stuff."

Liz glanced down at scattered papers, full of diagrams, notes and drawings. "You need help?"

"No!" Allie shoved the last of the papers into the binder and snapped it closed. "Just leave me alone. What are *you* doing here, anyway?"

"Following you." Liz frowned. "I saw you sneaking off."

"Yeah, well, let's both sneak out of here before the fire—"

"The fire's out."

"What?"

"Burke put it out. I heard my dad tell everybody right before I followed you. Brian ran into the classroom and put it out with a fire extinguisher," Liz said proudly, as if *she* had been the one to do it. "Never would have expected it from Burke, huh?"

"Um…right," Allie muttered, looking down on her white paint-splattered self and remembering her plan to "charm" Brian. *Yeah, right.* She laughed bitterly. *What a stupid idea.*

"So what happened to you?" Liz snickered. "You get pooped on by a vulture?"

"I got into an accident, okay?" Allie muttered. "And then I went to the bathroom to clean up, and then something weird happened."

Liz's eyes narrowed. "Like what?"

"I don't know!" Allie groaned. "I flipped the light switch, and then there was this *really* bright light, from the floor!"

Liz suddenly looked shocked. "From the floor?" she repeated. "Like a floodlight?"

"I don't know!" Allie said again. "There was something else, too...some kind of whirring sound."

"Like a saw?"

"Maybe. And then there was a hum, and a pop. Why?"

Liz looked troubled. "Come on," she said. "Let's go."

"Go? Where?"

"To the bathroom." Liz scooped up a flashlight from an abandoned toolbox. "To see what happened."

They walked down the hallway together. "By the way," Liz said. "I heard you wanted to talk to Burke. Why?"

"I just wanted to ask him something."

"Like what? I can pass it on to him—"

"No!" Allie shook her head wearily. "I just wanted to find out about the poltergeist, okay?"

"The *poltergeist?*" Liz looked startled. "Why?"

"It's not important," Allie mumbled. "And it doesn't matter now anyway," she added quickly, trying to change the subject. "I mean, Brian hates my guts, doesn't he? I don't know why—I even dressed up nice today so he'd like me..."

Liz looked amused. "Really. Well, if you wanted to charm *Burke,* you did it the wrong way."

"What's the right way?"

Liz rolled her eyes. "Try wearing pink and talking in a real soft voice and acting all snooty...here we go." They arrived at the girls' bathroom. Liz pushed the door open and turned on the flashlight.

Allie peeked over Liz's shoulder. She saw things on the floor: a floodlight, and a large electrical saw. "What are those doing here?"

"We were working here last night," Liz said impatiently. "But how did—"

"Liz!"

They both spun around. There was Mr. Simonelli, his face dark with anger. "Come here." he growled. "Both of you."

Liz looked scared as she followed Allie out of the bathroom. But she spoke as if she weren't. "Dad! Do you know what happened?"

65

"Yeah, I do," Mr. Simonelli said tightly. "What did I tell you to do last night? What did I say was *really important?*"

Liz seemed to shrink under her father's look. "You...you told me to make sure everything was unplugged," she said in a small voice.

Mr. Simonelli took the flashlight from her and shone it into the bathroom. "There are your tools," he said darkly. "All plugged in."

Liz looked shocked. "I *did* check them! I pulled them all out!"

Mr. Simonelli's eyes hardened. "Don't lie to me, Liz."

Liz's face reddened. "I'm *not* lying!" She stamped her foot. "I did! I unplugged *all* that stuff!"

"So what are you doing here?" Mr. Simonelli pointed at the bathroom door. "Trying to cover up what happened? Huh?"

"Excuse me."

A short, thin man with cropped grey hair walked up to them, holding a clipboard. "What's going on here?"

Mr. Simonelli's eyes widened in surprise. "Bickerstaff?" he said gruffly. "What are you doing here?"

"Building inspection," the man said carelessly. "Now, let's see..." He took out a pencil and scribbled something on his clipboard. "So far I got a fire and adolescents near high voltage equipment. Is this always the way you run things?"

"That's not what happened," Mr. Simonelli said quickly. "The kids weren't near anything dangerous. We don't—" He hesitated a second, and his eyes darted to Liz. "We don't know how the fire started. I turned the power off myself last night, and one of my employees, a licensed electrician, checked everything out before we left."

Mr. Bickerstaff scribbled some more. "What's the employee's name?"

"Hank—I mean, Henry Berringer. Like I just said, he's a licensed—"

"I've heard of him," the man said with another tight smile. "Ran into him a few months back. He did shoddy work then, too."

"Hey!" Liz glared at the man. "Don't talk about Hank that way!"

Mr. Bickerstaff looked amused. "And who's this?" He pointed at Liz with his stubby blue pencil.

"My daughter." Mr. Simonelli put an arm on Liz's shoulder. "She helps me out sometimes."

"How old is she?"

"Fifteen."

"So you had a child dealing with live, high-voltage equipment?"

"I'm not a child!" Liz snapped. "I'll be sixteen in a few months!"

"Quiet, Liz," Mr. Simonelli muttered.

Bickerstaff smirked a little as he tore a sheet off the clipboard. "This is a citation for violation of the county building codes. And I'll need to see the leaseholder, too...that would be Costain, correct?"

"Someone looking for me?" Mr. Costain walked up the hallway, a briefcase in one hand and a newspaper in another. "What's going on?"

"Mr. Costain," Mr. Bickerstaff said sternly. "It seems that there was an electrical fire on the premises."

"Yes, I just heard," Mr. Costain said. He glanced at Liz and Allie, and then at Mr. Simonelli. "Tammy told me we had a negative head count. What are these two doing inside?"

Mr. Simonelli scowled. "They came back in on their own. I've already called the fire department. They should be here any second."

"Mr. *Costain*," Bickerstaff cut in. "I'm obligated to tell you that I'll have to write a citation about this incident."

"Ah, Mr. Bickerstaff," Mr. Costain said mildly. "I'm a bit surprised to see you here again. We're not due for another inspection until November."

"This is a special inspection," Mr. Bickerstaff said. "in lieu of the construction permit you applied for—"

"And were approved for," Mr. Costain said gravely. "Has there been a change in our approval status? If so, I wasn't informed."

"That's not my concern," Mr. Bickerstaff said with a tight smile. "You got bigger things to worry about. I've only been inside this building for half an hour, and I've already seen numerous—"

"Excuse me," Mr. Costain arched an eyebrow. "Did you say *half an hour?*"

Mr. Bickerstaff's smile vanished. "Er...yes. But in that time I've noticed—"

"How did you get in?" Mr. Costain asked. "Did you announce yourself to anyone?"

Mr. Bickerstaff was taken aback. "Um...well, I'm sure I told *somebody*..."

"You didn't tell *me*." Mr. Simonelli growled. "I had no idea you were coming. Kind of rude, actually."

"That's all right," Mr. Costain smiled pleasantly. "But let's clear this up right away, shall we? We'll step outside and you tell me which of the adults here took your name and ID when you arrived."

Mr. Bickerstaff's face turned a little red. "Costain," he said angrily. "I don't think that's really necessary."

"Oh, but it is," Mr. Costain said gravely. "You see, as the principal here I'm obligated to keep track of all adults who come onto the premises. No adults are allowed to enter without visiting the school office. After all, there are children present. So, if you'll just step outside..."

Mr. Bickerstaff stared at Mr. Costain, looking dumbfounded. "Actually..." he said. "I just realized...another appointment. I better go. But I'll be back next week," he added, scowling. "To follow up on these violations."

"I'll be out of town most of next week," Mr. Costain said genially. "I'll be back Friday, though. Can you come by then?"

Mr. Bickerstaff snorted. "Fine. Sorry to intrude on your busy schedule."

"Don't worry about it." Mr. Costain smiled brightly. "We'll see you next Friday, then. Oh, and by the way..." He took the paper from Mr. Simonelli and handed it back to Mr. Bickerstaff. "Do you still want to issue us this citation?"

Mr. Bickerstaff's face turned purple. Without a word he snatched the paper and walked away stiffly. Liz glared at his retreating figure.

Mr. Simonelli turned to Mr. Costain, looking relieved. "Wow, Dan! Thank God you showed up when you did! I thought we were—"

"Later, Vince." Mr. Costain frowned. "I need to have a word with Miss Weaver here."

Allie looked up. "Me?"

"Yes, Allie. Come with me, please."

He led her up the hall into the school office without saying a word. After she walked in, he closed the door and looked at her a little sadly.

"Mr. Costain," she blurted out. "Am I in trouble?"

"No," Mr. Costain said gently. He unfolded the newspaper and gave it to her. "I have a few friends at the *Times-Herald*," he said, "And one of them tipped me off. This is tomorrow's paper. I think you have a right to see it before anyone else."

Allie's eyes widened as she stared at the front page headline:

THE NIGHTMARE IS OVER
Police ID Brandon Brock as Sparrow Hills Shooter

7

BLACK HOLE

She gasped as if she had just come out of deep water. Someone was shaking her. "Allie? Allie! Wake up!"

Blearily, she sat up and looked around. She was lying on the living room couch. It was dark. Her mother's face leaned over her, her face pale and anxious.

She rubbed her eyes. "What time is it?"

"It's late." Her mom sat down, her brow knitted with concern. "I came home," she said. "And I heard you. You were—"

"What?" Allie said, suddenly awake. She felt both embarrassed and angry, as if someone had walked in on her undressing. "What was I doing?"

"You were moaning. Crying. It reminded me of when...when you were little. Then you started tossing around, and...kind of whimpering." She looked at Allie, half-apologetically. "Do you remember what you dreamed about?"

Allie hesitated, and then looked away. "No," she lied. "I don't."

Her mom gave her an odd look, but didn't press the issue. "Okay." She stroked Allie's hair gently. "By the way, you got a couple messages. Ginger called for you again—"

Allie snorted.

"And Celia called too to see how you were. She wanted to know whether you're ever coming back to work camp. They're working tomorrow."

"Tomorrow's Saturday," Allie muttered.

"I know. Celia said that they need to make up for lost time. You want to go? You've been cooped in this house all week— you can borrow the car." Her mom smiled encouragingly. "So what do you think?"

"You *want* me to go?" Allie said grumpily. "I thought you wanted to keep me safe or something. What if there's another fire, or—"

"You need to get out of the house, honey. You need to see your friends."

"Don't tell me what I need, okay?" Allie snapped.

Her mom's smile vanished. "Okay," she said steadily. "Sorry. It was just an idea." She stood up. "You need to eat. I'll make something."

"I'm not hungry—"

"You're *eating*, Allie," her mom said sharply. "You're eating three full meals a day if I have to force you. Got it?"

"Okay, *okay*," Allie said irritably.

"Dr. Norris said you've lost ten pounds in the last month. He thinks you're starving yourself. *Why*, Allie?" her mom shook her head in frustration. "Why would you do that to yourself?"

"Don't start, Mom."

"Are you trying to punish yourself? Do you think it's your fault Nikki's—"

"I do *not* want to talk about it!" Allie snarled, jumping to her feet. "And since when did you start caring anyway? Why don't you just leave me alone? You're good at that!"

A vindictive thrill went through her as she saw the shocked look on her mom's face. She pounded up the stairs, down the hallway and into her room. She slammed the door and leaned against it, breathing hard.

Part of her was horrified at what she had done. But she shoved that part down. She *liked* the hot, fierce feeling coursing through her.

She started tidying up her room, more to keep busy than anything else. Grabbing a sheaf of papers off her bureau, she rifled through them. Some old school assignments: trash. A couple job applications her mother had picked up for her: trash.

And then she found the newspaper. She paused, and a chill went through her. She sat down slowly on the bed, and scanned through the article once again:

THE NIGHTMARE IS OVER
Police identify Brandon Brock as Sparrow Hills Shooter

After weeks of fear and anxiety, the saga of the Sparrow Hills shooting appears to be over.

Yesterday evening, representatives of the local police and the FBI announced that they have identified the Sparrow Hills shooter.

The announcement brought an end to this local tragedy that has attracted national attention. On May 29th, a gunman fired several shots into a crowded gymnasium at Sparrow Hills High School during a school dance, killing one and injuring three others. The gunman escaped the scene, and his identity has remained unknown—until now.

Brandon Brock, a 17 year-old junior at Sparrow Hills High School, allegedly shot himself last Wednesday. Responding to an anonymous 911 call of shots being fired, Officers Matthew Henley and Jerry Hichborn discovered Brock's body in a secluded, wooded area a few miles from his home. Brock had been killed by a single gunshot wound to the right temple. A pistol was found in his right hand.

There was nothing to connect Brock to the shooting at first. "It seemed like a pretty cut-and-dry case of suicide," Officer Matthew Henley stated.

But police took a second look after they discovered the pistol used by Brock, a 9mm Smith & Wesson, had the same serial number as one stolen from a local residence earlier in the year.

"If it hadn't been for that, I don't think we'd have looked further," Officer Jerry Hichborn said. "We served a warrant on the Brock residence, and discovered four other weapons, including a .232 Remington hunting rifle. This matched the caliber of the weapon used in the shooting. Finally, we found maps and diagrams on his computer of the school grounds. That seemed odd. But then we found more evidence on his laptop that was even more incriminating." Hichborn declined to elaborate on the 'other evidence.' "Let's just say that this kid was one sick puppy," he said.

Forensic tests confirmed what Hichborn had suspected—that the .232 Remington rifle was the same weapon used in the Sparrow Hills shooting.

Students at Sparrow Hills expressed relief at the announcement. "I'm just so glad it's over," said Courtney Myers, a sophomore who was present the night of the attack. "And I'm not surprised that it turned out to be Brock. He was always scary—him and his buddies. They used to beat kids up for no reason. I saw them do it once."

Others, however, expressed disbelief at the news, "There's no way Brandon shot Tyler," said Sparrow Hills junior Neil Flynt, a friend to both Getz and Brock. "We were like brothers. All three of us."

She crumpled the newspaper and threw it down. She couldn't bear to read any more. She remembered, with a kind of lurch in her stomach, how *she* had felt sorry for Brock when she had heard about his suicide. And when she had first read this story, four days ago, she hadn't believed it. She had agreed with Flynt—it didn't make sense! *Brock* an evil mastermind? One of Tyler's flunkies? She had hardly known him. She had never come close to suspecting that he was the guy.

But then Officer Hichborn had come to their house and told them everything. He had shown them the evidence they had found on Brock's laptop—the anonymous email accounts, the obscene photographs, the disposable phones—it was undeniable. *Brock* had been the one who had sent her those horrible emails and text messages. Had he guessed that everyone would blame Tyler? Of course he had...it was actually pretty clever.

So that meant it was Brock who had shot a gun at her in that hallway at Sparrow Hills, nine months ago. Brock was the hacksaw guy who had tried to get at George. Brock had been the one in the window, killing and then fleeing like a coward...

But it was over now. She was safe now. Now everyone expected her to be happy.

Well, she wasn't. It wasn't right. It wasn't *fair*. Brock had cheated. They—*she*—couldn't catch him now, and make him pay. The coward...

The hot, coursing hate rose up in her again. But it had nowhere to go. Brock was out of its reach. So the hate stayed inside, eating away at her like acid, leaving nothing. No plans, no goals, no mystery to solve, no hope of relief...just empty night.

She glanced down at her bed, where that stupid purple binder stuffed with her stupid notes lay. For a second, she wanted to throw it away or burn it or something.

But she couldn't. This was Nikki's binder. She picked it up and knelt down next to her bed. *Bye, Rufus. You did your best.* She pushed the binder underneath the bed and out of sight. *I can't pretend anymore. I can't make believe. I can't avoid the truth.*

The truth was that she had been kidding herself. Nikki was dead, and her death had meant nothing.

And no matter how hard she tried, Allie couldn't change that. She had been beaten. And now there was nothing left to do. Nothing at all.

She pulled up a chair to her bureau and sat down woodenly. "Bed head," she muttered, and picked up a hair brush.

This isn't fair, she thought sullenly as she brushed out the tangles. *Why'd Nikki even go to that dance? She didn't want to! Why she'd let me convince her? That's so typical—she was such a pushover! So weak! So easy to manipulate.*

"Stop it," she muttered, and the sullen mumble inside her ceased. Leaving nothing. No grief—no hate—nothing at all. She was hollow. Empty.

And in the emptiness a voice muttered to her, *you can't cry because you don't have any feelings…because you're a freak.*

James' empty, glassy stare…

A freak…a monster…that's why you have those dreams, you know. So full of hate. Deep down, you're as ugly as Brock was.

She closed her eyes.

Why? What are you scared of? Go ahead. Look at the freak.

She took a deep breath and opened her eyes again.

She saw a girl with a proud, pale face, framed by immaculately brushed blonde hair. Her eyes were a startlingly bright blue. Her lips were red. Her skin was unblemished. She wasn't ugly. She was pretty. Too pretty. It seemed unreal.

Allie realized, with a sort of dull astonishment, that she was beautiful. She still had her looks—and then some. Even without makeup, even with the dark circles under her eyes, she was prettier than many girls could ever hope to be. No wonder boys wanted her and girls envied her. No wonder she always stood out in the crowd.

She also realized that it didn't matter. No—it made it worse. There was something chilling about her beauty—something horrible. It was *too* perfect. Inhuman. It didn't have feelings inside. It didn't feel at all.

Like a mannequin in a store window. A realistic mannequin. No matter how beautiful it is, it's dead. Perfect and lifeless. Plastic…not real…not human…a freak…

She turned away and sank to the floor, hugging her knees, her eyes vacant.

Monster. Freak.

The black hole gaped wider, a huge, cavernous mouth. A window into nothing. She was falling…swallowed…lost…

"Jesus."

She whispered the word, threw it out like a lifeline, hoping someone would catch the other end.

"Jesus…help me."

There was a sharp knock on the door.

"Yeah," she said dully. "Come in."

Larry entered the room, carrying a dinner tray. "Your mom made this for you," he said, setting it down on the desk next to her. "And you're going to eat it."

Allie glanced up at the plate of spaghetti, salad, and diet soda. "I'm not hungry," she muttered.

"I don't care," Larry said sharply. He leaned against the wall. "Eat."

"What, and you're going to watch me?"

"Yeah. Your mom wants to make sure you actually eat."

"So that's why you're mad, huh?" She laughed bitterly. "You got someplace to go? Missing the ball game?"

"I'm mad because your mother's downstairs crying her eyes out."

"What?" Allie looked up, startled "Why?"

"Oh, I don't know. Maybe because you said she was a bad mother. Maybe because every day you get into a shouting match with her. Maybe because every time she tries to help, you give her lip and hurt her feelings."

Allie's mouth dropped open. She felt like a bucket of cold water had been dropped on her.

"Eat, Allie. Now."

Shooting him a resentful look, she started eating. She really wasn't hungry, but it still made her feel better. For the moment she forgot how miserable she was. Before she knew it she was wolfing the food down, and the plate was soon empty.

"Done." She held it up as evidence.

"Good." Larry stood up. "I'll let Diane know."

"Larry!"

"Yes?"

"Umm..." Allie stammered for a moment. "Do...you think...something's wrong with me?"

Larry's face softened a little. "What do you mean?" he said quietly.

Allie bit her lip. She had never talked much to Larry. Even though he had always been kind to her, she had never really gotten used to him being in the house, even after six years. He was never her *dad*—just mom's husband.

"Never mind," she said heavily.

Larry sighed. "Okay. You know what I think? You really need to get out of this house. Go and see your friends at that school. And call this girl Ginger back." He rolled his eyes. "At least that'll stop her calling every day."

"That's not *my* fault! I don't even know what she wants!"

"Well, maybe you should try returning her calls." Larry looked exasperated. "She told *me* when I answered the phone. She wants to talk about Nikki. That's why she keeps calling."

"Nikki?" Allie said, surprised. "But Nikki and Ginger weren't friends! They *hated* each other! Why would Ginger—"

"Why don't you call her back and find out?"

"But I don't *want* to talk about Nikki!"

"Why not? Is that so scary?"

She looked to the floor. "Yes," she mumbled. "A little."

"Then you *should* call her. Face your fears. Maybe it'll turn out okay."

"Really?"

A sad sort of smile flickered on her stepfather's face. "Well, kiddo…can it get any worse?" He handed her a yellow sticky note. "Here's her number."

He took the dinner tray and slipped out of her room. Allie stared down at the scribbled phone number.

He's got a point.

She picked up her cell phone.

8

THE ARTIST

"I'm very proud of you."

"I *know*, Mom." Brian yawned. It was eight o'clock on Saturday morning, and he would be spending the day at JP2 High. Work camp was taking over his weekends now, too. "You already told me. Five times. This morning."

"Well, I am!" his mom said enthusiastically, turning the van onto the highway exit. "And so is Dad! He was talking about it last night. This is the second time you've stayed calm under pressure. First at the shooting, when you helped to save that boy's life, and now this."

"Thank you," Brian mumbled. *Good thing she doesn't know what I'm doing today. She'd probably think I was a saint or something.*

Ever since he had extinguished the fire (or as J.P. had put it, "saved us all from certain, grisly doom") things had gotten...well, *weird.* For starters, he was nearly always the center of attention. The newer students looked awe-struck when he passed by. And every adult he met was always very, very proud of him.

"Here we are!" his mom said amiably as they pulled into the JP2 parking lot. "Make me proud, Brian!"

As the van drove away, Melissa turned to Brian with a smirk. "Make us proud, Brian!" she said in a squeaky voice. "Oh, Brian, you're so dreamy!"

Brian gritted his teeth.

"So, does *Mary Summers* think you're dreamy?"

Brian turned on her, but Melissa screeched with laughter and ran away. She disappeared into the school just as George walked up to him.

"Hey," he said. "You ready?"

Brian shrugged. "I guess so."

At that moment they heard a car door slam. Brian looked up and blinked. "Hey," he said. "Allie's back."

"What?" George spun around. Allie was walking up to the front door. She was wearing jeans and an old t-shirt, and carried a gym bag under one arm. *At least she's dressed decently now*, Brian thought.

"Allie?" George said. Allie looked up. Her eyes darted from George to Brian; then, to their surprise, she blushed and darted through the front doors and out of sight.

Brian blinked again. "What was *that* all about?" he said.

George stared at the front doors for a second, and then turned away, looking troubled. "I don't know," he said, pulling out his keys and heading for the car. "Come on, let's go."

Allie leaned against the front doors, breathing a sigh of relief. George and Brian were the last two people she wanted to see right now. George would ask a lot of awkward questions about where she'd been all week, and Brian—well, Liz had probably told Brian about Allie's plan to 'charm' him, so he probably hated her even *more* now.

She tried to collect her thoughts. She had told Ginger last night that she *might* be able to meet for lunch at the mall. But going to work camp *and* meeting Ginger Josslyn on the same day presented some problems.

On the one hand, she wanted to avoid any more static about her clothes. In fact, she wanted to 'blend in' as much as possible—hence the ill-fitting jeans and baggy t-shirt.

But on the other hand, you didn't meet a girl like Ginger Josslyn looking like a homeless person. She patted the gym bag. *I'll just change clothes in the bathroom, meet her, then change again before I come back here.* That was inconvenient, but Allie had long ago gotten used to balancing life at John Paul 2 High with life in the real world. JP2 High didn't have girls like Ginger and Madison who would rip you apart if you committed any fashion sins... At least she wouldn't get any grief for how she dressed today...

"Allie! You're back!" Miranda Costain ran up to her. "I missed you so—"

Miranda skidded to a stop, staring at Allie's clothes.

Uh oh. Maybe I was wrong. "Hi, Miranda," Allie said. "How's it going?"

"Um...fine." Miranda said. She kept looking Allie up and down, her eyes narrowed, until Allie started to get annoyed.

"I couldn't find anything else to wear," Allie said casually. "It's laundry day at my house."

"Oh!" Miranda looked a bit relieved. "Okay. Anyway—" She smiled brightly. "I really did miss you! Come on."

Miranda linked arms with Allie—her grip was surprisingly strong—and together they walked down the hallway. "I want you to meet some friends of mine," Miranda said eagerly. "New students, like me. Kristy and Vivian. I told them all about you. We're *totally* going to be best friends next year."

"Yeah, sure," Allie said testily. *Best friends? Like she even knows me. She's so fake...does she really expect me to believe her...*

Then a memory flashed through her mind—she, a freshman at Sparrow Hills, talking eagerly to Ginger and Madison, the cool upperclassman, trying to attach herself to them, getting on their good side...and Nikki hanging back, disapproving.

She stopped short, pulling herself free from Miranda's grasp.

"What?" Miranda said, but at that moment, two girls at the other end of the hall shrieked, "Miranda! Hi!!!"

"Kristy! Vivian!" Miranda emitted a similar shriek and ran up the hallway.

Allie leaned against the wall, frowning to herself. *Was I just like her when I was a freshman? All fake and shallow?*

She heard a quiet, barely audible scratching sound behind her, and turned around. She was standing next to an open classroom door. Inside, she saw a thin, slight boy with overlong wavy brown hair, sitting behind the teacher's desk and hunched over a notepad, writing or drawing something with a pencil.

He looks lonely, Allie thought. *Maybe I should...* She glanced back up the hall, where Miranda was chatting loudly with a tall blonde girl with a ponytail, blue eyeshadow, and huge earrings and a short brunette girl with trendy glasses with green wire frames. *That must be Vivian and Kristy. Maybe Miranda forgot about me. Good.* "Hey!" she said, walking into the classroom. "I'm Allie! What's your name?"

So," George said as they drove down the road. "How's the whole hero thing going?"

Brian rolled his eyes. "Everybody's proud of me. They tell me so all the time."

George chuckled. "Come on, it can't be *that* bad."

"No," Brian said grudgingly. "I guess not." At least he had actually gotten to speak with Mary Summers. *Twice.* Once to ask her for a pencil, and once because she noticed a piece of toilet paper stuck on his shoe. Not the best circumstances, perhaps, but it was *something.* And he had even managed to speak in complete sentences and get his name right. He grinned. *Not bad for a Three.*

"Hey, Brian?"

Brian looked up. They had pulled into the hospital parking lot, and George was gazing at him thoughtfully. "Look, all joking aside...you deserve it. You kind of are a hero."

Brian chuckled. "Oh, not you too. Look, all I did was—"

"Save the school from burning down. That's more than *I* did." George grimaced. "I panicked. You kept your cool."

"I didn't!" Brian said. "I didn't even think! I just reacted!"

"Come on, Brian." George reached over and poked Brian hard in the chest with finger. "I'm talking about what you got in *here.* Dude, you got *steel* in there."

Brian stared at George. "Okay," he said. "I have *no* idea what you're talking about."

"Really? Remember the shooting at the dance?"

"Yes. I thought I was going to lose it. I felt so—"

"Well, *I* remember what you *did.* How you helped me. I remember that you were calm the entire time." George chuckled.

"Never mind. You'll figure it out." He opened the car door. "Let's go."

They entered the hospital lobby, and George walked straight up to the receptionist. "Hi," he said. "Two visitors for Tyler Getz."

The wavy-haired boy looked up, saw her and smiled pleasantly. "Howdy," he said. "I'm Athanasius Courchraine."

"Oh," Allie said, thrown off. "That's an...unusual name. So what are you working on there?"

The boy shrugged and handed the notebook over. "Take a look."

It was a comic-book style picture of a large, burly figure with bulging muscles. He had a cape and a skin-tight costume, but he also wore a football helmet, and a large ornate crucifix hung round his neck. He was brandishing what looked like a futuristic bazooka.

Allie gaped at it for a second, and then giggled. "Wow. This is good." And it was; bizarre, but well-drawn. "What's it supposed to be?"

"Me," the boy said matter-of-factly. "It's a self-portrait. See?"

He pointed at the superhero character's head, where a stream of brown hair flowed out from the football helmet. "I can see how you would get confused, though," the boy added casually. "My hair's not that long yet. I plan to grow it out."

Allie stared at the boy, who was smiling wryly. "Hey," she said, amused. "Are you pulling my leg, Athanashee...Athanasee?"

"A-tha-nay-shus." The boy chuckled. "Just call me Athan. And I wouldn't pull your leg, at least not without asking."

"Oh, come *on*, Allie!" Miranda barged into the room, looking exasperated. "I want you to meet Vivian and Kristy, remember?"

There was a loud clattering sound. Athan had stood up suddenly, knocking over a jar of pencils and pens. Athan didn't appear to notice. He just stared at Miranda, his eyes wide.

"Athan?" Allie said, concerned. "Are you okay?"

Athan's face turned beet-red. "Sorry!" he said, diving to the floor and gathering up the pens and pencils on the floor. For the first time he looked very much like a freshman. "I just...uh...I just..." He slammed the jar back on the desk, and then snatched the notebook back from Allie and hid it behind his back.

Miranda watched all of this with one perfectly trimmed eyebrow raised. "Well?" she said to Allie. "Can we *go* now?"

Allie glanced at Athan, who still looked frazzled. "Miranda," she said, frowning. "This is Athan, and he's a great artist."

"Hi," Miranda said, waving a hand dismissively in Athan's direction. "Nice to meet you. Weird name. *Now* can we go?"

"It's short for Athanasius!" the boy blurted out, walking up to Miranda with his hand outstretched. "He was a saint! It's very nice to meet you...Miranda, isn't it?"

"Yeah." Miranda smirked a little as she shook hands with the boy. "Nice to meet you too, stud, but we gotta go. Come on, Allie."

As Miranda dragged her out, Allie looked back at the boy, who was rubbing his hand with a dazed, happy look. "Interesting guy," she murmured.

"Yeah, whatever!" Miranda laughed, steering Allie down the hall. "Loved the long hair. Bet that's against my dad's dress code."

"He was totally into you, you know."

"Really? Oh, whatever. He can take a number." Miranda shrugged. "Oh, watch out: Little House on the Prairie crossing right ahead."

Allie looked up just in time to see three girls coming up the hall, one short, one tall, and one heavy-set, all wearing long skirts of dark blue denim and print button-down blouses.

"Oh, hi!" Allie said. "Are you three new students too?"

Miranda gave a sniff but Allie ignored her.

The three girls halted and stared at Allie, looking wary.

"I'm Allie Weaver," Allie said, smiling in what she hoped was a welcoming, Celia-ish way. "I'll be a junior next year. So where did you go to school before? St. Lucy's?"

The heavyset girl spoke up after a moment. "I was homeschooled. I'm Josephine. And this is Mary Rose and Agnes. They were homeschooled too."

"Oh! Like Brian?"

The three girls burst into giggles. "Brian Burke?" asked the shorter one, a thin freckle-faced girl with braided red hair. "We were just talking about him!"

"Oh yeah, Agnes." Miranda snorted. "He's *such* a dream." She tugged at Allie's hand.

This made Allie even more determined to stay. "Yeah, Brian's great," she said.

As she spoke, tall, blonde Kristy walked up, along with short, glasses-wearing Vivian. "Hey Miranda," Kristy said in a haughty voice. "What's going on?"

"Just talking with the Amish," Miranda said. Vivian giggled.

"We're not Amish!" Josephine's eyes narrowed. "Stop it!"

"Hey, I was just joking." Miranda's eyes narrowed just a bit. "I know you're Catholic. Really, *really* Catholic. Unlike me, right?"

"Hey, we're all Catholic, right?" Allie said quickly, stepping in between Miranda and Josephine. "Come on, girls, let's go get some work done."

"Yeah, Miranda." Josephine glared at Miranda. "Are you going to work today? Or are you too busy leading your little clique?"

"Yeah, that's right," Miranda said disdainfully. "The clique of the well-dressed. Admission restricted. Come on girls," she said, turning to Kristy and Vivian. "Let's leave the Prude Patrol to their work, shall we?"

"What did you call me?" Josephine demanded.

"You heard me," Miranda said. "And I heard you telling Kristy and Vivian that their clothes were trashy."

Allie thought Josephine had a point. Vivian and Kristy's outfits looked just as trendy as Miranda's, but neither of them had Miranda's looks or sense of style. Vivian's legs were *way* too bony for her mini-shorts, and Kristy was just kidding herself if she thought she was small enough for that size two top. *They're trying too hard*, Allie thought. *Like they want to get noticed*. Then again, Josephine and her friends weren't exactly the height of fashion either…

"I said they were *borderline* trashy!" Josephine said. "And I wouldn't be surprised if someone starts giving out lectures on modesty because of them."

"Sounds like you want the job," Miranda said airily. "Like I said, Prude Patrol. I nominate you as Head Prude."

"Don't call her that!" Agnes yelled.

"Hey!" Celia hurried down the hallway, looking agitated. "What's going on here?"

"Nothing, dear sister." Miranda smirking. "Just talking."

"I know," Celia said acidly. "I heard the 'talking' from the gym. What happened?"

"She called us trashy!" Vivian pointed at Josephine.

"She called Jo a prude!" Agnes pointed at Kristy.

"She *what?*" Celia said sharply—and then she looked right at *Allie*, as if this was *her* fault.

"Um…yeah," Allie said uncomfortably. "Kristy said that. Not me."

"Okay, fine." Celia shook her head, looking exasperated. "Ladies, we got a *lot* of work today, all right? Come on, let's go."

"Yeah," Allie said. "Come on, listen to Celia. She's in charge."

The group broke up with muttering and dark looks on both sides and Allie used the moment to escape Miranda and attach herself to Celia. "Thanks for getting them moving in the right direction," Celia said to Allie. "It's nice to feel like I'm not trying to run the whole camp by myself."

Allie glanced at Celia warily. *Is she being sarcastic?* But Celia sounded just as cheerful as ever, even though she looked a bit tired.

"Honestly," Celia went on, "I just don't know what to do about these girls. I wish Miranda didn't have to come here. School hasn't even started yet and she already hates it here. I don't want to think about what she'll do next semester."

"Guess there's no chance of sending her someplace else?" Allie asked with a grin. "Like reform school?"

Celia laughed as she trudged up the hallway. "Are you coming, or do you have someplace to run off to?"

"Yeah, I'm coming," Allie said. "Sorry I've been out for the last couple days. I guess I haven't been much help in the Great School Cleanup Project."

"Um...yeah." Celia sighed. "Well, you're here now. That's what's important."

9

BAD GIRL

"How many times have you seen him?" Brian said to George as they walked down the hospital hallway.

"Four times," George said. "So far."

Brian mulled this over. Even though George had saved Tyler's life during the shooting, he doubted that the two of them had become friends. Neither of them were likely to easily let go of a grudge. He wondered what they talked about when George visited...and why George kept coming.

They arrived at Tyler's room. "You ready for this?" George asked. "I know you probably don't like Tyler...I mean, after what he did..."

He trailed off, and Brian's mind went back to the day when Tyler and his two friends had jumped him and dressed him up in a bra, lipstick and a wig. Anger flared briefly up at the memory, along with a vindictive thought: *Well, Tyler's paid for that now.*

Ashamed, he pushed the thought away. "I'll be okay," he assured George. "Let's go in."

George took a deep breath, and knocked on the open door.

There was Tyler Getz, sitting on a hospital bed, his midsection wrapped in bandages. The room was full of gifts from well-wishers: the bedside table was laden with cards, there were flower arrangements on the windowsill, and a couple of balloons tied to the foot of the bed.

Tyler had looked up hopefully as they entered, but now his face darkened. "Oh," he grunted. "Hey, Peterson. And Burke. Come on in." He motioned listlessly to a couple chairs.

Brian walked over and offered his hand. "Hi Tyler," he said, holding out his hand.

Tyler took his hand slowly. His arm was shaking slightly, and his grip was much weaker than Brian had expected. In fact, Tyler had lost of lot of weight during his two-month-long stay in the hospital. His forearms were skinnier, his chest looked pale and thin, and his face looked hollow.

Tyler's face twisted in a smile. "Yeah, I'm not really in shape right now." He let out a short, barking laugh. "You don't need to worry about me jumping you for a while, Burke. Not yet."

"You look terrible," Brian said bluntly.

Tyler shrugged. "Yeah, I've lost some weight. Apparently the bullet nicked some things on its way through, and I can't eat any solid foods for a while. But don't worry, I'll be back to my old self soon." He glared at both of them, as if daring them to contradict him. "I guarantee it. Once I get out of here, I'm gonna start training again. But maybe I'll keep some of the weight down," he mused. "Maybe I can slip into the 160 class."

Brian and George exchanged skeptical looks. "Tyler," George said in a low voice, "I heard Dr. Nutt say that you couldn't work out for...for at least a couple years."

Tyler scowled. "Yeah," he admitted grudgingly. "They say I got to start taking physical therapy or something. But whatever it is, I'll get over it."

The room lapsed into gloomy silence. The bravado slowly faded off of Tyler's face, replaced by a sad, dead look. Brian found himself feeling sorry for him. What did Tyler have, really, besides wrestling? Brian didn't know. He didn't know Tyler well at all, and he doubted that George did, either.

The silence lasted for a long time, broken only by the quiet beeps from the medical equipment. Brian's eyes wandered across the room. The flowers on the windowsill were withered. The balloons were losing helium. There was a thin coating of dust on the table with the cards. *Tyler's been in here two months*, he thought. *Probably doesn't get a lot of visitors anymore.*

"Why do you keep coming here, Peterson?" Tyler muttered.

George looked up. "I have to," he said quietly.

"No, you don't," Tyler said bluntly. "Seriously, dude, I know you feel guilty and all, but you don't have to keep coming here, okay?"

"Yeah, I do," George said. "It's what Christians are supposed to do. Visit the sick."

"Christian, huh?" Tyler said savagely. "Was it *Christian* to get me kicked off the squad? And try to drown me?"

"Hey!" Brian said, unable to contain himself. "You got *yourself* kicked off the squad!"

"It doesn't matter," George mumbled. "He's just mad."

"Hey, I can hear what you're saying, you know," Tyler snapped. He started to sit up, winced, and flopped back down with a curse.

"Watch your mouth," Brian snapped.

Tyler gaped at Brian. Then he shook his head and chuckled. "Well, *you* haven't changed a bit, Burke. Give me a break, okay? I'm in a little bit of pain here."

Feeling both embarrassed and resentful, Brian stared at the floor.

"Huh," Tyler said after a moment. "So you're doing the Christian thing, huh? You're always taking care of people. You took care of *him*," he gestured at Brian. "And now you're gonna take care of those two kids, right? Flynt told me."

Brian gave Tyler a puzzled look. *What is he talking about?*

"But you got it wrong, Peterson. As usual. You should be taking care of Allie."

"Allie?" George frowned. "Why bring *her* up? What do you care?"

"You don't understand. Allie and Nikki—they were tight. *Real* tight. She's got to be taking it hard, even if she won't admit it."

George and Brian both gaped at Tyler. Then George's eyes narrowed. "Okay, Tyler," he said. "What's the angle?"

89

Tyler sighed heavily. "There's no angle. I'm just telling you to *take care* of Allie, okay? She needs you more than me; but she's too proud to ask you. Besides...that shooter guy is still out there."

George and Brian looked at each other. "Er...Tyler," Brian said. "Have you watched the news lately?"

"Of course I've watched the news!" Tyler snarled. "I'm just not dumb enough to believe it! There's no way Brandon shot me! And Flynt agrees with me!"

Brian shook his head and sighed. Of course, denial was to be expected. *He's not thinking clearly.*

"Um...sure, Tyler," George said after a moment. "So...did you hear about Feist?"

"Matt Feist?" Tyler looked surprised. "No. What about him?"

"Coach is gonna make him squad captain this year."

"Really?" Tyler sat up, looking a bit more interested. "Hmm. Yeah, that makes sense. What class is he in now?"

"160. You remember he had a great record last year..."

Brian watched as George and Tyler embarked on a discussion of the different wrestlers on the Sparrow Hills squad, their records, their tactics, and whether Feist was the right choice for captain. He had never seen the two of them just talking like this. They may not be friends now, but the old hostility wasn't there anymore.

Maybe they aren't enemies anymore, Brian mused. *Just maybe.*

So what are we working on today?" Allie asked in a deliberately helpful, cheerful voice as she followed Celia down the hallway.

"The bathrooms," Celia said. "I sent you an email...but I suppose you missed it?"

Again Allie wondered if Celia was being sarcastic, but the anxious look on the other girl's face made that unlikely—besides, this was *Celia.* Allie doubted she knew how to be sarcastic.

"Well, no," she said. "To be honest, I haven't even checked my email since Monday."

"Really?" Celia said, sounding confused. "Why not?"

Allie bit her lip. She couldn't explain the depression she had sunk into in the last couple days—at least not to Celia.

"Um…I've been busy," she said lamely. "Anyway," she added jokingly, "No human being could possibly keep up with the amount of emails you send me!"

"Oh," said Celia in a strange voice. "So…you haven't been reading them?"

"Um…hey!" Allie ran up to a stack of paint cans just outside the gym. "Are these for the bathroom?"

"Yeah," Celia said quickly. "They are. If you could help me run them down to the girls' bathroom…that is, if you're feeling okay…"

"I feel fine," Allie muttered, and grabbed a couple paint cans.

"Good," Celia said. "Jacinta's waiting for us there. She's been helping me a lot in the last couple days." Together, they made their way to the girls' bathroom.

As they approached the bathroom door, Jacinta ran out to meet them. "There you are, Celia! Come on!"

"At least you have a reliable second-in-command," Allie said to Celia.

Celia gave her a funny look, but Jacinta grabbed her arm and pulled her into the bathroom. There Isabel waited, clutching a sketchbook to her chest.

"So we're gonna paint everything sky-blue, like you said," Jacinta said. "Except for right *here*." She pointed to a space on the wall between the sinks and the toilet stalls. "That's where Isabel comes in. Isabel?"

Isabel came forward with a happy smile and held up a notebook. They all stepped closer to see.

On the notebook was an intricate pencil drawing of a nun, framed by an elaborate border. The nun held a white rose in one hand and a blue bird perched on another hand. Behind her, lambs and bunny rabbits frolicked in a field of yellow flowers. "Wow!" Celia said. "Who's that?"

"Clare of Assisi," Isabel said happily. "She's my favorite saint."

"And you want to paint her here?"

Isabel nodded rapidly, sending a few strands of hair flopping into her face.

"I think that's an awesome idea," Celia said. "Really a lot more doable. Okay, everyone, let's get to work!"

As Celia and Jacinta started preparing the paint trays, Allie edged closer to Isabel. "You know," she said. "I found another artist. His name's Athan."

"Really?" Isabel looked thrilled. "Thanks! Maybe he can do a matching picture of St. Francis in the *boys'* bathroom!"

Smiling to herself, Allie pulled a bandanna out of her gym bag and wrapped it over her head just as Liz walked into the bathroom.

"Hey Allie," Liz balanced a stack of paint trays in one hand. "Nice bandanna."

"Yeah, I don't want to get paint in my hair," Allie said, tossing her gym bag into one of the stalls and covering it with a tarp. "Not after what happened last time."

Liz snickered. "Good point. You should wear one of *these.*"

Allie looked at Liz again. She was wearing what looked like a white jumpsuit, covering her from head to toe.

"What's that?" Allie giggled. "A spacesuit?"

"Painting coveralls!" Liz said proudly. "My dad got them for me; they're super useful. Keep you from messing up your clothes. Anyway—" She dropped the trays on the floor with a crash and said in a low voice. "Before I forget— The Burkes are having a movie night at their house tonight. You coming?"

"At *Brian's* house?" Allie hesitated. "I don't know if I can come..."

Liz shrugged. "Don't matter to me; I just need to let everyone know." She headed back into the hallway.

Just then, Vivian and Agnes came in, both looking rather sulky. Vivian's trendy clothes were covered by a painting smock, and Agnes looked uncomfortably warm in her long skirt and blouse.

"We'll start with white primer," Celia said. "Then we'll let it dry during lunch and put the blue coat on this afternoon. It's a big job, but I know you can do it, as long as you work *together.*"

Work together? Allie glanced doubtfully at the scowls Agnes and Vivian were giving each other.

"No problem," Jacinta said cheerfully. "Thanks Celia!"

She planted herself between Agnes and Vivian and started on the wall. "Hey Vivian," she said, "I just love those green eyeglasses. Where did you get them?"

"Huh?" Vivian looked suspiciously at Jacinta.

But Jacinta was serious. "I have contacts, but every once in a while I see a really cute pair of glasses, and I totally want them."

"Oh," Vivian said. "Well, I have astigmatism, so I can't wear contacts."

"Really? That's too bad. Agnes, can you hold this pan for me for a sec—what about you, Agnes? Would you wear glasses just for fun?"

"I don't know." Now it was Agnes's turn to look startled. "I guess I never thought about it...but they make people look smart. Like you," the short redhead said to Vivian. "I think they look super on you."

Vivian giggled. "That's funny, because I'm not smart at all!"

All three freshmen started laughing, and Allie looked at Jacinta with respect. *She's pretty good at breaking the ice,* Allie thought.

The door banged open, and Mary and Liz came in, looking daggers at one another.

"Hey!" Jacinta said. "Come on in and join the party!"

"I'd rather just paint," Liz growled.

"Same here," Mary snapped.

Allie glanced from Liz to Mary. *What's going on with those two?*

With Jacinta keeping up a steady patter of small talk, the assorted girls painted throughout the morning. It was a big job—the bathroom was bigger than it looked, and there was a lot of space to cover.

Allie joined in the conversation as best as she could, but mostly she painted in silence, glancing from time to time at her cell. The hours crept by slowly, until they finished at 11:30.

"Awesome!" Celia said when she came by to check on them. "Good job, everyone! Let's take a break before lunch—"

Allie looked up hopefully.

"—and then you can start on the second coat!"

A few of the girls groaned. "Do we *have* to?" Vivian whined.

"Come on," Celia said bracingly. "Just think: tonight we'll all be at the Burke's house for movie night."

"Movie night?" Mary said. "What's that?"

"It's when we watch a *movie*," Liz said dryly. "At *night*."

"And it's tonight?" Jacinta looked dismayed. "Why didn't anybody tell us?"

"You didn't hear?" Celia turned to Liz with a frown. "Liz, I told you to spread the word."

"I did," Liz said blandly. "I told everyone I saw. You guys all heard, right?"

Everyone in the room nodded. "Well, *we* didn't," Mary snapped.

Liz shrugged. "Sorry. My bad."

"So can you come?" Celia said. "It would be a great way to get to know the school community."

"Well..." Jacinta glanced at Mary. "If Mom could drive us..."

"She won't," Mary said bitterly. "Her schedule's packed, and she won't change it now."

"No problem," Celia said. "I'll drive you."

Mary and Jacinta exchanged embarrassed looks. "The thing is," Jacinta said apologetically. "My mom doesn't like us driving with teenagers."

"Oh." Celia looked startled. "Well, maybe I can talk to her about making an exception..." She ducked out of the bathroom.

Mary shook her head. "She's wasting her breath. Mom won't budge on her rules."

Liz snorted. "Typical."

"What was that?" Mary snapped.

"Your mom." Liz smirked. "She's got a tight leash on you two, doesn't she?"

"Mind your own business!"

"I will if *she* will," Liz retorted. "She cornered me yesterday and told me I should stop working with all the *boys* because it wasn't *feminine* or something. Is she always that preachy?"

"Are you always this rude?" Mary fired back.

Allie's cell phone buzzed. *Text message—maybe from Ginger?* She turned away and checked.

"Come on, Mary," Jacinta said anxiously. "Forget about it."

"Yeah, let's go to lunch already!" Vivian said impatiently.

`Ill be at mall @ 12:15,` the text said. `Meet me by Geoffreys.`

It's 11:45 now! Allie thought anxiously. *Great—barely have time to change.*

She hung back until the others had left, then ducked into the stall where her gym bag was hidden.

She was almost done changing when she heard the bathroom door bang open again. "Allie? Are you still in here?"

"Yeah, Seal." Allie said, buttoning up her blouse. "Kind of busy."

"Oh...well, I just wanted to let you know we can't have lunch in the gym because of the paint drying—so we're eating in the classrooms in the other wing."

"Great." Allie tucked in her blouse, wondering why Celia had come back here just to tell her *that*. She also remembered, awkwardly, that she hadn't actually told Celia she was going out for lunch.

"Actually, Allie..." She heard footsteps walking up to the stall. "There's something else I wanted to talk to you about."

"Can it wait?" Allie shoved her old t-shirt, jeans and sneakers into the bag.

"Well...it's important, actually."

"Fine," Allie said tensely, pulling her makeup kit and hair brush out of the bag. "Just make it quick."

95

"Okay." Celia sighed. "See, I've been...struggling with something, but it's kind of embarrassing. You'll probably think it's stupid, but—"

Allie pulled open the stall door and walked past Celia to the mirror. "Okay," she murmured, brushing out her hair. *Just a quick brush, then maybe some lipstick and blush, and then—*

She noticed Celia in the mirror, staring at her, mouth open.

"Oh." She turned around. "I'm sorry, Seal. Didn't mean to interrupt you. What..." She giggled. She couldn't help it—Celia looked so flabbergasted. "What were you saying?"

Celia blinked. "Um...well, I don't know if this is the right time."

"No, go ahead." Allie turned back to the mirror and resumed her brushing. "By the way, what time is it?"

"Um...five minutes to noon."

"Good," Allie murmured. "Still got time."

"Time for what?"

"Nothing. I'm just meeting someone." She put down the hairbrush and glanced down at her makeup kit. *Maybe I don't need it. I look pretty good already.* "Hey Seal..." She turned around. "How do I look?"

Celia hesitated. "Um...you look..." She smiled faintly. "You look *beautiful*, Allie."

"Really?" Allie said distantly, turning to gather up her things. "Thanks."

"You're welcome," Celia said quietly. "So...you're leaving again?"

"Yeah, but I'll be back."

Celia turned away quickly. "Okay. See you later then." She walked out of the bathroom.

Allie frowned. *That's funny. She didn't even want to know why I was leaving.*

Whatever. She turned back to the mirror. *Then again, maybe I do need the makeup...*

Five minutes later she was done, and stepped back to view the results. *Wow.* Celia was right; she looked good. Sexy, actually. She turned around slowly. The pink blouse was just snug enough, and the denim skirt really complimented her legs. *I could be back at Sparrow Hills.*

But that was the problem—she wasn't. If Josephine's gang saw her like this...or worse, Mrs. Summers...*Okay. Better make a discreet exit.* She slipped out of the bathroom and walked down the hallway; but the door at the end was locked. *Great. Well, I can always go out through the gym.*

But when she got to the gym, she heard voices. Glancing in, she saw a few women sitting there, talking—Mrs. Summers, Mrs. Burke, and...Celia.

Maybe if I just pass through, they'll ignore me.

She walked by quickly, keeping her eyes ahead. She heard the conversation in the gym falter, but no one called her name. *Phew,* she thought, passing through the double doors and walking past the school office. *Okay, I can get out through the front doors.*

She turned the corner and glanced down the main hallway. There were voices coming from the classrooms—kids having lunch—but the hallway itself was empty, and the main doors were at the end. She groped for her phone to text Ginger and realized it wasn't in her purse. *Darn, I must have left it in the bathroom...*

"Stop right there!"

She gulped, and turned around. Mrs. Summers was walking up to her, her grey-streaked hair up in a bun, looking furious.

"Uh...hi, Mrs. Summers," Allie said casually. "I was just..."

"Why are you dressed like *that?*"

Mrs. Summers' voice echoed down the hallway. A few kids spilled out from the classrooms, looking alarmed.

Allie stared at Mrs. Summers. "I'm...meeting somebody," she stammered.

Mrs. Summers smiled tightly. "Allison," she said, "this is a Catholic school. Your manner of dress is *not* Catholic. It's offensive, the way you're carrying yourself. Would the Blessed Mother dress like that? Would she approve of how you're tempting the young men here to sin?"

"What?" Allie gaped. "I'm not trying to—"

"Oh, yes you are," Mrs. Summers snapped. "Every time I've seen you, you've dressed indecently. Now I'm seeing other girls dress the same way. Do you enjoy being the ringleader?"

"The what?" Allie giggled nervously.

Mrs. Summer's eyes narrowed. "You think this is funny?"

"No!" Allie said hastily. She glanced down the hall, which was filling with students emerging from the classroom. Everyone seemed be watching them now—Josephine's group, and Miranda's...

"Look," Allie said in a low voice. "It's Miranda who's the ringleader. Right over there; Miranda Costain. Ask Celia, she'll tell you."

Mrs. Summers' eyes remained hard. "Celia," she said, "is the one who brought this to my attention."

Allie's mouth dropped open. "What?"

"I was talking to her just now, and Cecelia told me how disappointed she was in *you*. She said you were a bad example to the other girls."

Allie felt like she had been punched in the gut. She glanced down the hall, at the other girls watching her. Some of them looked shocked; others looked embarrassed. But no one spoke up to defend her.

She looked down at her sandals, her face burning, as Mrs. Summer's voice came pounding down on her: "—*example* is the most important thing we can set, Allison, and I don't think you're doing that—"

And then, abruptly, she felt nothing. Nothing at all. Except hate. Hate for all of them: Mrs. Summers, Celia, the whole bunch. She didn't feel fragile or afraid anymore. She felt strong.

Mrs. Summers was still talking: "I would talk to your mother, but—"

"You're *not* my mother." Allie snapped, looking up and glaring at Mrs. Summers.

"I wish I was!" Mrs. Summers retorted. "You wouldn't be allowed to—" Then she seemed to catch herself. "Listen, I'm telling you this in love. We love the sinner and hate the sin here—"

Allie laughed harshly. "Sure you do."

"Don't you talk back to me!" Mrs. Summers said angrily. "You should know better...but given your family background..."

Celia told her about my parents too. Nice. Allie laughed bitterly. Then she turned and walked away.

"Hey! Stop right there! I'm talking to you, Allison!"

Allie ignored her. *I'm getting my phone and I'm leaving.* She walked back the way she had come, leaving the crowd of whispering students behind.

When she entered the gym again, the other women came up to her, looking concerned. "Allie?" Mrs. Burke said. "What happened?"

Allie barely heard her. She had seen Celia. For a second the two girls stared at each other. Celia looked shocked, her face pale, her eyes wide. Allie glared at her for a second, then tossed her head scornfully and walked away.

I don't feel anything. Nothing.

She walked until she found herself next to the girl's bathroom. Snatching her phone from the sink, she sank down and sat on the filthy floor, hugging herself. *Don't feel anything. Don't. Nothing—*

"Why?" she whimpered. "Why, Seal? Why did you set me up?"

Grow up, the cold voice inside her answered. *You don't need her. You don't need any of them. You're better than them. Stronger. Unique.*

Alone. Like an Ice Queen. Like Ginger.

"Yeah," she muttered. Ginger Josslyn, the coldest Ice Queen, sneering, sarcastic...Ginger, who probably never darkened the doors of a church in her life, who was cruel and cold and strong...

Ginger wouldn't stand by and let herself get humiliated or insulted. Ginger wouldn't be the good little girl, like Nikki.

Ginger would get *back* at them.

Boom.

She looked up, frowning. She had barely heard it—a deep, muffled sound. And other sounds, barely audible—water. Water swishing.

There. It was coming from a battered metal door a few feet away.

Hmm. Allie walked up to the door. *Interesting.*

Brian and George were almost back to the school when George's phone rang. "Hand that to me, would you?" George said ruefully. "I bet it's Seal. We're late."

Brian handed George the phone and then looked out the passenger side window, frowning to himself.

"Hello? Hey Seal. Yeah, we're driving back now. What? Oh, you're *kidding!*"

Brian glanced up, startled.

"Okay," George said heavily into the phone. "Calm down, Seal. We'll be back in a few minutes." He tossed down the phone. "Guess what?" George said gloomily. "The furnace room's flooded."

"What?"

"Whoah!" George slammed on the brakes.

Brian braced himself against the seat. They had just passed Sparrow Hills, and had run into traffic.

"Why is there always traffic here?" George said irritably and then resumed the conversation. "Yeah, they just found out. Apparently the boiler broke or something and flooded the whole room. Cool, huh? I think our school is jinxed."

"Don't be superstitious," Brian said automatically. He turned back to the window, his brow furrowed in thought.

10

NEW (OLD) FRIEND

"Hey!" As Brian and George walked into the school, Celia ran up to them, looking frantic and tearful. "It just happened! I was trying to find Allie, and I heard water running...the furnace room's just *flooded*, George! There's a big crack in the boiler, and..." She covered her face in her hands.

"Hey, calm down," George said, startled. "I mean..." He laughed awkwardly. "It's just a boiler, right?"

Celia looked away. "You'd better get down to the boiler room," she mumbled. "I think Mr. Simonelli needs all the help he can get. By the way, have you seen Allie?"

Brian and George exchanged looks. "Not here," Brian said. "I think she drove past us as we came in."

"Hey!" a shrill voice came out of one of the classrooms. "Don't talk about my mother that way!"

Brian, George and Celia glanced into the classroom. There was Mary Summers and Liz, glaring at each other, as a bunch of other students looked on.

"I'll say whatever I want!" Liz shot back. "Your mom's nuts! She's not gonna stop until we're all in frilly dresses! Well, guess what? I don't *like* frilly dresses!"

"That's right!" J.P. chimed in, equally indignant. "Why, if she ever told *me* to wear a frilly—"

"Shut up!" Liz and Mary said together, so fiercely that J.P. actually looked scared and backed away.

"This is all my fault," Celia said in a small voice as Liz and Mary's argument continued with increasing fury. "This is all my fault. Oh, I need to call Allie right away. Please, George, do something!"

"What?" George looked startled. "What can I—?"

"I don't know, just stop them from fighting before something worse happens!

"Okay, okay!" George glanced at Brian. "We'll split them up and talk them down," he said tersely. "You take Liz; I'll take Mary. Okay?"

"No!" Brian blurted out.

George frowned. "What?"

"I mean..." Brian stammered. "Let's switch. *I'll* talk to Mary."

George shrugged. "Whatever. Okay, girls! *STOP!*"

He bellowed the last word so loudly that Liz and Mary froze and stared at him.

"Liz," George said in his normal voice, "Can you come over here a second? Let's talk. And the rest of you," he added, glancing around at the others. "You should be getting back to work. Come on, get out of here."

Now or never, Brian thought wildly, and ran up to Mary. "Hey, Mary," he said. "Let's go and...talk."

Out of the corner of his eye he saw Liz give him an angry look as she left with George. The classroom emptied quickly, and soon he was alone with Mary and Jacinta.

Mary threw herself down on a chair and crossed her arms. Jacinta hovered near her, looking anxious. Brian glanced at Mary, and a wild thought popped into his head: *She looks kind of cute when she's angry.*

"So," he said, sitting down next to Mary. "What happened?"

"Ask your girlfriend!" Mary snapped. "Ask her what she has against my family!"

"Um...she's not my girlfriend. Just my friend."

"Why are you always hanging out with her?"

"Well...um..." He laughed awkwardly. "I'm friends with everyone. I'm a...friendly person."

Jacinta giggled shakily, and Mary's lips twitched a little.

"Seriously though, what happened?"

"I'll tell him, Mary," Jacinta said. She blurted out the whole story. "It was horrible! I felt so sorry for Allie!"

"What was she dressed like that for?" Mary said stubbornly. "She *changed* clothes, Jacinta! Why?"

"I don't know! But Mom still shouldn't have singled her out like that!"

"I think," Brian said, "That Jacinta may have a point."

"Well..." Mary looked a little troubled. "Maybe. But wasn't my mom *right*? Allie was trying to get attention! Did you see how short her skirt was? What if any of the boys saw her in that?"

"Oh come on, Mary!" Jacinta waved a hand airily. "Don't be so cynical! These aren't like the boys at Vernon! They're Catholic boys!"

"They're still boys," Mary said darkly. "And Allie knows it."

"But they're *gentlemen*!" Jacinta said earnestly. "Like Brian here! He'd never look at Allie like that! Would you, Brian?"

"Well..." Brian hesitated. The correct answer was *Yes*, followed by *Duh*. But that wasn't exactly diplomatic. "I think..." he said cautiously. "That Catholics should welcome everybody, no matter how they, uh, dress—"

"So it doesn't *matter* how girls dress?" Mary said.

"No!" Brian said. "I mean...we should *encourage* her to dress modestly, of course..."

"So you *do* agree with my mom?"

Brian stared at Mary. Her golden brown hair was tied back loosely in a bun, framing her oval face and long, graceful neck. Her skin was milky white, and her cheeks were a little flushed. Her big brown eyes looked back at him hopefully. He couldn't look away.

Just say yes.

But then he remembered Allie's face on the day of the meeting, pale and sad, as she stood alone outside the school.

"No," he mumbled. "I'm sorry, but I don't." He gritted his teeth. "Allie's part of this school. When she first came here, she didn't really fit in. But now she's like part of our family. We shouldn't just...throw her out. We should help her."

Mary's face fell. "But my mom *was* trying to help her!"

"I know!" he said hastily. "But I think...some kinds of help aren't as...helpful...as others."

Mary scowled. "Fine." She turned away.

Great. That's what I get for doing the right thing.

He stood up woodenly. "Um...you girls coming to movie night?"

"We can't go," Mary said irritably. "Liz 'forgot' to tell us."

"What?" Brian said angrily. "Great. Well, um...bye." He left the classroom and closed the door.

He stood in the hallway, trying to process everything.

"Hey!" Liz ran up to him. "What were you doing with *them?*"

"What are you talking about?"

"Since when do you side with the newbies?" She poked him hard in the chest. "What's the deal? You ditching me?"

"No," Brian retorted. "Looks like I'm stuck with you."

Liz looked surprised. "Oh," she said. "Um...good. Don't you forget it!"

"I won't," he muttered.

Allie slammed the car door and started across the mall parking lot. She was late—thanks to Celia and everyone else at that stupid place. *I can't believe her nerve,* she thought savagely. *I wish I could see her face when she looks into that furnace room...*

But even as she thought it, she felt a twinge of guilt. It made her angry. *She deserved it. After humiliating me like that...Ginger wouldn't take it either. She'll understand.*

Ginger Josslyn. Curly blond hair, perfect figure, eyes like steel. The terror of all the geeks, the ugly girls, and the misfits at Sparrow Hills. The kind of girl who could kill with a glare or a single, cutting remark.

The kind of girl who knew how to get revenge. Allie winced. Last spring, when Ginger had been with Bobby Henderson, she heard a rumor that Bobby had been cheating on her—that he had hooked up at a party with some freshman girl, Brittany Stello.

Ginger had cornered Brittany in the cafeteria. She had asked if Bobby was good. Then she had listed Brittany's faults—physical and otherwise—in a loud, cold voice that everyone heard.

It ended with Brittany running away in tears. They found out later that the rumors weren't true. Bobby had been hitting on Brittany, but she had rejected him; because she was scared of Ginger.

Had Ginger apologized? No. She just dumped Bobby, and spread her own rumor that he had given her herpes.

Allie laughed awkwardly to herself. Sure, it was a nasty story, but it just showed how tough Ginger was. Tough, smart, ruthless, and beautiful—that's what you needed to survive in Sparrow Hills. That's why Allie had fought so hard to get close to Ginger and Madison. Better to stick close to the bullies. That was the safest place.

Hmm, she thought, stopping at a crosswalk. *Kinda wimpy of me, now that I think about it.*

Nikki must have thought so. Maybe Nikki had despised Allie, deep down. She had definitely despised Ginger...and Ginger had despised her right back. Called her their mascot, their resident prude. She had a point, though; Nikki was so naïve. She never even had a boyfriend.

And now she never will.

Allie stopped short, her heart in her mouth.

She closed her eyes. *No. I don't care. I don't feel sad. I don't feel anything.*

She walked into the mall and sat down at a bench just outside of Geoffrey's. It wasn't surprising that Nikki and Ginger hated each other; they were complete opposites. The regal, haughty upperclassman and the wholesome girl-next-door. Miranda versus Celia. Bad girl versus good girl.

"Allie?"

"Ginger!" Allie jumped up as the slim blonde in a black capris and a short green tunic walked up to her. "How *are* you? You weren't waiting too long, were you?"

"Yeah, I was." Ginger smiled wryly. "But no big deal."

Allie sighed in relief. "So...um...you look nice! You get your hair done?"

Ginger laughed. "You like it?"

"Yeah! It's...different." Ginger had always curled her hair in tight ringlets and let it grow really long. The new style was simpler: straight and graceful and shoulder-length. "It makes you look older," Allie said. "More mature, you know?"

"Really?" Ginger laughed again and tugged at her big hoop earrings. "Cool. That's what I was going for."

"Did Madison like it?"

"She hasn't seen it. We don't hang out anymore."

"No way! You guys have a fight?" *Now* that *would be interesting.*

"Eh..." Ginger shrugged carelessly. "I just got tired of her."

"But..." Allie hesitated. "I thought you were best friends."

"Nah. She's a snob."

Allie giggled. "I *know*, totally! Just like you!" She felt a stab of panic as a look of anger flashed across Ginger's face. "I mean..." she said awkwardly, "that...um...sorry..." She sank back down on the bench, feeling awful.

"No, no," Ginger sighed heavily and sat down next to her. "I probably deserved that."

Allie blinked. "What?"

"For gossiping. About Madison." She shook her head. "Sorry."

Allie stared at her. Ginger Josslyn was *sorry* for something? That was like Celia being mean...or George being wimpy...or Brian being stupid. It didn't make any sense.

Ginger noticed her staring and chuckled. "What's wrong?"

"You're...wrong," Allie said blankly. "I mean...never mind..." She looked away, totally confused.

Ginger stood up. "So what do you want to do first? Talk about old times, or shop?"

"Shop," Allie said. "Let's shop. I know shopping."

They wandered through the mall for the next few hours, stepping into different clothing outlets. Gradually, Allie started enjoying herself. She found, to her surprise, that she *liked* Ginger now. Ginger wasn't nearly as bad as she expected; a bit dry and sarcastic, but not cold and sneering. She asked Allie about school, about her family...and she really listened when Allie answered. She laughed a lot more. She didn't seem to care about being cool. Oddly enough, that made her even cooler. It was weird. The whole thing was weird, and she still felt suspicious...but she couldn't help liking it as well.

"So Ginger," she said as they stepped out of a clothing store. "You still smoke?"

"Nope," Ginger said proudly. "I quit."

"I figured." Allie grinned. "It's been a couple hours, and you aren't twitching. How did that happen?"

Ginger took a sip from the iced coffee she'd been carrying. "Nikki."

She took another sip, and then noticed Allie's puzzled look. "Oh, yeah." She shook her head. "I keep forgetting. You don't know."

"What are you talking about?"

"Hmm." Ginger glanced at Allie. "So now you *do* want to talk about the old times?"

"I *know* the old times," Allie said, halting in her stride. "This isn't the old times. This is different. You're different."

"Really?" Ginger looked gratified. "Is it a good different?"

"It's a weird different! And what does this have to do with Nikki?"

"It's almost four," Ginger said, pointing. "There's the food court. Want to get something? My treat. And you can ask me anything you want."

I love Chinese," Ginger said, sitting down with a plate of steaming noodles and vegetables. "Don't you?"

"Um...sure," Allie said warily. She was even less hungry than usual. "So how does this work?"

To her surprise, Ginger reached into her purse and pulled out a little digital camera. "You ask. I answer." She put the camera on the table. "Simple as that."

"And what's with the camera?"

"Never mind," Ginger said blandly. "We might need it later. Ask away."

"How did Nikki help you quit smoking?"

Ginger chuckled. "If you were weirded out before, I don't know how you'll take *this*." She deftly picked up a noodle with her chopsticks and popped it into her mouth. "She told me…to ask Jesus for help."

Allie's eyebrows shot up in surprise. "Jesus?" she said. "You mean…*the* Jesus?"

"Yeah," Ginger laughed. "*The* Jesus. The man who died for me. The Son of God, the Alpha and Omega, all of that." She sighed happily, a radiant smile on her face.

Allie just stared at her. For the millionth time that day, she was rendered speechless.

"You're a Christian."

"Yeah," Ginger said quietly. "I am. And you know what?" she added, breaking into that radiant smile again. "I don't care what people think anymore. I don't care what Madison says. I'm not ashamed of it."

Allie just stared at her. *This is a joke. Some sort of mean, sick prank. It's got to be.*

"So what do you think?" Ginger said brightly. "Still weirded out?"

"I…er…you're a *Christian?*" Allie leaned forward, her eyes narrowed.

"Come on, Allie!" Ginger reached across the table and took Allie's hand. "Isn't this great? I mean…I just wish everybody could be as happy as me right now!"

"Hmm." Allie pulled her hand away. "That's great. Good for you. Yippee. Whoop-de-doo."

Ginger flinched. "Wow. Sarcasm. That's original."

"Well, I learned from the best," Allie snapped. "You. Remember?"

Avoiding Ginger's eyes, she tried in vain to snag a piece of chicken with her chopsticks. *Stupid things! Why didn't I get a fork?*

"Here," Ginger said. "You're holding the chopsticks wrong. Let me show you—"

"I got it, okay?" Allie snapped at the chicken one more time and missed. With a snarl, she threw the chopsticks down and walked to the condiments bar to get some silverware. She didn't know why she was so angry. *I didn't expect this. It's not fair.*

She glanced back at the table. Ginger wasn't looking so freaking happy anymore. She actually looked kind of shocked. Maybe even hurt.

"What?" Allie walked back, hitching a smirk onto her face. "You gonna cry now? Is that part of the act?"

Ginger didn't reply.

"You really thought I'd believe you?" Allie said coldly. "You think I'm that stupid?"

Ginger shook her head. "I don't care if you believe me or not. It's true."

"It *can't* be!" But suddenly Allie knew, somehow, that it *was.*

And it made her even angrier.

"I can't believe it," she sneered. "I used to look up to you, you know. I used to think you were *tough*, not another Jesus nut. I get enough of that at school, thanks."

Ginger flinched. She picked up the camera and put it back in her purse.

"So you're leaving? Good." Allie picked up her own purse. "We're done here."

"No. We're not." Ginger looked up. For a moment she was the Ice Queen again, her face hard and menacing.

"Sit down," she said coldly. "And shut up."

Her eyes glittered. Allie blinked...and sat down without a word.

"And eat that Chow Mein. I paid good money for it."

"Fine!" Allie stabbed at her chicken sullenly.

For the next few minutes, they ate in silence. Allie kept glancing at Ginger, wondering. *Is it really true? It can't be. Ginger, of all people...*

"I was wondering," Ginger said in a serene voice, wiping her mouth with a napkin. "How did you and Nikki meet?"

"Me and Nikki?" Allie mumbled. "Um...in the third grade." She wiped her mouth. "At Woodhaven."

"And you've been best friends ever since?"

Allie nodded. "We were *more* than friends. We were like sisters." She took another bite of chicken. "My folks split up when I was ten, but it was pretty rough before that. Lots of fights. Lots of screaming. Sometimes my dad would leave and not come back for days. It was pretty bad."

"And Nikki helped out?"

"Yeah. And her parents. I stayed at their house for a while."

"Really?"

"Yeah. I mean," Allie said evasively. "After school and stuff. It wasn't like I ran away from home. I just didn't want to *be* home very much. You know what I mean?"

"Yeah, totally. My dad split when I was nine. Keep going."

"Well, I *loved* staying at the Millers. Her mom and dad are totally in love, and they were so nice to me." Allie smiled wistfully. "They *liked* me. I used to tease Nikki about it. I said we must have been switched at birth, or I was her long-lost sister, or something." She sighed. "I just wanted a normal life. Like hers."

"Yeah. Who wouldn't?"

"But it's all over now," Allie said heavily. "She's dead. I guess nobody's got a perfect life."

"Nobody does."

"Then why are *you* so happy?" Allie said brusquely.

Ginger shook her head, a smile playing on her face. "Sorry," she said. "But I can't help it. You know, that was the funny thing about Nikki; she was always happy. She always seemed to have it together. It got on my nerves."

"I know, me too!" Allie laughed despite herself.

Ginger arched an eyebrow. "*She* got on your nerves too? Your best friend?"

110

Allie smirked and leaned in closer. "She wasn't so normal as she liked to pretend. She had a weird streak."

Ginger frowned. "What do you mean?"

"Well…" Allie paused, savoring the words. "She was into psychic stuff. Unicorns and magic and things…She even thought she could predict the *future!* Seriously! Like when I met her, she told me…" She closed her eyes, remembering. "…that she dreamed about me, and that she knew we would be friends forever." She grinned. "Pretty weird, huh?"

To her surprise, Ginger looked neither amused nor skeptical. "Really?" she said quietly.

"Um…yeah." Allie said, disconcerted. "This was in third grade, though. Kids say weird stuff. No big deal."

"Did she do it again?"

"Do what? 'Predict the future?' Of course not! That would be…Ginger, what's wrong? You look like—"

"She gave her jewelry away."

"She…what?"

"A couple days before the dance." Ginger lowered her voice. "She brought her jewelry box into school and told us to take whatever we wanted. She acted like it was no big deal, saying it was mostly junk in there anyway. But it wasn't. Some of it was really nice, and looked expensive. There were these ruby earrings—"

"*Those* earrings?" Allie gasped. "Her dad gave her those! She loved them! She wouldn't let *me* borrow them!"

"Yeah, well, Madison has them now."

"*What?*" Allie said, outraged.

"Well, Nikki insisted. She said she didn't want them."

Allie felt a chill go through her. *This doesn't make sense.*

"There's another thing." Ginger hesitated. "She kept mentioning you."

"What do you mean?"

"She kept saying things like 'I want to have one last talk with Allie.' It was freaky. It was like she knew."

"No. No way." Allie shook her head. "She couldn't have. It was just a coincidence. She couldn't have known about Brock."

Ginger's brow furrowed. "Yeah. If it *was* Brandon Brock, she couldn't have known. She wouldn't have gone to the formal otherwise. She wasn't planning on it; but she changed her mind at the last—"

"Hey, hey, we're getting off the subject," Allie said hastily. She pointed her fork at Ginger. "You. How'd you end up like this? And what does this have to do with Nikki?"

Ginger sighed and ran her fingers through her hair. "Well, it's a long story..."

Allie's cell phone buzzed. She dug it out of her purse and glanced at it. *Celia. Has she found out yet? Probably—but there's no way she knows about me...she probably just wants to smooth things over.* She silenced the phone. *I don't think so.*

"Who was that?" Ginger asked.

"Just Celia. She's a girl from my school." Allie tossed her phone back in the purse. "You'd like her; she's a Jesus nut too. So are you gonna tell me what happened? Or just sit there grinning like you swallowed a bottle of happy pills?"

Ginger chuckled. "Okay. Lay off the sarcasm, though. Leave it to the pros."

Allie grinned. "Start talking."

11

GHOST STORIES

"So then I heard someone yell 'fire!'" Mr. Simonelli said. "And I ran back to the classroom, and there was this guy—" he placed an arm round Brian's shoulders, "—standing there as cool as a cucumber, and the fire was out."

The crowd of parents beamed at Brian. "Good for you!" Mrs. Simonelli said in her high, sing-song voice. "What went through your mind?"

"I don't know," Brian muttered, his face red. "I just reacted."

Mr. Simonelli chuckled. "I know what *my* reaction would be: *Holy sh—*"

"Vince!" Mrs. Simonelli said severely.

The kitchen rang with laughter. Brian looked down at the brown-tiled floor, wishing he could sink through it.

His dad seemed to sense what Brian was going through. "And that reminds me: what did the fire chief say?" He steered the conversation away from his son. Brian was grateful.

He felt a tap on his shoulder. "Burke." Liz was standing at his elbow. "Come on," she whispered. "While they're distracted."

"Oh!" He glanced around furtively, and then followed her out into the front hall. As the door swung closed behind him, he heard his mother say, "Brian? Now where did he go?"

He heaved a sigh of relief. "Thanks."

"No problem." Liz grinned. "You looked like you needed an escape plan."

He grinned back—and then he remembered that he was mad at her. "Yes," he said stiffly. "Well…I better go."

"Hang on a sec." Liz took a deep breath. "Burke, we need to talk."

"Okay."

"Not here. Can we go someplace private? I don't want to be overheard."

Brian arched an eyebrow. *Maybe she wants to apologize for what she did to Mary. I hope so.* He didn't like being mad at Liz. "Okay," he said. "Follow me."

He led her to a door by the stairs that opened onto a narrow hallway. "Not the living room!" Liz said. "They're watching a movie in there."

Brian smiled. "We're not going there. We—"

But at that moment Celia emerged from the door at the end of the hallway. "Hey Brian," she said anxiously. "Can I use your home phone? My cell phone doesn't get any reception, and I need to call Allie…"

Brian shrugged. "Sure. It's in the kitchen."

He waited until Celia was safely gone, and then led Liz up to a side door. "Check this out." He pulled a key out of his pocket and unlocked the door.

They entered a large, stately room. On one side was a large desk and computer; on the other were some leather armchairs grouped round a walnut coffee table. The walls were lined with bookshelves, pictures and corkboards. A small table lay nestled in one corner, covered in blueprints. Behind the desk, a row of arched bay windows looked out into the woods.

Liz whistled. "Wow. What is this place?"

"My dad's study." Brian closed and locked the door. "He meets clients here. It's always locked."

Liz whistled. "We should have movie night *here*. Too bad there's no TV."

Brian grinned. "Well, actually…" He walked over to the opposite wall and pulled open a set of double doors. "There is."

"No way!" Liz ran over to the huge flat screen TV inside the closet. "What's this for?"

"Oh, presentations, video conferencing…" Brian shrugged. "That sort of stuff."

Liz chuckled. "I keep forgetting that your dad's loaded. What a cool hideout! How'd you get a key?"

"My dad let me have a copy. He—"

"Wait a sec." She grabbed his arm. "You hear that?"

Brian heard it too: voices. Voices out in the hallway. He glanced at the door and saw, to his horror that the knob was turning.

Liz shoved him hard to one side of the narrow closet, and then pulled both doors closed, plunging them into darkness. A moment later they heard the door open and the sound of footsteps.

Liz's hand grabbed his wrist. "*Quiet!*" she hissed.

It all started a year ago," Ginger said. She hesitated. "I had a little…thing over the summer."

Allie cocked an eyebrow. "Did this *thing* have a name?"

Ginger nodded. "Michael."

"Was he cute?"

"Yeah," Ginger laughed. And then her face clouded, and she actually blushed.

"He was the love of my life," she whispered. "He stole my heart."

Allie blinked. *Wow. She got it bad.* "So you really fell for this guy, huh?" she said lightly.

"Yeah. You could say that."

"But it didn't work out. Is that all?" Allie shrugged. "Well, you know what they say…better to have loved and lost—"

"I didn't lose Michael. I ditched him."

"Really? Why?"

Ginger scowled. "Because he wanted too much from me!" she said hotly. "He wanted a lifetime commitment!"

Allie smirked. "The needy type, huh?"

"I'm serious!" Ginger said hotly. "It was...crazy. He was changing me, Allie!"

Allie's smile vanished. "What are you talking about?"

"Look..." Ginger leaned forward and tapped the table. "This guy was *not* in my plans, okay? He came out of nowhere, swept me off my feet, but...I was ashamed to be with him! He wasn't—" She laughed bitterly. "He wasn't the kind of guy you'd expect *me* to be with. You get the picture?"

Allie stared at her—and then remembered James giving her those flowers—how she had hugged him, and the thought had crossed her mind...*ugh!*

"Really?" She shook her head. "You were *with* a guy like that?"

"Yeah!" Ginger said coldly, as if daring Allie to make fun of her. "Pretty funny, huh?"

"Um...no," Allie mumbled. "Sorry. So how long did it last?"

Ginger closed her eyes. "About two and a half months. But I kept it under wraps. I didn't tell anybody. And finally I wimped out. I killed the thing. It was just too much."

Allie took a bite of chicken and chewed it thoughtfully. Now *that* sounded like the Ginger she remembered—tough. Brutal. But the old Ginger would have moved on pretty quickly. Ginger had hooked up with so many different guys...the only time she was serious was with Bobby, and even that hadn't lasted long. And now she was...love struck? Broken-hearted? Why?

"Um...well, if you like this guy, can't you get him back?" she said awkwardly.

"No," Ginger said softly. "He won't be back. I made sure of that."

Allie sighed. "Fine. So why can't you just move on?"

"I thought I had. I was fine for a long time. But then one day, two weeks before Christmas, I lost it. Had a total nervous breakdown during biology class. Next thing I know I'm in the bathroom crying my eyes out. And that's where Nikki found me."

"Nikki?" Allie looked up, startled. "What'd *she* do?"

"Nothing. She just listened. I couldn't believe it. I always thought Nikki hated me."

I thought so too.

"And now she's hugging me as I'm bawling my head off, telling her my miserable life story." Ginger's mouth twisted in a painful smile. "I miss her," she finished sadly.

"Yeah," Allie murmured, feeling a sort of pain inside; but a *good* kind of pain, more like an ache than a stab. "Me too." She chuckled. "Nikki always had a soft spot for criers. One time when I was eleven my dad didn't show up for a visit, and I lost it. I called Nikki up, and she actually biked over to my house—we lived a mile away. She didn't even tell her mom and dad—they almost called the cops, and she got grounded for it. But that didn't matter—all she cared about was—"

She looked away, her stomach churning. The grief had come out of nowhere, like it always did, and now it was so much stronger. *No, no, no! Not in front of Ginger!*

"...about you," Ginger finished quietly.

"Yeah," Allie muttered. "Sorry."

"It's okay." Ginger said quietly. "It's okay to miss her. You were so lucky to have her."

"Yeah, I know." Allie played with her food fretfully. "Sure, she was kind of a pushover, and she was weird, and she nagged me a lot...but if you *really* needed a friend, she'd always be there. Always." She let out another rueful chuckle. "I'm kind of surprised she didn't ever turn into a Jesus freak like you."

"What are you talking about?" Ginger looked astonished. "Didn't you know?"

"Know what?"

"Dude! Nikki *was* a Christian! She's the one who converted me!"

For a moment the two girls stared at each other. Then Ginger grinned. "Wow. That's kind of funny."

"How?" Allie said blankly. "Why didn't...she never told me!"

"Well, it happened after you left," Ginger said. "She started going to this big church. It's called Cross Bridge. Ever heard of it?"

"No," Allie said. "What's it like?"

"It's *awesome*," Ginger said. "It's not like church at all. They have this great music, and they have small groups, and the pastor is so cool—"

"Yeah, yeah, whatever," Allie said impatiently. "So when did she start going to this place?"

"I don't know. November, I guess."

"I was already in John Paul 2 High by then."

"You know, she mentioned that. She said that's why she started thinking about Jesus and God. Because you started talking about it too." Ginger shook her head. "Sorry. I just assumed you knew all this."

"How could I? She never told me!" Allie felt betrayed. *How could Nikki not have told her?*

But her mind was already racing back, revisiting the past, seeing it in a new light.

After she had started at John Paul 2 High, she had still talked to Nikki a lot...but as the months went by, they hadn't talked as much. Sure, there was the occasional email or IM or phone call...but it wasn't the same.

Well, I was making new friends. Celia. George. I didn't need her as much.

Ginger gave her a shrewd look, as if she guessed what Allie was thinking. "Don't beat yourself up," she said. "Nikki didn't tell anyone about it at first. I didn't know till January, when she started asking me to go."

"*She* asked *you?*"

"Yeah. Constantly. Every time I saw her, it was all 'Come to Cross Bridge. See if it's legit. Come on. Come on.'"

Allie smiled faintly. "Now *that* sounds like her."

"Yeah. I finally gave in. Went just to shut her up."

"Yeah." Allie snickered. "Nikki was *such* a nag, you know? She was always bugging me to do the 'right thing.' Always trying to reform me."

Ginger frowned. "Reform you?"

Allie smirked. "Nikki didn't even want to hang out with you guys at first. I did. *I* convinced *her*. And she didn't like me dating Tyler either; she thought I was too young. She was always *pestering* me like that. Looks like she did the same thing to you, getting you to go to this Cross Creek place—"

Ginger looked a bit troubled. "Cross Bridge."

"Whatever. So what was it like?"

"Well...to be honest, it was a little creepy at first." Ginger took a deep breath. "The preacher—Pastor Holtz—he preached this sermon, and it was exactly what I needed to hear. He talked about kindness. And treating people right."

"And you *listened?*"

"I had to," Ginger mumbled. "After what I did to Michael...I had to. Even though it hurt."

"Um...okay. What else did he talk about?"

"Jesus," Ginger said in a low voice. "About how much Jesus loved me, no matter what I did. About how He could take away all the bad stuff and just...*fill* me up with love."

Allie blinked. "What was that? Fill you up?"

"Yeah." Ginger sighed. "You ever feel like you're just...empty? Like, you have nothing inside of you?"

Allie just looked down at her hands. "Um...what happened next?"

"Well, I went again. I just had to."

"Sounds like a cult." Allie forced a laugh. "You *had* to come back? What, did this Holtz guy brainwash you? Is *that* why you're so different?"

Ginger chuckled. "First of all, I'm not *that* different. I still got the same issues, but, Allie..." She smiled that radiant smile again. "You're right! *Everything's* different now!"

"Why? How?"

Ginger closed her eyes. "It happened the third time I came. I finally let him in. And he *did* fill me up. I wasn't empty anymore."

She smiled that radiant smile again. She looked so unbelievably happy...as if the peace and joy on her face shone out like light...and everything the light touched became as beautiful as her.

Allie just stared at her, unable to put her thoughts into words. "Wow." She laughed awkwardly. "It's like you're...in *love* or something."

"I am."

Allie's laugh faded. She looked down at her hands, embarrassed. "You're in love, huh? With Jesus?"

"Yes!" Ginger took Allie's hands. "And you can be too, Allie!"

"No, I can't!"

"Why not?"

"Because…" Allie opened her mouth, intending to tell Ginger how she'd *never* be a good girl like Nikki and Celia, all mushy and wimpy. But this was *Ginger*. Ginger was as far from Celia or Nikki as you could get. Tough. Confident. Regal.

And she still was now. She *hadn't* changed that much. She was just more…real. A strange thought flitted through Allie's mind: *Maybe this is the real Ginger. Maybe the Ginger I knew before was a fake. This is what she's supposed to be.* And then another, even stranger thought came: *Maybe I can be real too. Not a pretty mannequin. Not dead. Not fake. Real.*

"Okay," she said slowly. "Let's pretend I actually believe you. What's the trick to all this? What do I need to do?"

Ginger chuckled. "Don't be an idiot. There's no trick. You don't need to *do* anything."

"Then what—"

"Don't you get it? You got to give up. Surrender. Let go. Let Jesus in."

"I…don't know what that means."

"Why don't you come to Cross Bridge and find out? There's a service tonight."

Allie looked down at her hands. "I don't know…"

But what else could she do? Go back to John Paul 2 High? Every time she went there, something horrible seemed to happen. Or go home and creep back into her room? She was so *sick* of her life. She felt so trapped. And here was an escape. Maybe.

Don't go, an alarmed voice said inside her. *It can't be real. She's nuts. And you'll be nuts if you go with her.*

I don't care. It can't be worse than what I'm in now.

"Sure." She looked up. "Why not? I'll go."

Brian froze, dumbfounded, listening through the closet door.

"...and by the time I got to it, the damage was already done," came Hank's voice. "I honestly can't figure it out, Mr. Burke—"

"Call me Dennis," His father said. "Vince? What do you think?"

"I think Hank's being too hard on himself," Mr. Simonelli's gravelly voice replied. "That boiler's thirty years old. But coming right after the fire—"

"Exactly," came a fourth voice: Mr. Costain. "This just looks bad."

"Let's get out of here," Brian whispered. "It's just my dad—"

"Shut *up!*" Liz hissed.

"I'm not going to stay here and eavesdrop!"

"Brian Burke, if you don't shut up," she hissed back. "I'll...I'll say we were making out!"

"What?" he said, aghast.

"Shut *up!*"

He did. But he still wanted to see what was going on. Carefully he moved to the crack between the double doors. "I'm just going to watch," he whispered. "I'll be quiet."

"You better!"

He peered through the crack and saw his dad sitting behind his desk, and Mr. Costain, Mr. Simonelli and Hank sitting in the armchairs.

"—if we could just get the blueprints we could be sure," Mr. Simonelli was saying. "But we can't. The only copies are in the state archives."

"So let's get them," his dad said.

"We need a court order." Mr. Simonelli snorted. "Don't you love bureaucracy? Never mind. Hank and I are keeping the power off until we figure this out. And I was hoping that when Dan's in Harrisburg..."

"Yes, that's what I was thinking," his father said. "When are you leaving, Dan?"

Mr. Costain sighed. "Emily and I are leaving Monday; along with Danny, Jeremy and Sophia."

The other men glanced at him curiously. "Wasn't this supposed to be a business trip?" Mr. Simonelli said.

"Yes." Mr. Costain sighed again. "But my wife and I decided to make it a vacation too. We really haven't had a break since the school started. So we're staying at my in-laws and taking along the kids, except for Celia, Miranda and John Mark."

"John Mark's staying?" his dad asked.

"Celia insisted on it. She volunteered herself and her sister to babysit him." Mr. Costain smiled wryly. "I'm not sure if she told Miranda beforehand. Anyway, this shouldn't change things on the business side. I'll be meeting with your lawyer on Monday, and the hearings on Thursday. In the meantime we just got to make sure there are no more incidents."

"And for that we need the blueprints." His father pulled out a business card and scribbled something on it. "I'm going to give Pete a call."

"Pete?" Liz whispered. "Who's that?"

"Pete Hegseth," Brian whispered back. "He's a state senator. My dad knows him."

"—and we don't really need power now, do we?" His dad cracked a smile. "You can keep the kids busy with drywall and painting until this gets sorted out. But Vince, I don't think you should depend on Liz to double-check things."

"Don't worry," Mr. Simonelli said gruffly. "I fired her."

Brian winced. Liz's hand had tightened painfully on his wrist.

"But then there's the matter of inspections," Mr. Costain said. "Not totally unexpected—the city has always been hostile to us. But in any case, we need to be up to code by next Friday."

"Then we'll need a new boiler," Mr. Simonelli said. "It'll cost at least five grand, maybe more."

Mr. Costain glanced at his dad. "Dennis," he said. "If you can't contribute this time, I understand."

His dad smiled warmly. "Dan. We all have our part to play in this endeavor, and I know mine." He stood up. "Vince, me and you will go get the boiler next week. I'll pay for it."

The other men looked startled. "Dennis," Mr. Costain said. "I can cover this loan in the fall...when the tuition checks come in—"

His dad chuckled. "I never lend money, Dan. You know that. Just keep doing what you're doing. That's payment enough for me."

The four men shook hands. "God bless you, Dennis," Mr. Costain said.

"He has. Now let's get back to the party."

The four men left the desk and passed out of sight.

As soon as he heard the click of the lock, Brian pushed the doors open and tore himself away from Liz. "What is *wrong* with you?" he said furiously.

"Hey!" She looked outraged. "I was just trying to save your butt! Didn't you say no one was allowed in here?"

"I am. But if my dad finds out I was hiding here, listening..."

"Yeah, that *was* kind of interesting," Liz said thoughtfully. "Do you know what it means?"

"I don't *want* to know! Don't you get it? My dad *trusts me*, Liz! But if he finds out I was eavesdropping..."

"Okay, fine!" she retorted. "I didn't realize you had such a cozy relationship with your dad! I don't with mine, in case you hadn't noticed! I was only trying to help!"

"Like you helped with Mary Summers? Keeping her and Jacinta from coming here?"

"What? Um..." A flicker of guilt showed on her face. "Who told you that?"

"She did! Don't deny it!"

"All right! All right!" Liz held up her hands. "I admit it. But I did it to help *you*, Burke. Honest."

Brian scowled. "You really want to help me? Then stop treating me like an idiot. Let me make my own decisions! I can take care of *myself*, Liz!"

Liz gaped at him for a moment. Then she looked down at her shoes, blushing. "Brian," she said in a small voice. "I'm sorry."

Brian's eyes narrowed. "Really?"

"Yeah." She sighed. "You're right. I shouldn't have gone behind your back. From now on, I'm gonna play it straight with you." She held out her hand. "Okay?"

Brian frowned. "Okay." He shook her hand.

"Good!" Liz looked relieved. "Now we can talk."

"About what?"

"I think you *know* what." Liz walked over and sat down in the same armchair her father had used. "Because I've been thinking the same thing. And after what we just heard, I'm thinking even harder."

Brian stared at her. Then, slowly, he walked over and sat down too.

"I *have* been thinking," he said hesitantly. "First there was that fire last week...then the boiler broke down today..."

"Yeah!" Liz nodded. "Too much of a coincidence, doncha think?"

"So what are you saying?"

"I'm saying," Liz said solemnly, "that the poltergeist is back."

12

JESUS WEPT

"What's on your mind, Allie? Having second thoughts?"

Allie looked away from the rain-drizzled car window. "No," she said. "Actually, I was thinking about what you said."

"Which part?" Ginger grinned. "I said a lot." She'd convinced Allie to drop off her car at her mom's house and drive to Cross Bridge with her.

"About Brock. You said, 'if it really *was* Brock.' What did you mean?"

Ginger drummed her fingers on the steering wheel. "Well...I know those guys pretty well, obviously."

"Whaddya mean, obviously?"

Ginger gave her a funny look. "Neil's my cousin. Didn't you know?"

"You're related to *Flynt?*" Allie laughed harshly. "Wow. Sorry."

Ginger scowled. "Quit it. Neil's not as bad as the other two."

"Sure, whatever." Allie smirked. "So you don't think Brandon Brock did it? Why not? Because he was too nice?"

"No," Ginger said flatly. "He was too dumb. No disrespect to the dead, but Brandon Brock was slightly less smart than a pack of crackers. They all were. Tyler was the smartest of those three; and Tyler ain't that smart."

"Hmmph." Allie frowned to herself. She had thought the exact same thing...but Ginger didn't know what she did. It had to be Brock. The evidence said so. "Well, it doesn't take a lot of brains to shoot up a dance, does it?" she said sulkily.

"Maybe not," Ginger admitted. "All I know is that *I* was really surprised when they fingered Brock."

"So was I," Allie muttered. "But I was relieved, too. I was happy."

"Why?"

"Because he's dead."

The words came out in a flat, merciless voice. It sounded strange to her own ears.

"Um...wow," Ginger said after a long, painful pause. "He killed himself, Allie!"

"He deserved it," she retorted, and turned away, glaring out the window into the rainy, windy darkness.

"Are we there yet?" she said after a few moments.

"Yeah," Ginger said, looking troubled. "Here it is."

They pulled into a large, nearly full parking lot. "There's the church." Ginger pointed at a large, sleek-looking building. It didn't look like any church Allie had ever seen. There were no stained glass windows, no big wooden doors...but there *was* a big metal cross on the top, lit by spotlights. The whole thing looked kind of...*cool*, actually.

They exited the car and walked up to the church. Under a wide steel porch was a row of glass doors, and inside there were couches, coffee tables, carpets...and people. *Lots* of people talking, laughing and generally looking pleased to be there.

Wow. This is a church?

The poltergeist," Brian muttered. "Are you sure?"

"What else could it be?"

"Okay, let's think this through," Brian said. "How did the fire start? Hank and your dad didn't say it was sabotage."

"They don't know *what* it was," Liz snapped. "They can't figure out how it happened. But *I* did."

"Really?" Brian said skeptically.

"Yeah." Liz leaned forward. "The fire started when Allie flipped the light switch in the girls' bathroom, right?"

"Right..."

"That bathroom and the classroom are linked. They're on the same circuit. Hank took out the fuse for that circuit the night before— I saw him. So later that night, the poltergeist gets into the school—"

"How?"

"Hank's keys," Liz said with a satisfied smile. "I bet he swiped them from Hank at some point, used them to unlock the doors, and then left them in the school so we'd all think Hank had just lost them again."

Brian smiled. "Or Hank really *did* just lose them."

"Really? Then explain this: on the morning of the fire, the front doors were unlocked. And I *saw* my dad lock them the night before."

"Oh." Brian's smile faded. "Well, that's..."

"Let me finish. The poltergeist gets into the school. He sees that we're working on that classroom. So he goes to the fuse box and...well, he probably screwed a penny in it."

"He what?"

"You know how a fuse works, right? If the voltage gets too high, the wires heat up. The fuse is made of metal that melts at a lower temperature. So it melts *first* and breaks the current. But if you take the fuse out and put a *penny* there instead, you can overheat the circuit. Copper is a high conductor; it won't melt like a fuse will."

"So the poltergeist puts a penny in the fuse box," Brian said slowly. "What then? He goes to the bathroom and plugs in your tools. Why?"

"He also took off my 'out of order' sign." Liz arched an eyebrow. "You see?"

"No."

"Dude! You know that light switch in the bathroom? It doesn't just turn on the lights—it turns on the outlets! *Now* do you see?"

Brian frowned...then his eyes widened.

"Yes. He set a trap."

"Exactly!" Liz said eagerly. "And a pretty good one too. All he needed was a penny. Then he just had to wait for some girl to go inside the bathroom, flip the switch, and..."

"And all those outlets turn on," Brian finished. "and with your tools plugged in..."

"...and all those high-voltage tools start up, the wires turn red-hot, and voila! You got a fire!" Liz concluded triumphantly. "Pretty clever, actually."

"Yes..." Brian's brow furrowed. It *was* clever. It was also ruthless. He thought of the smoke billowing out of the classroom door, with his mom and sister and brother in the building, and he shuddered. *This is bad stuff. Evil stuff.*

"Have you told your dad about this?" he said.

Liz's eyes shifted slightly. "Of course I did."

"What did *he* think?"

"He...well...he looked at me like I was nuts, and told me to make sure I unplugged my tools next time."

"Oh." Brian blinked. "So...*did* you unplug your tools?"

"Yeah! I did!" she said hotly. "I may be a lot of things, but I'm not *stupid*, Burke!"

"Sorry!" But he was secretly relieved. It was obvious Liz *thought* she had unplugged her tools. But maybe she hadn't. That seemed more likely than some sinister villain with evil plans to kill them all.

"How about the penny thing?" he asked. "*Was* there a penny in the fuse box?"

Liz scowled. "No," she admitted. "I checked the next day. The socket was empty. They *still* don't have an answer to why there was power in the bathroom at all—since they won't listen to me," she added bitterly. "Obviously the poltergeist came back after the fire—maybe that night—and took the penny out again."

"With Hank's keys," Brian said dryly. "Maybe he 'swiped' them again, right?"

"He could have made a copy!"

"Why not just hold onto them?"

"So no one would get suspicious!"

"Well, the *fire* is even more suspicious."

"Okay, I get it. You don't believe me." Liz stood up. "That's why we need to take a look at that boiler."

"We?"

"Aw, come on, Burke!"

"Why me? Why not J.P., or—"

"J.P.'s too stupid for this!"

"No he's not," Brian retorted. "He almost caught the poltergeist the first time, remember?"

"Yeah, but nobody's gonna take him seriously! Nobody takes *me* seriously! But you're different. People respect you. Including my dad."

Brian sighed. "What do you want me to do, Liz?"

"Well, for starters you can find out when they're going to replace that boiler. And maybe you can come look at it with me. Please?"

"I don't know…"

Liz smirked. "*Pleeeze?*" she said in a soft, breathy voice, almost exactly like Mary Summers. "If I talk like *this*, will you do it?" She pranced over and batted her eyelashes. "*Pweeze, Brian?*"

"Quit it!" He pushed her away, both irritated and amused. "I'll think about it, okay?"

"All right, all right." Liz grinned. "But don't think too long, Burke. I can be *way* more annoying than this."

"I believe you," he said dryly.

Allie and Ginger walked through the front doors and into a crowd of teenagers. "Wow," Allie laughed. "This feels like a rock concert."

"Oh, I forgot!" Ginger said. "There's gonna be a band here tonight!"

"Really?"

"Yeah! They're called Forgyven. They're *really* cool, and you know who the lead singer is? Keenan Clearwater!"

"No way!" Allie said. "Simone's older brother?"

"Yeah! Simone's here too. So you've met Keenan?"

"Once or twice," Allie said. Simone and her friend Tara were the captains of the cheer squad. As a matter of fact Allie had only met

Keenan once; the only thing she could remember about him was that he was extremely cute.

They passed into a circular auditorium, with seats—not pews, but real padded seats—going down in descending rows. At the bottom there was a stage, with a drum set, microphones, and speakers. A bare wooden cross hung on the back wall. Above the stage hung a jumbo screen, blazing the message **WELCOME TO CROSS BRIDGE!** in big orange letters.

Meanwhile, people were filing down the aisles and taking their seats. It looked like the service—or concert, or whatever—was about to start. Feeling slightly confused, Allie followed Ginger down the aisle.

Then she bumped into someone, a slender girl with sandy blonde hair. "Oh, sorry—Simone?" she said, amazed.

"Allie? Is that you?" Simone Clearwater laughed. "Man, I haven't seen you in, like, forever!"

"Is Tara here too?"

"Yeah, she's saving us seats in the front. Come on!"

Allie followed the other girls, shaking her head. Two more Ice Queens. She wondered if Madison would show up, or Brad Powell. She grinned. *So THIS is where the cool people go to church.*

They came down to the front row. "Hey, Allie!" Tara, a thin, slight girl with black hair, waved at her with a warm smile.

"Hi," Allie said hesitantly. This was different too. Tara was always quiet, aloof and a bit of snob. She had certainly never been as friendly as she was now.

It felt like old times. Soon she was chatting with the two other girls, and found out what she had been curious about: how they had ended up at Cross Bridge.

"I've always come here," Tara said shyly. "Even before Nikki. I kind of grew up here."

"So did I," Simone said. "But I stopped going a long time ago. Then Ginger convinced me to come back after Nikki died."

"So you're not just here because your brother's playing?" Allie said.

130

"Nah—he's been playing here for years." Simone chuckled. "Keenan's always been the holy roller of the family."

"But do you *like* it here?" Allie said.

"Oh, yeah!" Simone said.

"Why?"

"Because *Jesus* is here!" Simone said enthusiastically.

"He is?" Allie said. "You mean, like in the..." she laughed nervously. "In the Eucharist?"

"The what?" Simone looked puzzled. "No, I mean he's here because the Bible says so. *Where two or three come together in my name, there am I with them.*"

"*You* know the Bible?" Allie blurted out.

Simone giggled. "Well, not as much as I should. I'm kind of a Bible ignoramus. Keenan's a lot better."

Allie gave a tentative smile in return. It was nice to not be the only Bible ignoramus in the group.

The crowd suddenly roared. Some guys had come onto the stage. They looked young; maybe teenagers or a little older. One of them sat behind the drums—the others slung on electric guitars.

The screen above the stage flashed the word **FORGYVEN**, and the lead singer strolled up to a microphone in the center, an acoustic guitar slung round his neck. There he was: Keenan Clearwater, Simone's holy roller brother.

Holy or not, Keenan was as cute as she remembered. He had shoulder-length brown hair, a goatee and a pleasant, boyish face. "Hey there!" he said into the microphone. "How y'all doing tonight?"

The crowd roared in response, and Keenan flashed a big smile. He really had a great smile. "Are you ready to praise God?"

"*Yeah!*"

And then the music started, loud and exuberant. Keenan started singing, and everyone joined in.

After a while, Allie found herself singing along with everyone else, following the lyrics as they appeared on the jumbo screen. It sure was different...nothing like the boring, sappy music at St.

131

Bridget's. This music was *fun*. No, more than fun; joyful. Like a love song. A happy, joyful love song.

The song ended with a huge drum roll and thunderous applause. "All right!" Keenan yelled into the microphone. "Praise God!" The crowd roared back in response, and there were cries of "Amen!" "Praise God!"

Keenan held up his hands, and the cheers subsided. "Okay, we're going to pass into a spirit of prayer now. Please welcome the wisest man I know...Pastor Mark Holtz!"

A man in a blue polo shirt and khaki pants walked onto the stage to thunderous applause. He looked like he was in his 30's, with straight black hair, and he smiled warmly at the crowd. He didn't look like a creepy cult leader. He looked normal.

"Thank you, thank you!" Pastor Holtz said in a deep, clear voice. "Welcome to all of you! First I'd like to thank Forgyven for leading us in worship tonight. Come on, let's give them a big hand!"

Keenan Clearwater waved and bowed. There were a few wolf whistles, and general laughter. Allie grinned. Apparently she wasn't the only one who thought Keenan was cute.

"Okay, okay!" Pastor Holtz said, chuckling. "Control yourselves, ladies! Now...I'd like to talk to you a bit. I want to talk about *healing*."

The crowd subsided. Allie frowned. *Healing? Is that all? That doesn't sound very life-changing.*

"Let me ask you something. Who here has ever gotten cut or bruised or something? Go on, raise your hands."

A forest of hands went up. Pastor Holtz strode across the stage, microphone in hand. "What happens when you get a little cut? You bleed a little, but you heal up fine on your own. But sometimes..." He stopped and looked out over the crowd. "Sometimes you get a *bad* cut."

"I got a bad cut once, when I was seven years old." He chuckled. "You know how Keenan just said I was 'the wisest man he knew' or something? Well...wait until he hears *this*."

Pastor Holtz rolled his eyes and sighed, drawing chuckles from the crowd. "The thing is...I *really* liked pirates when I was a kid. So I always used to take a stick and pretend it was a knife, and hold it in my mouth, like a pirate!"

Pastor Holtz bent down suddenly, and when he straightened, he was holding a stick in his hand. The crowd laughed and applauded. "A stick just like this! The thing is...I didn't quite have the right idea. I didn't bite on the stick like this—" he bit down on the stick, pirate-style. "No, I bit down on it like *this*—" he stuck one end of the stick into his mouth and bit down, so that the other end stuck out. "Thee?"

The crowd roared with laughter. Pastor Holtz gave them a mock bow. "I know, I know! Pretty slick, huh? Anyway, we had a tree house in the back yard, and I used to pretend that it was my *pirate* ship, y'know? So one day, while I had that stupid stick in my mouth, I decided it would be a really *cool* idea to jump out of the tree house! Well, you can guess what happened. I hit the ground, and that stick *jabbed* up—"

He illustrated the motion with his hand, drawing some appreciative gasps from the crowd. "—And gave me a big old cut all over the roof of my mouth! I'll never forget the look the emergency room doctor gave me! 'What happened to *you?'* he said. 'I fell out of a tree,' I said. 'Yes, the *stupid* tree,' he said. 'And you hit every branch on the way down!'"

"Now," Pastor Holtz went on after the laughter died down. "On that day I got hurt bad; so bad that I had to go to the hospital." He chuckled. "I *definitely* couldn't handle that on my own! I had to go to a professional!

"You know something? There are spiritual hurts. Our souls can get cut and bruised just like our bodies. And sometimes you get a *bad* cut. Sometimes you have to go..." He turned and pointed to the bare wooden cross. "...to a professional."

There was absolute silence. Pastor Holtz stood, head bowed, for a moment.

"Recently," he said quietly, "we got one of those bad cuts. We lost someone. Her name was Nikki Miller."

No. Allie suddenly felt cold. *No! Don't talk about this!* She turned to Ginger. "What's he doing?" she whispered furiously.

133

Ginger looked taken aback. "Calm down," she said. "It's no big deal—"

"It is for me!" Allie hissed.

"I got to know Nikki," Pastor Holtz said, "In the last few months of her life. I first met her in December, when she came here; and she told me of her own wounds...her loneliness, her sadness. I told her about Jesus and the redemptive power of the Cross. Nikki believed. She listened. She gave her heart to Christ, and He saved her."

Allie scowled. *This guy is full of it. Nikki didn't* need *to be saved. She wasn't messed up. She was happy*—

"And then, two months ago..." Pastor Holtz paused, and for a moment grief—real, heart-felt grief—showed on his face. "Nikki was taken from us. Taken in an unspeakable act of violence."

He sighed heavily. "Now on one level, I can take comfort from the cross. After all, Nikki gave her life to Christ, and surely Christ has her now."

Allie felt anger well up in her stomach. *She* didn't feel comforted. She felt angry, sad and confused, all at once. Maybe Nikki *had* found Jesus, but so what? Maybe Jesus was only for people like her, good people with good families, sheltered, safe, free of real hardship. Anyway, Nikki was gone now, gone forever...and Allie was alone. Alone, in a world without Nikki, without Jesus, without *anyone...*

She felt the dark wave come again, and suddenly she was afraid...afraid that she would be swept away by it, that she would...freak out or something in front of everybody.

"That's it," she hissed, and stood up. "I'm leaving."

"No!" Ginger grabbed her arm. "Allie, please, don't—"

"But what about us?" Allie froze. Pastor Holtz's words rang through the silent church, angry, anguished, and bitter.

"*What about us?* It's not fair! Nikki didn't deserve this! Neither do we! What does God say to that? How does he answer our complaint when we look at him and say—" Pastor Holtz turned and pointed at the cross accusingly, "This is *your* fault! If you had just *done* something, Nikki wouldn't have died!"

Pastor Holtz turned back to the crowd. "Did you know," he said. "That somebody asked Jesus the same question once?"

He held up a bible. "It's in the story of Lazarus. Let's read it."

Allie sank back in her chair. The dark wave was gone, for now; all she felt was surprise.

Pastor Holtz began reading in a deep, clear voice. Allie had heard about Lazarus before, of course: the guy in the tomb that Jesus raised from the dead. But she still found herself hanging on every word, compelled to listen by the sheer strangeness of the story: Jesus hears that His friend Lazarus, a friend whom he loves, is sick. Lazarus' two sisters, Martha and Mary, want him to come.

Jesus tells his disciples that Lazarus is now dead; and he's *glad* that he's dead; but still He goes to the house of Lazarus, defying danger to get there.

By the time he arrives, Lazarus has been dead four days. Lazarus' sister, Martha, comes to see Him, and then...

Pastor Holtz looked up. "Now," he said. "Listen carefully to this part in John chapter 11. This is important. Remember what I said about wounds. Martha and Mary are both wounded. Wounded badly. And Jesus is the doctor.

'Lord,' Martha said to Jesus, 'if you had been here, my brother would not have died. But I know that even now God will give you whatever you ask.'

Jesus said to her, 'Your brother will rise again.'

Martha answered, 'I know he will rise again in the resurrection at the last day.'

Jesus said to her, 'I am the resurrection and the life. The one who believes in me will live, even though they die; and whoever lives by believing in me will never die. Do you believe this?'

Do you?" Pastor Holtz gazed at the crowd, and for a second Allie thought his eyes lit on her. "Do you believe that Jesus can bring you back to life? That He *is* life? In other words...do you *trust* the doctor? 'Cause that's the first step: trust. Listen to Martha:

'Yes, Lord,' she replied, 'I believe that you are the Messiah, the Son of God, who is to come into the world.'

135

Martha trusts Jesus." Pastor Holtz said. "Even when she's hurt, she trusts the doctor. She believes."

Yeah, Allie thought bitterly. *Like Ginger. But not me.*

"But maybe you're not like Martha." Pastor Holtz said quietly. "After all, it's not easy to trust when you're in pain. But Jesus knows this!" His voice rose, echoing through the room like a trumpet. "Jesus *knows* that it's hard to believe when you're hurt, and you feel betrayed, and you're angry! And *that's* when we need to just...cling to our faith. And it ain't easy. Being a follower of Jesus is always tough, but toughest when you have to believe blindly, in the dark, with no comfort or hope. That's how Mary must have felt. When she sees Jesus, look what happens:

She fell at his feet and said, 'Lord, if you had been here, my brother would not have died.'

Mary's not as strong! She doesn't understand? She just...cries out to Jesus! Now that's the normal reaction! That's what *I* felt after I heard about Nikki! Why, Lord? Why did this happen—to her?"

Yeah, why?? Allie thought. And suddenly she realized that she had been asking this every day since Nikki's death.

"But listen to what happens next:"

When Jesus saw her weeping, and the Jews who had come along with her also weeping, he was deeply moved in spirit and troubled.

"Where have you laid him?" he asked.

"Come and see, Lord," they replied.

Jesus wept.

"Jesus wept!" Pastor Holtz said. "He was the Son of God, the Alpha and the Omega, present from the beginning of time, and yet He wept. He wept because He loved His friend, and He wept because he saw the pain of Martha and Mary. Jesus...knows about grief. He knows about pain. He took our pains for Himself on the cross."

"So, if you're feeling hurt tonight...if you're feeling angry, if you're feeling like your heart will just...burst from all the pain, but you just...can't let go, or lose control...look at Jesus. Tell Him your pain. Give it to Him. He understands. Jesus wept...why can't you?"

Allie's heart swelled in her chest. She thought about Jesus weeping...and then she thought about Nikki's mom and dad crying at the funeral, and how *she* had cried too.

Then she remembered how she had wanted to cry so many times since then, but she hadn't. She couldn't. She had to be strong...

No. You have to give up.

Maybe I just don't want to. Maybe I'm too proud. Proud? Of what? I've got nothing. Nothing left. Maybe that's what I...deserve...

Shuddering, overwhelmed and totally helpless, Allie sank down in her chair. She looked up to the bare wooden cross behind Pastor Holtz. For a moment she hesitated...and then she shut her eyes.

"Okay," she mumbled. "Um...Jesus...Truth Guy...can you help me? Do you really...want to?"

Music suddenly floated through the air: a guitar, softly strumming. The music was soft, sweet, and heartbreakingly beautiful.

"So I'm asking you tonight," Pastor Holtz said in a hushed, urgent voice, "to give Jesus a try. Wherever you are, whoever you are, you need Him. If you're hurting...He can heal you. If you feel lost...He'll find you. If you feel like no one cares...*He* does!"

"Please help me, Truth Guy," she whispered. "Jesus, help me. I'm so scared."

The music swelled. "Jesus wept," Pastor Holtz whispered. "He *wept*. He knows how you feel. He can help you. All you have to do is believe in Him like Martha...and cry out to Him like Mary. Just cry out to Him." His voice dropped to a whisper. "Cry out to Him."

Allie covered her face in her hands. "Why?" she whispered. "Why does it have to hurt so much?"

And then, as if in answer, a voice broke out into song.

137

I'm giving you my heart,
Take everything I have.
I give it all to you
And I give up
I give up
I give up everything to you.

The words washed over her, echoing through her mind...and then the whole church was singing.

I'm giving you my heart,
take everything I have,
I give it all to you...

And then she was singing with them, singing in a mumbling, broken voice:

And I give up
I give up,
I give up everything to you.

Tears were trickling down her cheeks. *Can't take it anymore...so hard...so alone...and nobody cares, nobody notices...*
I do.
The voice came into her head suddenly. She recognized it. She had heard it before.
*I love you. I died for you, and I'm **not** going to leave you alone. Ever.*
And then suddenly her heart broke, and she was crying, sobbing into hands, her whole body shaking.
She felt hands on her shoulder, and then Ginger was hugging her, whispering, "It's all right...it's okay, Allie..."
And then she was hugging Ginger round the waist, and she stayed like that for a long time, weeping like a child.

13

SUNDAY MORNING

The drops of water shone like diamonds on the windshield. With one hand the girl brushed back a strand of blond hair; with the other she turned up the volume on the car stereo. Praise music blasted from the speakers, music about blessing the name of the Lord, about surrender and perfect joy...

"How do you feel?"

"Great," she whispered. "Really great. I mean...wow! Praise God!"

Ginger chuckled. "I never expected to hear *you* say that."

"I know!" Allie laughed. "It's so weird!"

But it didn't feel weird. She *wanted* to say it. She sighed happily and snuggled into the car seat. It was after midnight, her stomach was growling and her whole body ached...but she didn't care. How could she? How could anything make her unhappy now?

God loved her. And that changed everything. Everything seemed beautiful: the raindrops glistening on the windshield, the yellow street lamps flashing by...even the darkness wasn't dark anymore. Light was everywhere.

They pulled into the driveway of Allie's house. "By the way," Ginger said, "There's a Bible Study on Wednesday, if you want to come..."

"Sure!" Allie said. "I'll see you there!"

Ginger took her hand. "If you want to talk or anything, before Wednesday...just call, okay? I'm here for you."

Allie squeezed Ginger's hand. "Thank you," she whispered. "You have no idea what that means to me."

She hardly recognized the face in the bedroom mirror. It wasn't Allie Weaver. Allie would never let her hair get so scraggly...or her cheeks red and puffy and wet with tears. Those blue eyes weren't Allie's—they were far too peaceful. And that smile wasn't Allie's—it was far too real. Far too joyful.

The joy of the Lord is our strength. That was from the Bible, wasn't it? She needed to start reading the Bible. She had to learn more about Jesus. The Truth Guy. The one who had saved her.

"Saved," she whispered, and the Allie in the mirror beamed.

She snuggled under the covers and closed her eyes. A few moments later she was asleep.

She didn't have any dreams.

Brian's eyes snapped open. He glanced at the clock radio. **6:30**. *It's early,* he thought hazily. *Good.* He got up and walked to the window. The woods and fields behind the house were lit by the rosy glow on the horizon. *Hmmm...maybe I can go out to the shrine and say my Rosary.* It would be nice, praying alone in the woods, just before sunrise.

Hurriedly he put on a Sparrow Hills hoodie and sweatpants, grabbed his sneakers and a pair of socks, and tiptoed out of the room. The stairs creaked on his bare feet as he went downstairs. He sat down on the bottom stair and put on his socks and shoes, singing quietly to himself, "*Hail, Holy Queen enthroned above...O Maria...*"

"Hi!"

Brian looked up. There, in the doorway at the end of the hall, was Liz.

"Oh!" he said blankly. "Liz!"

"Oh! Burke!" Liz grinned at him. Her dirty blond hair was rumpled, and she wore pajama pants and a long-sleeved shirt.

"What are you *doing* here?" Brian said.

She shrugged. "Well, last night my dad left and I told him I'd get a ride with George, but forgot to tell George about it. Then George left before I knew it, and I was stranded. So your mom said I could sleep over as long as I called home to let them know. So I called home and my mom said okay, and I bunked with Melissa. We stayed up late talking—"

"What did you talk about?"

"Oh, nothing," Liz said breezily. "Just girl stuff. You wouldn't be interested."

Brian reflected on this, and then nodded. "You're right. I wouldn't." He walked past her into the kitchen.

Liz followed him. "Where ya going?"

"Out. To pray." He took his rosary off a hook on the wall.

"Cool! I'll come with! You got an extra set of those prayer beads on ya?"

He sighed, and gestured to the wall where the other rosaries hung. "Go ahead, take one. And hurry up."

He walked briskly through the back-yard garden. "So where are we going?" Liz said, jogging after him.

"The woods." Brian pointed to the beginning of a path between two large spreading oak trees. "We have a Marian shrine back there."

It was a cool morning for late July. The mists hung about the garden and the surrounding woods like a curtain. They walked along the narrow path, hearing nothing but their own footsteps and the occasional birdsong.

"It sure is quiet out here," Liz said. "I don't even hear a car. Why do you guys live out so far in the country?"

"My dad wanted to. He built our house here. He built the path we're on, too. And the shrine."

"Wow! How long did it take him?"

"Never mind that now." Brian stepped over a fallen log. "Let's quit talking, okay?"

"Why?"

"Because...I'd rather listen."

141

They entered a clearing in the woods with a small statue of Mary in the center. The beams from the rising sun shone through the beech trees, filling the air with green and golden light.

Brian pulled out his rosary, crossed himself, and knelt. Liz copied him, a little self-consciously. "Um…what are the mysteries today?" she whispered. "Is it the Joyful, or the Sorrowful, or the…"

"It's Sunday," Brian murmured. "The Glorious Mysteries. First decade's the Resurrection. I believe in God, the Father Almighty…"

As they went through the prayers, Brian felt better and better. Usually it was a bit of a struggle to pray the rosary…but today it was easy.

He sank deeper and deeper into prayer, his eyes closed, his hands, clasped, the words washing over him like clear water.

"…we may imitate what they contain and obtain what they promise, through the same Christ Our Lord. Amen." He crossed himself slowly and took a deep breath, his eyes still closed, the sunlight gently stroking his brow.

"Man!" Liz stood up with a groan. "My knees are killing me! Can we go back now?"

Brian chuckled. "Sure."

They walked back through the woods together. The sun was now fully risen, and it was starting to get hot.

"Do you pray every day?" Liz asked, jumping from rock to rock over a little stream that crossed the path.

"I try to. It's really easy to pray out here, though. It's so peaceful. No distractions."

"I know! It's so pretty!" Liz balanced on a rock and gazed up at the trees, looking wistful. "Like a fairy tale," she said softly.

Brian rolled his eyes. "Um…right. But there's disadvantages too. No cell phone coverage, for example. I wish I could get one of those Thunderbolt phones. They're so cool…"

"Don't start geeking out on me, Burke." Liz nimbly jumped back onto the path. "So you come out here to pray all the time?"

"Yes. Mostly the rosary."

"Why? The rosary's so boring!"

Brian shrugged. "I just like how structured it is."

...Liz snickered. "Surprise, surprise. But doesn't it bother you praying to Mary? A *girl?*"

"Um, it's a bit *different* with Mary. She's the mother of God."

"Wow. You got high standards. Hey, I bet *that's* why you like Mary Summers! Her name! It can't be her personality."

Brian's good mood evaporated instantly. "What's your problem with Mary, anyway?" he said. "Why do you hate her so much?"

"I don't *hate* her. I just don't *like* her."

They emerged from the woods and into the garden. A whiff of cooking sausage came from the house ahead.

"Well, she doesn't like you either." Brian said gloomily. "And she definitely hates *me*."

Liz frowned. "You think so?"

"Yes," Brian said bitterly. "She got mad at me just because I wouldn't agree with her about Allie. Maybe you were right about her."

"Um...right. Maybe." Liz tugged on his arm. "Come on, Burke. I'm starving."

You got any more of those eggs?" Allie said eagerly, holding out her plate.

Her mother chuckled incredulously and scooped some more eggs onto the plate. "Sure, honey. So you're still hungry?"

"Yep." Allie grinned. "Thanks for making breakfast. You're so nice."

"Oh! Um...thanks!" her mom said, looking both startled and pleased. "You know, I haven't made eggs for you since you were little."

"Yeah, I know," Allie said. "I don't know why I stopped liking them. You're such a good cook!"

"Hmm." Her mom turned back to the stove. "There's something different about you."

"Like what?"

143

"You're happy."

Allie grinned. "Yeah. I guess I am," she said playfully. "That's okay, right?"

"Oh, honey," her mom turned back to her, and her eyes looked a little bright. "That's all I want you to be."

Allie looked back at her. Then, without a word, she walked over and hugged her mom tightly.

They held on to each other a long time, and Allie heard her mother sniffle once or twice. "Mom," she said hesitantly. "I'm sorry."

"Oh...that's fine, honey," her mom said, wiping her eyes. "But you better get going; you'll be late for church."

"Actually," Allie said. "I went last night. Besides, I got to clean out my closet and pack up winter things."

"You're finally doing that?" her mom said. "I've been asking you all week—"

"Yeah, I know, I'm sorry about that," Allie said truthfully. "Don't worry about the dishes; I'll take care of it."

Her mom stared at her again. "Allie," she said. "What church did you go to last night?"

"Um...well..." Allie hesitated. "Well, Mom, it's..."

"That's okay," her mom said. "If you want to keep it to yourself, that's fine. But whatever happened yesterday...I'm glad it did." She gave Allie another hug, then left the kitchen.

After she was done cleaning up the dishes, Allie went up to her room, pulled open the closet and surveyed the vast amount of clothes inside. *This could take all day,* she thought ruefully. But she wasn't tempted to go back on her promise. She was actually enjoying being the good girl...

Celia! Allie gasped. *Omigosh, I never told her!* She pulled out her cell phone.

She got Celia's voice mail: "Hi! This is Celia. Say something!" *BEEP.*

Darn it. "Um...hey, Seal. It's Allie. Look, um...I got to tell you something. Something about the school. Give me a ring, okay? Bye..."

144

She checked her missed calls and saw a number she didn't recognize. *Hmmm...maybe that's Celia's home number...?*

So what church are you going to again?" Liz said.

"St. Stanislaus," Mrs. Burke said, loading Liz's plate up with pancakes and sausages and handing it back to her. "It's the only church for miles around here that has an indult Mass in the Tridentine Rite."

"Oh. Okay." Liz glanced at Brian. "Um...what's that?"

"It's a traditional Latin Mass," Brian said.

"Latin Mass?" Liz said blankly.

"Well, that's the way all Catholic Masses were said prior to 1962," Brian said. "It's really beautiful, but it's different from what you're used to. Some of it might seem...old-fashioned."

"Eh." Liz shrugged. "I kind of like old-fashioned stuff. There won't be any guitars, right?"

Everyone burst into laughter. "You don't know my dad," Melissa said. "If there were guitars..."

"I wouldn't go there," his father said solemnly. "No, for me it's the organ or nothing."

"And it's in *Latin*," Brian repeated, sure that Liz hadn't really understood. "Not in English, okay?"

"I got that part." She gave him a quizzical look. "Do *you* like it?"

"Yes," Brian said. "I really do."

"Then I'll come along," Liz said. "That okay, Mrs. Burke?"

"Of course it is," his mom said, beaming at Liz.

"You can borrow some of my clothes!" Melissa said eagerly.

"Wait a sec." Liz looked alarmed. "I need special clothes?"

"You can't go in my pajamas, can you?" Melissa pulled Liz to her feet. "I got a dress that might fit you..."

Grinning to himself, Brian carried his plate and silverware into the kitchen. The phone rang as he passed it, and he answered it. "Burke residence, Brian speaking."

"Celia?"

"No," he said, puzzled. "Brian. Who's this?"

"Brian, this is Allie. You know, from school?"

145

Brian rolled his eyes. "I know who you are," he said, walking to the sink. "What's up?"

"Well, somebody called me from this number last night, and—"

"That was probably Celia." Brian cleaned off his dish. "She was trying to get a hold of you."

"Oh. Darn. Hey Brian…" Allie hesitated. "Did anything…bad happen at school yesterday?"

"Bad?" Brian frowned slightly. "Well, yes. The boiler broke down. How'd you hear about—"

"How bad was it?"

"Pretty bad, actually. Look, I can't talk now—we're going to church. Have you gone yet?"

"Oh! I did!" Allie said. "Last night! I went to this awesome church called Cross Bridge. It was *so* awesome! The preacher was incredible, and so was the music, and…well, I just had this incredible experience! I mean, I really felt God's love for the first time, and…well, I really felt Jesus in my heart. I've been wanting to tell somebody about it since it happened, but my mom wouldn't really understand, I guess…"

Brian was barely listening—He could hear Melissa and Liz talking in the hallway.

"You can borrow one of my veils!"

"Um…veils?"

Brian grinned to himself. "Um…that sounds really neat, Allie," he said, glancing at the kitchen clock. It was almost eight—they would all need to hustle. "But was this a *Catholic* church?"

"Well…no. But it was still church. So I'm good."

"Actually, you're not," Brian said. "You have to go to *Mass* on Sunday. At a Catholic Church. If you miss Sunday Mass, it's a mortal sin."

There was a long silence on the phone. "Allie?" Brian said. "You still there?"

"Yeah. Sorry. Okay. Well…I guess I better go then. See ya." There was a click, and then a dial tone.

Brian looked at the phone for a moment, feeling vaguely troubled. Then he shrugged, hung it up and walked away.

146

Fifteen minutes later, Brian was waiting on the porch with his dad. Everyone else was in the van, except for Melissa and Liz.

"Looks like your friend's going to make us late," his dad said, smiling wryly.

"I know," Brian said fretfully. "What's taking them so long?"

"Well, you know girls," his dad said. "They're probably chatting, or doing their hair…"

"No way. Not Liz."

"Really? Why?"

"Because she's *Liz!*" Brian said impatiently. "She's not girly like that!"

His dad chuckled. "Brian, I can't say that I totally understand women, but I've never known one who didn't attend to her appearance. Speaking of girls…You ever solve your homework riddle? Why did Dante choose Beatrice to represent God's love?"

Brian sighed. "Um…Beatrice was cute?"

His dad shook his head. "Close. But no cigar." He stood up. "I'm getting in the van. Why don't you go and remind those two of the time?"

Brian rolled his eyes. "Sure."

He ran inside and yelled up the stairs, "Hurry up!"

"Chill out, Spock!" Melissa yelled back. "We're almost ready!"

He paced back and forth in the hall fretfully. *Beatrice…*Mary's face popped up in his mind. *If only I'd said yes. Yes to whatever she wanted…* He sat down glumly. *But that would be wrong. Just another temptation…but why can't I stop thinking about her?*

He heard footsteps on the stairs. "Finally!" he said, turning around. "What took you so—whoah!"

Liz and Melissa were at the foot of the stairs. "What do you think?" Melissa said proudly.

Liz wore an long ruffled green dress, trimmed with white lace. She had on black stockings and black slipper shoes, and a white lacy veil on her head. She was also blushing furiously.

"What do you think?" Melissa said, beaming.

"Um…" Brian felt a crazy urge to laugh. "Wow."

"I look stupid," Liz muttered.

147

"No!" Brian, grinning. "No, you look really nice."

Liz scowled. "Wipe that grin off your face, Burke," she growled, pushing past him to the front door. "Or I'll do it for you."

Allie walked quickly out of the front doors of St. Bridget's, made her way through a crowd of people, and got into her mom's car. "Well, I went to Mass," she muttered. "Did my duty. Not in mortal sin. Happy, Brian?"

It had been almost impossible to get there in time, what with traffic, and having to change and beg her mom for the car. This all just seemed so...wrong. Missing Mass was a mortal sin...so if she hadn't happened to find this little fact out from Brian by accident, would she have gone to hell? Was that what God was like?

No way. Not the God I met last night. Jesus wouldn't do that...

But Brian *did* know what he was talking about. He was smart, no doubt about that. She gritted her teeth. *If he's right, than what does that mean about...the Catholic Church?*

She had always assumed all religious people were like Catholics: follow a bunch of rules and stuff, or you go to hell. It seemed so small, so narrow...so unlike what she had felt last night.

She groaned and put her head on the wheel. It was all so confusing. Maybe Celia could help...but when she told Celia what she had done, wouldn't Celia be upset? Brian had said it was pretty bad...what did that mean?

I have to make it up to Celia somehow. I have to tell her how I've changed. How everything's changed. With a sigh, she started the car up. It took her forever to get out of the parking lot.

She was almost home when her phone finally rang. She snatched it up eagerly. "Hello?"

"Hi Allie! It's Simone Clearwater."

"Oh," Allie tried to hide her disappointment. "Hey Simone. What's up?"

"There's a party at my parent's house tonight. You want to come? It's a party for Keenan—"

"Keenan's going to be there?" Allie said before she could help herself.

"Yeah," Simone sounded amused. "It's his party, you see. It's funny you asked, 'cause it was his idea to call you."

"It was?" Allie felt a tiny bit excited.

"Yeah. Me and Tara were talking about you, and he overheard us. He said it's important for new Christians to be around other Christians. So anyway, the party starts at eight. I'll email you the directions, okay?"

"Yeah! Sure!" Allie said, and gave Simone her email address. Then she hung up, feeling light and buoyant. Keenan had asked about her? Really? She felt a thrill of excitement. *He's cute.*

Et verbum caro factum est et habitabit in nobis; et vidimus gloriam eius gloriam quasi Unigenti a Patre, plenum gratiae et veritatis."

"Deo Gratias," Brian murmured with the congregation, feeling that serenity that almost always came to him at the end of Mass. Bowing his head in prayer, he crossed himself. Out of the corner of his eye he saw Liz stand up.

"Ave Maria, gratia plena..."

Liz sat down again, looking annoyed. Everyone joined in saying the Hail Mary three times, and then the St. Michael prayer, and then the Litany of the Sacred Heart...

"Hey!" Liz said in a stage whisper. "Can I take the veil off now?"

He chuckled. "It's almost over."

His mom and dad got up, crossing themselves, and they all followed suit, filing out of the pew.

"So, what do you think?" Brian asked Liz as they walked out the front doors. "Did you like it? I know it's not what you're used to, but—"

To his surprise, Liz laughed and twirled around like a ballerina in the borrowed dress. "It *is* different," she said. "But you know what? I don't care. Not that I'd want to make a permanent habit out of it."

"Really?"

"Yeah," Liz said. "It's kind of warm though, especially in July—"

"I suppose so," Brian said, remembering that the church's air conditioning had broken down a few weeks before.

"—and these black stockings just don't work. But the rest...it's cool. It's like wearing a costume. Do you like it?"

"Sure I do..." Brian faltered. "Wait. What?"

"I was telling you what *I* think. So what do *you* think?" she said, and did a little mock curtsy. "Of my new look?"

"Um...you kind of look like one of my sisters."

"I know!" Liz climbed into the van. She turned around and whispered in a conspiratorial tone: "It's like I'm dressing up as a Burke for Halloween!"

Brian gaped at her, and she grinned. "Kidding!" She clambered to the back seat.

"It's so nice that you two said the rosary together this morning," his mom said, walking up to the van. "She seems like a really nice girl."

"Yes." Brian frowned. "She does *seem* like it." *A costume?* Shaking his head, he clambered into the van and sat next to Liz in the back seat.

"Liz," his mother said from the front seat. "We can drop you off on the way home if you like. You can return Melissa's clothes later."

"Thanks, Mrs. Burke!" Liz said brightly. "And thanks for letting me come along. It was really cool!"

Brian's eyes narrowed. *Is she 'acting' again? Is this some kind of joke?* Then a new, disturbing thought occurred to him: *Is she just trying to get more info about the boiler? Is that the real reason she's here?*

"Brian!" Liz whispered.

"What?" he snapped.

Liz pointed to the front of the car. "Listen!"

His dad was talking on his cell phone. "Tuesday? Are you sure? Great! Thanks, Vince." He snapped the phone shut.

"What was that about?" his mom said.

"Let's discuss it later." His dad angled the van expertly into the traffic.

In the silence that followed, Liz leaned closer to Brian. "You know what that was about, right?" she whispered.

"I do," Brian muttered. "Congratulations: now you know when they're going to replace the boiler."

"Exactly!" Liz whispered eagerly. "Now let's see…if they're going to replace it Tuesday…"

"…then you only have one day. Good luck."

Liz's face fell. "Oh, come on, Burke! Can't you help me out?"

He bit his lip. *She's not going to let up. Just agree with her.* "Okay," he said tightly. "Sure."

Liz sighed. "That's a relief. Honestly, I don't know who else to ask. No one else knows about the boiler, except for George and Celia—"

"And Allie."

"Allie?" Liz frowned. "What are you talking about? She was gone by the time the boiler blew."

"Well, she knows about it. She called this morning and asked how bad the damage was. Seemed pretty anxious about it, too."

"Hmm." Liz's brow wrinkled. "That's…weird. I didn't think she'd—wait." Liz put a hand to her mouth. "No way. I just had a crazy idea."

Brian frowned. "What?"

Liz scooted closer to him. "What if…" She looked around, and lowered her voice to a whisper. "What if it's Allie?"

Brian blinked. Then he chuckled. "You're joking, right? We *saw* the poltergeist, back in the fall, remember? He was a guy! Not to mention Allie was standing there with us too—"

"Shhh!" Liz clamped a hand over his mouth. Luckily Melissa and Lucia were talking loudly in the seat in front of them.

"Maybe," she whispered. "But maybe I was wrong about the *poltergeist* being responsible for this stuff. Listen: I saw Allie right after the fire. She had snuck back in. You know why? Because she had left this binder inside. A binder full of notes, and diagrams, and plans. She acted like she didn't want anyone seeing them. And another thing: remember how she had wanted to talk to you that day?"

"Yes…"

"She told me why. She wanted to ask *you* about the poltergeist."

Brian blinked. "Me? Why?"

"Why do you think *I* wanted to talk to you about it? You're smart. Maybe she wanted to size you up, see if you could stop her!"

"From what?" Brian snorted. "Sabotaging the work camp that *she* helped to start? That's cra—"

"I *know* it sounds crazy!" Liz whispered furiously. "But you can't deny the facts! Right after Mrs. Summers yells at her…boom! The boiler blows up! Coincidence?"

"Yes!" Brian whispered back, exasperated. "Come on, Liz, think! Why would Allie do anything like this?"

"Hmmph." Liz crossed her arms. "It was just an idea. I mean, I always thought Allie was the poltergeist back in the fall— before we saw him, I mean. Remember that broken gym window?"

Brian thought back to that day. Somebody—*the poltergeist*, he told himself firmly—had thrown a brick through the gym window. Later on, Liz's mom had accused Allie of the crime, after everyone else's whereabouts had been accounted for. Allie was the only one without an alibi. Of course it was *possible* that Allie, not the poltergeist, had thrown that brick, but…

"But why would she *do* it?" Brian whispered back. "This is still crazy."

"I don't know. Maybe she went crazy after the shooting thing. You got to admit she's been acting a little weird!"

"This would be more than a *little* weird," Brian muttered.

"Well, all I know is that the two times Allie's come to work camp, we've had a major catastrophe." Liz shook her head.

"Even if she didn't do it, I kind of hope she doesn't come back. Just in case other people start to think the same thing."

Brian shook his head. "She didn't do it."

But all the same, the prospect of Allie not coming back to work camp didn't bother him that much. Allie had been nothing but trouble for him this summer.

14
SUNDAY NIGHT

Allie walked up to the door of the small red-brick house and knocked.

The door opened, and Keenan Clearwater was there. "Hi!" he smiled broadly at her. "You here for the party?"

"Oh! Um...yeah! I am!" Allie said, feeling flustered. Keenan looked every bit as handsome as he had looked on the stage last night, dressed in cargo pants and a green t-shirt, his face open and friendly.

"Um...I'm Allie Weaver," she said shyly.

"I know! I saw you at Cross Bridge last night!"

"You...*saw* me?" Allie laughed nervously and played with a strand of hair. *Great, he saw me bawling my eyes out...*

"Quite a night, huh?"

She looked up. Keenan looked sympathetic. "Yeah," she said honestly. "But...it was good."

"Awesome. Praise God!" Keenan returned her smile. "Come on in!"

Simone and Ginger met her in the living room. "Allie!" Ginger gave her a hug. "I'm so glad you made it! Come on, we're all hanging out in the back yard."

Allie followed the two girls and Keenan through the house. The back yard was full of people; mostly teenagers, but some adults as well. There was a barbecue set up and picnic tables loaded with food.

"What's the occasion?" she asked Simone.

"Graduation party for Keenan," Simone said. "We were supposed to have it in June, but...well..."

She trailed off. Allie's stomach twisted uncomfortably. "Yeah..." Ginger said quietly. "I canceled my party too—I mean, graduation was only a few weeks after..."

"Well, congratulations anyway!" Allie cut her off.

Keenan smiled. "Thanks. It's all thanks to God, really. I was having trouble in junior year, but Pastor Holtz encouraged me, and—"

"And you did great!" A short, balding man walked up and threw an arm around Keenan's shoulder. "Didn't you, son?"

Keenan and Simone both looked embarrassed. "Allie, Ginger," Keenan said, "this is my stepfather, Sam."

"How're you doing? Good to see you here," said the man loudly, grinning from ear to ear as he shook their hands. "Make yourselves at home! Go get something to eat!" With another smile and a wave, he walked off.

Allie glanced at Keenan's red face, and thought about Larry, who also had a tendency to be loud at inopportune times. *I know exactly how Keenan feels.* "Actually, I *am* kind of hungry," she said. "Why don't we get some food?"

"So Keenan," she said, picking up a paper plate and getting in line for the barbecue, "What are you gonna do now? College?"

Keenan shrugged. "I don't know," he said. "We're not rich, and I didn't get any scholarships..."

"Oh, Keenan, you *have* to go to college!" Simone said from her place in line behind them. "You'll do great!"

"Yeah, but there's a lot of temptation out there," Keenan said seriously. "I don't know if I'm ready for it yet, to be honest. I think I need to wait and see what God says about it."

"You'll do fine," Simone said dismissively. "No *way* you'll get into trouble. Not my holy-roller, bible-thumpin' bro."

Keenan laughed and ruffled his sister's hair. "You're taking this hero-worship a little too far, Simone."

Allie felt a twinge of envy as she watched them. *I wish I had an older brother.* But Keenan was fascinating anyway. As good-looking as George, as wholesome as Celia…and he was *cool*.

"Do you really mean that?" she asked Keenan. "I mean…waiting for God to tell you whether to go to college or not?"

"Sure I do." His brown eyes gazed at her steadily. "Don't you?"

"I…I don't know," Allie stammered. She mused for a moment. "I want to go to college," she said. "I want to study business administration."

"But you should still pray about it," Keenan said. "Always pray, Allie. *Always.*"

They came to the barbecue, where a burly man in a white apron was flipping burgers. "Hey Keenan!" he roared. "What'll you have?"

"Hey, Mr. Lamar! You got any hot dogs left?"

"Sure do!" The man slapped a hot dog into a bun and handed it to Keenan. "And what about you, Miss?"

"I'll have a cheeseburger," Allie said eagerly.

"Sure thing. Hey…" The man peered at Allie thoughtfully. "Don't I know you from somewhere?"

"I don't think so," Allie said, surprised.

"Got it!" The man snapped his fingers. "You're George's friend! From the Catholic school!"

"George?" Allie stared at the man, and suddenly recognized him. "Coach? Coach Lamar?"

The Sparrow Hills wrestling coach chuckled. "You got it!" he said. "How's George doing, anyway? And Brian Burke?" Without waiting for a reply he slapped a cheeseburger on her plate and handed it back. "Tell them I said hi!"

As they walked away, Allie turned to Keenan. "How do you know him? You didn't wrestle, did you?"

Keenan laughed. "Nah, I know him from Cross Bridge. He goes there too."

"Really?"

"Sure. There's a lot of Christians out there, Allie—if you just know where to look."

Allie glanced around at the other party goers. There were certainly a lot of familiar faces. *So they're all Christians*, she thought in a sort of happy bemusement. Most of these people were...normal. And she felt normal too. She fit in. *Maybe this is where I belong.*

*F*ire, Brian typed. *Electrical. Furnace.*

He drummed his fingers on the desk for a moment, then typed *Entry? Hank's keys?*

He frowned, turned on bold and italic, and typed **MOTIVE??**

That's what really didn't make sense. What possible motive could anyone have for attacking their tiny, run-down school?

He stood up, suddenly furious with himself. *Of course it doesn't make sense. What's wrong with you? You're starting to actually believe Liz's stupid ideas. First she thinks the poltergeist is back; then she thinks Allie's the poltergeist... this is all just coincidence. And Liz, trying to get even with her dad.*

He shook his head. *Well, it'll all get cleared up tomorrow morning when we look at that boiler—assuming that we actually go—*

The laptop made a soft chime. He sat back down and pulled it closer.

ArglyeSocks435: CHOCOLATE THUNDERRR RR!!!!!

Brian shook his head and chuckled. *Just when I need a voice of reason, look who shows up.*

brianburke3: Hey J.P.
brianburke3: you pea-brained potato-muncher
ArgyleSocks435: hey no fare
ArgyleSocks435: u racist!
ArgyleSocks435: and stop spelling things rite
ArgyleSocks435: ur makin me feel inferior
ArgyleSocks435: anyways...
ArgyleSocks435: a crtain crazy italian lady says
ArgyleSocks435: u 2 need a ride to school 2mrrow
ArgyleSocks435: just wanted 2 tell u im takin care of it
ArgyleSocks435: JPnater is on da case

Brian raised an eyebrow.

> **brianburke3: You didn't steal a car, did you?**
> ArgyleSocks435: flattery will get u nowhere
> ArgyleSocks435: my big bro eddie can give us a ride
> ArgyleSocks435: be ready at 8
> **brianburke3: Okay.**
> **brianburke3: I will see you then.**

So Rich walks in, right?" Ginger said. "And he screams, 'that chick *maced* me!'"

Allie, Keenan, and Simone burst out laughing. Ginger grinned. "And I was like, 'Um, okay, Rich. Did you get her name, or was it just a drive-by?' And he just stares at me and yells: 'My girlfriend! That Catholic school chick!' And I had met Liz once, and I was like, 'You're lucky that's *all* she did!'"

"Omigosh..." Allie gasped, wiping her eyes. "He *was* lucky!"

Ginger got up off the porch swing and stretched. "Well, it's getting late. I better take off."

"Really?" Allie said, and suddenly realized that it *was* late. All the partygoers had left, except the four of them on the porch. *Maybe I should get back...*

Then she glanced at Keenan leaning back in his chair, his legs crossed, his long brown hair looking handsomely disheveled.

"I'll stay a little longer," she said. "That okay, Simone?"

Simone shrugged and walked to the door. "Sure. Mom and Dad are already in bed. I'm gonna go inside. It's getting a bit cold for me."

As Ginger and Simone left, Keenan yawned and stretched. "Quite a party, huh?"

Allie glanced at him and felt a little quiver in her stomach. "Yeah."

"It was Sam's idea." Keenan frowned. "I didn't want to have a party—not after the shooting—but he insisted. At least he delayed it a bit."

"Do you..." Allie hesitated. "Do you *like* your step-dad?"

Keenan stared down at the wooden slots of the porch. "He's alright, I guess," he said. "But he'll never be my *real* dad."

"When did your real dad leave?"

"When I was two. I hardly remember him. Maybe I'll track him down someday."

"My dad left when I was ten."

"Your folks are divorced too?"

"Yeah," she said, suddenly apprehensive. "Is that okay?"

Keenan gave her a puzzled smile. "What do you mean?"

"I…I don't know," Allie said. "I mean…Catholics don't like divorce."

"Neither do we."

"Yeah, but Catholics *really* don't like it. I mean, you can't be a good Catholic and be divorced."

"Really? Why?"

"I…don't know," Allie stammered. Even though Keenan's voice was mild, there was something about his calm, steady gaze that made it hard to think.

"Church teaching?" she said lamely.

Keenan looked thoughtful. "Hmm. Church teaching," he said. "That sounds so legalistic to me. So rules-driven. I just go to the Bible and do what Jesus would do."

Allie's brow furrowed. James' sneering face floated into her mind. *He'd probably call Keenan a heretic or something.*

"All right," she said. "What does the Bible tell *you* about divorce?"

"Well…" Keenan stroked his goatee thoughtfully. "I know that it's not *your* fault your parents split up. It doesn't mean God loves you any less…or your parents. Look—" He put a hand on her shoulder. "Some Christians are really into acting big and condemning people, but that's not what Jesus did. In John 3:17, Jesus said: 'For God did not send the Son into the world to judge the world, but that the world might be saved through Him.' That's what I believe, Allie."

Allie felt another quiver go through her stomach. His brown eyes were earnest and kind. *He means it*, she thought. *I don't know if he's right, but I know he really does care about me. He wouldn't condemn me...he's...kind of like Jesus.* She chuckled, shaking her head.

Keenan grinned. "Am I coming on too strong? Just like Simone always says, old holy roller Keenan."

"No, no, it's cool." Allie laughed again. "It's just—well, I wish I could be like you. I just wish it could be so simple."

"It *is* simple!" Keenan said eagerly. "All you have to do is believe in Jesus, and you'll be saved!"

"That's *all* you have to do?" Allie said playfully.

"Yep." Keenan grinned. "You ever read Romans 10:9?"

"Um...what?"

"If you confess with your mouth, 'Jesus is Lord,' and believe in your heart that God raised him from the dead, you will be saved."

Allie's brow wrinkled. "That *does* sound simple," she admitted. "Are you sure about this?"

"Sure I'm sure! You want more proof? Acts 15:11: 'We believe that it is through the grace of Lord Jesus that we are saved.' Acts 16:31: 'Believe in the Lord Jesus, and you will be saved.' And in First Corinthians—"

"Okay! Okay!" Allie laughed and held up her hands. "I got it! It's just weird!"

"Why?"

"Because Catholics do a lot of other things besides that."

"Like what?"

Allie hesitated. A bunch of things popped into her head: confessions, Latin, theology, the saints, rosaries...

"Well," she said. "There's the Rosary."

"Oh," Keenan said. "That's where you pray to Mary, right? How does that work?"

"Um...hold on." Allie scooped her purse off the floor and pulled out her rosary. She felt a vague disquiet as she handed it to Keenan. "Here," she said. "You say one Our Father and ten Hail Mary's—"

"What's a Hail Mary?"

"Hail Mary, full of grace, the Lord is with you..." Allie recited the rest. "You say fifty of those. I got a friend, Celia, who says it all the time. She loves it. What do you think?"

Keenan didn't speak for a moment. He had a pained expression on his face, as if he was afraid of offending her. "Um…to be honest, it just seems wrong."

"Really?" Allie said, surprised. "Why?"

"You're saying ten prayers to Mary. But only one to Jesus."

"But…" Allie struggled for words. "But Mary's the mother of Jesus! Doesn't the Bible say to honor your father and mother?"

"Sure it does," Keenan said. "But the Bible also says that you shouldn't say the same prayers over and over."

"It—what?" Allie said.

"I think it's in Matthew," Keenan said thoughtfully. "It says…hmmm…'Do not use meaningless repetition as the Gentiles do, for they suppose that they will be heard for their many words.'"

Allie felt a sinking in her chest. "Um…" she stammered. "Well, that's…I don't know as many bible verses as you do, okay?" She turned away irritably. *At JP2 High, we read more about Church history than we read the Bible,* she thought. *How is that right?*

"Allie, I'm sorry," Keenan said hastily. "I didn't mean to attack your faith."

Allie was silent. *I always had trouble praying the Rosary…I thought it was my fault…maybe it's not…Maybe he's right.*

"Maybe it's not my faith," she muttered. "I've been Catholic my whole life, but I never really *felt* like a Christian until last night. Am I really a Christian?"

"Do you believe in Jesus?"

"Of course I do!"

"Do you want to give your life to Him?"

"Yes!"

"Just say 'Jesus, you are Lord. I give my life to you.'"

"That's—that's it?" Allie said.

"Yep. Go ahead. Say it. Just make sure you mean it."

Allie stared at Keenan. He looked serious.

She took a deep breath, closed her eyes, and clasped her hands together. "Jesus…" she whispered, "You are Lord. I give my life to you. Amen."

She looked up. "Will that do?"

Keenan was beaming at her. "Yes." He took her hand.

"Um...wow!" Allie stood up, and he stood up with her. She suddenly felt giddy. "That's it! That's it!" She hugged him. "Oh...thank you!"

She looked up into his eyes...those big, brown eyes...

She kissed him. Then she kissed him again.

And then her cell phone rang. They both jumped and broke away from each other. "Omigosh!" Allie gasped. "Um...wow!"

Keenan looked a little dazed. "Yeah!" he said. "Wow!"

Allie pulled out her cell phone, giggling. "Sorry!"

"Allie?" A familiar voice came from the phone.

"Celia?" Allie blinked. "Oh. You called back."

"Um...yeah," Celia said uncertainly.

There was an awkward silence. Allie sat down on the porch swing. *Where should I start?* So much had happened in a few days.

"Allie, about what happened with Mrs. Summers—"

"It's okay."

"I wanna explain why I told Mrs. Summers that stuff—"

"It's *okay*, Seal," Allie smiled sadly. "I don't care why you did it. It's in the past. Whatever it was, I forgive you."

There was a moment of silence. "Really?" Celia said cautiously.

"Yeah, really," Allie said quietly. "I have to. Jesus forgave me, right? Don't worry about it."

"Well, um...thanks." Celia sounded confused. "But I'd still like to tell you..."

"No, I got to tell *you* something first." Allie took a deep breath. "Celia, about the boiler at school..."

"Oh, you heard?" Celia said. She chuckled. "Yep, it broke down."

"Oh," Allie said blankly. "That's...bad, right?"

"Well, yeah," Celia said. "But it turns out that Mr. Burke's going to buy a new one for the school! So I guess it's actually a blessing in disguise!"

It took a few seconds for this to sink in. Allie felt a weird mix of relief and...disappointment? It turned out her big revenge on Celia hadn't hurt her at all. *But then again, she never needs to know.*

162

"That's...super, Celia," she finally said. "So no harm done?"

"Nope! Just a couple more days off from work camp while they replace the boiler." Celia sighed. "We're really behind schedule, Allie. I don't know if—"

"So you're free tomorrow?" Allie said as an idea struck her. "There's something I need to tell you, and I need to do it in person. Something really good."

"Really? That's...great, Allie," Celia said. "I can't meet tomorrow though. Mom and Dad are away with the older kids and I'm babysitting John Mark. Let me think. I bet I could get Miranda to watch him: it's about time she took a turn. Do you want to go and get coffee or something? Maybe on Tuesday?"

"Sure. Tuesday's good." Allie glanced at Keenan. "I'll tell you everything then. Bye."

She flipped the phone shut. "Sorry about that."

Keenan didn't reply. He was staring into space, still looking dazed.

Allie giggled. "Okay...well, I better go."

Keenan turned to look at her. "Hey!" he blurted out. "You coming to Bible Study on Wednesday?"

Allie giggled again. "Yep. I can't wait." She picked up her purse.

"Oh!" Keenan said, grabbing her arm. "There's something else: a Bible Camp. It's starting in a couple weeks. I'm leading music for it. You want to go?" He looked at her eagerly.

Allie smiled. "Maybe," she said coyly, pulling her arm free. "I'll think about it. See you Wednesday, okay?"

15

UNDERCOVER

Brian shifted from foot to foot while waiting in front of his mailbox. He checked his watch. 8:10 AM. *Where are they?*

He was about to give up and start the long walk back to the house when a red sports car roared up the road and screeched to a stop right in front of him.

The front passenger-side window opened and J.P.'s freckled, red-haired face appeared. "Burke!" he yelled, his eyes bulging crazily. "Get your bony butt in here!"

Brian sighed and, knowing J.P, took his time walking around to the other side of the car. "I was starting to get worried," he said as he opened the door and got in the back seat next to Liz. "You said you would be here at eight."

"Oh, that's my fault." Liz grinned at him. She was dressed in a black t-shirt, black parachute pants and black sneakers. A black backpack lay next to her on the seat. "Once I knew we were going to be late, I made Eddie slow down so we would get here at 8:10. I know how much you like round numbers."

"She ain't kidding," said a drawling voice from the front seat. Eddie Flynn, J.P.'s older college student brother, turned around with a lazy smile. He looked like a taller, thinner version of J.P, only with black hair and no freckles.

"Hi Eddie," Brian said warily. "Thanks for the—"

Eddie gunned the engine and the car shot down the road. "Woohoo!" J.P. yelled.

Brian gulped and hastily buckled his seat belt. "So how are we gonna get into the school?" he asked Liz. "Isn't it locked up?"

"Come on, Burke, give me some credit!" Liz pulled a set of keys from her backpack. "I swiped my dad's spare keys. He won't need 'em today—he's off with your dad to pick up the new boiler."

Brian glanced at Eddie. "Does *he* know anything?"

"Nope."

"How about J.P.?"

"Oh, *he* knows. So what? I thought you said he wasn't stupid."

"Come on guys!" J.P. cranked down his window. "Bug catching contest! First one to eat ten wins!" He opened his mouth and stuck his head out the window.

"Perhaps I spoke too soon," Brian muttered as Liz smirked. "So what's in the backpack?"

"Everything we'll possibly need," Liz said serenely. "For example…" She pulled out a camera. "To take crime scene photos."

"I see," Brian said dryly. "You didn't 'swipe' that too, did you?"

"Yeah, it's my mom's. She won't miss it for a few hours."

"Hey!" J.P. pulled his head back inside and gave them an injured look. "Why aren't you playing?"

"Sorry," Liz said dryly. "We're playing another game."

"Really? What kind?"

"We're guessing on how you'll die. Will you choke on a bug? Will your head get knocked off by an oncoming truck? Will your—"

"Your game stinks! Mine's better!" J.P. stuck his head out the window again.

"You know," Brian said with a grin. "I don't believe J.P. is taking this seriously."

Liz zipped her backpack up with a sour look. "Well, he should! This *is* serious!"

Brian smiled to himself. *Sure it is.*

In a few minutes they drove into the JP2HS parking lot. "Okay," Liz said. "Now we…Eddie! Stop!"

Eddie slammed on the brakes, stopping the car halfway into the parking lot.

"Look!" Liz pointed. A battered red van was parked next to the front doors.

"Oh, great," Brian gave Liz an exasperated look. "Is that your dad? I thought you said—"

"No! It can't be!" Liz snapped. She looked worried, though.

"Uh...guys?" Eddie drawled. "We're kind of blocking traffic. Just so you know." A car had pulled up behind them and beeped impatiently.

Liz hopped out of the car, dragging her backpack with her. "Brian! J.P. Out!"

Too surprised to argue, they got out and stood on the grass next to the lot entrance. Liz turned to Eddie. "Drive over to the SpeedEMart," she said crisply. "It's that way. Make a right, then another right, then it's on your right. Wait there for us. We'll be about twenty minutes."

Eddie shrugged. "Whatever." He backed back into the road and roared away.

Liz shouldered her backpack. "Let's get under cover!" she hissed to the two boys.

They ducked into the woods that lined the parking lot and crouched together behind a clump of bushes. "What now?" Brian said.

"Zip it, Burke." Liz pulled a small set of binoculars out of one of her pants pockets. She stood up and trained them on the van. "Wait a sec..."

She lowered the binoculars and grinned. "Phew! It's only Hank!"

"Oh," Brian said, not feeling very relieved. "What now?"

Liz tapped her chin with her finger thoughtfully. "All right, we got to split up," she said. "J.P., get to the back of the school and go in through the gym doors. Take my backpack with you. But I'll need some stuff first." She turned around and rummaged through her backpack. Brian and J.P. exchanged confused glances.

"Here." Liz turned around and handed J.P. the backpack. "Go through the woods. Keep out of sight. Get to the boiler room and start taking pictures. I'll meet you there. Quick!"

As J.P. plunged into the woods, Brian turned to Liz. "What about me?"

"You need to get out of here," Liz said tensely, turning around. She looked as if she was hiding something behind her back. "Go over to Hank, and *stall* him."

"Stall him?" he gasped. "How?"

"I don't know, Burke! Improvise!"

"I can't do that!"

"Yes you can!" Liz put a friendly hand on his shoulder. "Trust me, Burke. You only need to stall him for a few minutes."

"Why?"

She grinned. "You'll see. Now go!" She shoved him. "Go go go!"

Brian stumbled out into the open. He looked around, but Liz had already disappeared behind the bushes. He glanced at the van—there was Hank, unloading equipment out of the back.

"I can't believe this," he muttered. Taking a deep breath, he walked slowly across the parking lot.

Hank was struggling with a large dolly when he got there. "Um...Hank?" he said tentatively.

Hank looked up. "Brian? What are you doing here?"

"Oh..." Brian licked his lips, thinking furiously. "I just came from..."

"Sparrow Hills, maybe?" Hank grinned. "Yeah, Joey went up there too. Good luck!"

"Er...thanks." Brian said, trying not to sound as confused as he felt. "So...what are you doing here?"

"Taking out the old boiler." Hank heaved a propane tank out onto the curb. "It's a big job; I got to turn the water off, then dismantle the plumbing, then cut it up with a propane torch...cool, huh?"

"Hiya, Hank!"

Brian spun around. His mouth dropped open.

A girl walked up to them. For a second Brian's eyes took her all in, from the high heels to the white miniskirt to the bare midriff to the pink halter top...to the vacant face framed by two ponytails of dirty blond hair.

"Liz?" he gasped.

"Liz?" Hank looked baffled. "Why are *you* here?"

Liz cocked her head to one side and put one hand on her hip. "Oh, I'm such a goof!" she bubbled. "Y'see, I'm supposed to meet my friends Hally and Sally today, and I was just *about* to call them, when I couldn't find my cell phone! And, like, I looked all over the house, and I *couldn't* find it, so Hally gave me a ride here to look for it—"

"Really?" Hank frowned. "I didn't hear anybody drive up..."

"But it's a good thing *you* were here," Liz prattled on. "Because I *totally* forgot that it would be locked up. Can you let me in? *Please?*"

Hank rolled his eyes. "Yeah, yeah, sure. Just stop acting like an idiot."

"But I can't *help* it!"

Hank walked to the front doors, fumbling for his keys. Liz pranced after him. Brian leaned against the van, feeling dazed. *Okay. Stay calm. Don't give it away...just keep him occupied while Liz and J.P. are inside.*

"So," he said in a breezy voice as Hank walked back. "Why don't we just...wait out here for a while?"

He winced. *Okay. Maybe that's too obvious.*

But to his surprise, Hank sat down on the curb, looking surly. "Good idea," he grunted.

"Um...really?"

"I'm not going anywhere *near* her," Hank muttered. "That chick's bad news."

He pulled out a phone and started pecking away at it. Brian looked on, interested. "Is that a ThunderBolt?" he said.

"Yep." Hank grinned. "Greatest phone ever. I'm just checking out this new game. Wanna see?"

"Sure!" Brian sat down next to Hank and took the shiny black phone. For a few minutes they played the game together. Brian started to relax a little—he almost forgot why he was there.

"How long is she gonna be?" Hank said suddenly, glancing back at the doors. "I got to get started."

Brian hesitated. *Come on, improvise. Change the subject.*

"You sure got a lot of tattoos," he said wildly. "Where'd you get them?"

Hank chuckled. "Each one's got a story. Most of them I got while I was doing time."

"What?" Brian stared at him. "You were in jail?"

"Yep. And I'd probably be back there now if it wasn't for Vince. He gave me a hand up when I was in a bad place. Good guy, Vince. Too bad his kid turned into such a ditz."

"You really think so?" Brian said hopefully. *At least he's not suspicious.*

"Yeah," Hank said. "I don't know why a smart kid like you hangs out with her. Unless it's because..." He stopped, and gave Brian an appraising look. "How old are you, anyway?"

"I'll be sixteen next week."

"Huh. Well, you're still too young to be with a girl like *her.*"

"But she's three months younger than me!" Brian protested. "And I'm not *with* her! She's just my friend!"

"Is that why she didn't even look at you just now?" Hank shook his head. "She's using you, Brian."

"No she's not! She's just..." Brian stopped himself and clamped his mouth closed, feeling helpless.

"Yeah, she is. That's what chicks like her do." Hank gave him a sympathetic look. "Trust me. I've seen it a million times."

"I found it!" Liz emerged from the school, waving her cell phone. "Thank you *so* much, Hank—oh! Hi Brian!"

She skipped right up to him. "I didn't see you there," she said coyly, leaning over, her hands behind her back. "How you doing?"

For a horrible moment, Brian's eyes darted to a place he did *not* want to look. Then he turned away, his face red. Over Liz's shoulder, he saw Hank giving him an I-told-you-so look.

"Brian," Liz cooed, "You wanna walk me over to the SpeedEMart?" She winked.

"What? Um...yes. Of course."

She took his arm and steered him away.

"See you later, Brian," Hank said dryly.

Once they were around the corner and out of sight, Liz let go of his arm. "Let's go," she whispered.

"What happened? Did you—"

"We can't talk here." Liz kicked off her high heels and picked them up. "J.P.'s waiting for us at Chimney Rock. That way." She pointed. "I'll follow you."

Brian obeyed without any more argument. *Good. She's behind me. I can't see her then.*

J.P. leapt to his feet as they walked up to Chimney Rock, a cluster of boulders in the woods roughly halfway between JP2 High and the SpeedEMart. "You made it!" he said.

"Obviously," Liz snapped. "Backpack?"

J.P. jerked a thumb over his shoulder. "On the other side of the Chimney."

"Good. You two wait here." She ran out of sight behind the biggest of the boulders, her bare feet slapping on the stone.

Brian breathed a sigh of relief. "So what happened?" he asked J.P.

"Well, I got inside the school from the back and got in the boiler room. I was taking pictures, when Liz walked in." J.P. grinned. "Why's she dressed like that? And more importantly…how can we get her to *always* dress like that?"

"That's not funny," Brian snapped.

"Aw, come on dude! You had to enjoy that a little."

"No! I didn't!"

"Aw, Burke. I'm hurt." Liz walked up to them, grinning broadly. She was back in her black shirt and pants. "We did it!" she crowed, hugging Brian and J.P. in turn. "We have proof!"

"What proof?" Brian said waspishly. "All you did was take some pictures."

"You didn't tell him?" Liz gave J.P. an exasperated look.

"What? Oh yeah!" J.P. dug into his jeans pocket. "Look what we found! By the fuse box."

"It was in the corner, under a rag," Liz said proudly.

J.P. dropped something small into Brian's hand, and Brian stared down at it: a blackened circle of metal, about the size of a...

"It's a penny," he muttered.

"Yeah," Liz said, a gleam in her eye. "A *burnt* penny."

Liz and J.P. were both in high spirits on the car ride home, recounting their war stories with relish. "I can't *believe* we pulled it off!" J.P. chortled.

"Of course we did," Liz said scornfully. "Hank's about as sharp as a marble. All I had to do is act like I was back on the cheer squad. And you did fine too, Burke. We make a cute couple."

"You were a cheerleader?" Brian muttered.

"Yeah. Eighth grade at St. Lucy's. Lucky for us...and lucky I packed my ditz outfit." She patted her backpack fondly. "Like I said: everything we would possibly need."

"You could have warned me," Brian snapped. "About the...ditz outfit."

"That wasn't for you! It was for Hank! I *had* to dress like that!"

"Why?"

"So Hank would get scared! I knew if I dressed skimpy, he wouldn't want to come near me. And I was right! He stayed outside until I came out." Liz smirked. "Boys. They're so simple."

She's using you, Brian.

He scowled. "That was wrong, Liz. The ends don't justify the means."

"What if the 'ends' are to keep the school from burning down?"

He looked down at the blackened penny in his hand.

"It makes sense now," Liz said smugly. "It's all coming together. *Allie* put that penny in. *That's* why she snuck into the school—to get it back. Luckily I interrupted her."

"Wait a second." J.P. gaped at Liz. "You think *Allie's* the poltergeist?"

"No!" Brian snapped, throwing his arms up. "You're crazy, Liz! This is all just a coincidence! It has to be!"

"Coincidence?" Liz looked outraged. "How much more proof do you need, Burke! Stop making excuses! Stop pretending!"

"Stop pretending? What were you doing back there at the school, huh?"

"I was pretending for a *reason!* I was playing a part!"

"Really?" he retorted. "What part are you playing now?"

"What?" Liz said sharply.

For a moment they glared at each other. "Hey, hey," J.P. said with a nervous laugh, "Why don't we all *pretend* that everything's *fine*, okay?"

"Shut up," Liz snapped. "Things aren't fine. Burke—I'm playing myself. I *always* play myself with you." She turned away. "I figured you knew that."

Brian turned away, feeling angry. He didn't know why.

16

MIXED SIGNALS

Allie sat down on a bench in the food court and pulled out her phone. She had two messages: one from Celia and one from a number she didn't recognize. *Hmm. Well, let's check Seal's message first.*

"Hey Allie." Celia sounded irritated. "This is a pain, but I'm afraid I'm going to have to bring John Mark with me after all. Miranda can't watch him. Long story. Old story." She sighed. "Anyway, I'm sorry I'm running late. Hopefully I'll be there at 12:30."

Allie sighed. *It's noon now...I guess I can just hang out.* She went to the next voicemail.

"Hey Allie. This is Keenan."

She grinned. *I thought he might call.*

"I got your number from Simone. Sorry...I was just thinking about what we talked about before. You know...the rosary thing. Well, I still think you should pray to Jesus before you pray to Mary. I think that's what God would want. I know your friend loves the rosary, but she's wrong. No offense—"

Allie felt a twinge of sadness.

"—but I hope this helps. I'll tell you more at the Bible Study tomorrow; hope you're still coming! Oh, by the way...a group of us from Cross Bridge are going to the beach next weekend. You're invited."

The beach? Cool! Her sadness was quickly eclipsed by excitement.

"I'll see you tomorrow. God Bless! Bye."

Allie flipped the phone closed. *I haven't been at the beach in forever! I need to get a new swimsuit! Hmm...I saw some cute red bikinis at Geoffrey's...* She giggled. *He'll like that.*

"Allie?"

She looked up. There, of all people, was...

"George!" She shoved her phone back into her purse. "What are *you* doing here?"

"Going shopping." George held up a plastic bag. "Brian's birthday's coming up; I thought I'd get him some decent wrestling gear."

"Oh! Well..." Allie looked her ex-boyfriend up and down. "Um...wow! It's great to see you again!"

"What are you talking about?" George frowned. "I saw you Saturday. For a second."

"Oh...right." She laughed ruefully. "Sorry I blew you off then. But a lot has happened since."

"Like what?"

Allie smiled. "Sit down and I'll tell you."

And that's it," Allie finished. "That's the whole story."

She watched George anxiously. He didn't look happy—in fact, his frown had grown more and more pronounced as she went through her story.

"Um..." He drummed his fingers on the table.

"What are you *thinking*, George?"

"I'm thinking...that this is all my fault."

Allie blinked. "Your...fault?" She chuckled. "Why?"

"Because I wasn't there for you. You asked for my help, and I wasn't there."

Allie's grin faded.

"It's okay," she said awkwardly.

"No, it's not," he mumbled. "I messed everything up. You asked me for help, and I tried...but I said all the wrong things."

He hung his head. Allie watched him, touched.

"George." She reached over and took his hand. "You didn't say the wrong things. I just wasn't ready to hear them. You were

174

right, George. God's love— that's what I needed. And now I have it!" She chuckled. "Don't you get it yet? I'm happy!"

He looked up, incredulous. "Happy?"

She smiled affectionately. "Yes. Happy." She squeezed his hand. "For the first time in a long time. I've never been happier."

"Allie? George?"

They both looked up. Celia stood there, holding a squirming little boy with black curly hair and staring at them with a bemused expression.

George pulled his hand away, looking nervous. "Hi, Seal. We were waiting for you."

"Oh," Celia said. "Sure. I'm—I'm sorry I'm late." She looked as though she felt she were intruding.

Allie looked from George to Celia, and giggled.

Celia's brow wrinkled. "What's so funny?"

"Nothing," she said. "It's just that you look so confused."

At that moment the toddler squirmed extra-hard in Celia's arms. "Lemmee go! I wanna see George!"

"Put him down, Seal. Hey, John Mark!" George knelt down as John Mark ran happily up to him. "You want to go check out the toy store?"

"Yeah!"

George took hold of John Mark's hand. "I'll take care of him, Seal. You can meet me at the toy store when you two are done talking."

Allie watched George disappear into the crowd with little John Mark. "He's such a great guy," she murmured. "The one that got away," she added with a laugh, turning to Celia. "Right, Seal?"

Celia was looking at her shoes, a sad, almost sulky expression on her face. *Uh oh.* Allie felt like kicking herself. She had seen Celia look that way many times, back when she and George were together. It made Allie feel ashamed, but also irritated—Celia was so passive about these things.

"Hey, I was joking," she said, smiling. "That's all in the past, right?"

"What?" Celia looked up, surprised. Then she let out a shamefaced laugh. "Oh…right. Sorry. I was just reminded of…you know…the past."

"Well don't!" Allie said, laughing again. "Don't worry, I'll never be interested in George again. He's all yours!"

"Um…thanks," Celia said, a little stiffly. "But I don't know what you mean…"

Allie sighed. "Let's go get some drinks," she said. "My treat."

Celia seemed to be having a hard time getting comfortable. Her face was still red five minutes later as they sat down together with their drinks.

"So…what was that all about?" she finally asked.

"George and I were just trying to make you jealous," Allie said before she could help herself. "KIDDING, Seal!" she quickly added as Celia's brow wrinkled. "Come on, lighten up! We just ran into one another and hung out, waiting for you."

"Oh," Celia said, and finally looked a little less troubled. She even smiled weakly. "Sorry if I got upset. I'm just tired, and I'm having a hard time with Miranda. So what did you want to tell me?"

Allie took a deep breath. "Well…where do I start?" She took a long sip of her iced latte. "It all started when I met Ginger…"

Allie launched into the story of what had happened at Cross Bridge. As she told the story, she could tell that Celia was interested —and then moved. When Allie told her how she had broken down and cried at the service, Celia looked almost ready to cry herself.

"Wow," she said softly, her eyes glistening. "That's…oh wow, Allie, that's so awesome." She grabbed Allie's hand and squeezed it. "Praise God."

Allie laughed shakily. "Yeah. Praise God." She felt herself blush. "So that's it," she said shyly. "Hard to believe, huh?"

"Oh, Allie…" Celia wiped her eyes. "It's more than I hoped for."

"And that's why I wanted to tell you in person, Seal. Because this is all because of you. This never would have happened if I hadn't had you as an example..."

Celia giggled. "I don't know about *that*. I mean...you know what?" She brightened. "You should come with me to Eucharistic Adoration tomorrow night. Come and see Jesus with me. Wouldn't that be awesome?"

"Oh..." Allie suddenly remembered. "I can't. Not tomorrow. I promised Keenan I'd go to Bible Study at Cross Bridge."

"Keenan? Who's that?"

"Um...nobody." Allie hesitated. "Just some guy I know— well, I *barely* know him, really. I know his sister. But I really want to go to this Bible Study. I want to learn more about Jesus."

She saw a flicker of worry pass over Celia's face. "Learn about Jesus? At Cross Bridge?"

"Yeah. Why, what's wrong with that?"

"Nothing!" Celia hesitated. "Well, I mean...gosh. It's not Catholic, is it?"

"Who cares?" Allie laughed. "It's about Jesus, right? Isn't that the most important thing? Encountering him?"

"But that's why I want you to come to Adoration with me." Celia looked a little more worried. "The Eucharist—that's Jesus. He's really there. And I really *feel* him there. Maybe now you will too."

"Well..." Allie thought about St. Bridget's, and the underwhelming experience she had there on Sunday morning: how *less* excited she had felt compared to Cross Bridge. "I don't know, Seal. This is different. Maybe I'm different. Maybe..."

Maybe I'm not meant to be a Catholic. The thought struck her. But she didn't say it.

Celia sighed. "Oh, I wish my dad were here. He'd know what to tell you. I just don't want anything to happen to you that will hurt your faith..."

"Hurt my faith?" Allie shook her head. "You don't understand Seal. I finally *have* faith now!"

"What do you mean?" Celia said anxiously. "Didn't you have faith before?"

"Well...a little," Allie said hesitantly. "But it's different now, you know? It's simpler. It's personal. Just me and Jesus."

"Oh," Celia said. But she still looked anxious.

Allie sighed. "Hey, why don't you come to this Bible Study too? There's lots to do at this church. They even have a Bible camp. Anyone can go. It's like a retreat, like the one George went on, in the woods and everything..."

"That sounds great," Celia said distantly. Her eyes darted over Allie's shoulder. "Uh oh. Look."

Allie turned to see George approaching, holding a bawling John Mark.

"Looks like John Mark had a meltdown." Celia stood up and shouldered her purse. "He's due for a nap anyway...Allie, can I talk with you about this later?"

"Sure," Allie said, disappointed. She wanted to talk more with Celia—there was so much more she wanted to tell her—and ask her. "Come to Bible Study," she said. "Tomorrow night, eight o'clock at Cross Bridge. I'll text you the directions. We can talk more then, okay?"

"Okay. Thanks so much for telling me, Allie. I'm happy for you."

They exchanged hugs, and Allie watched as Celia walked away with George and the crying boy. Despite Celia's last words, she hadn't *looked* very happy. And Allie didn't feel too happy either. But she didn't know why.

17

HEAT WAVE

A blast of hot air rushed into the van as Brian pulled open the sliding door. He glanced up at the blazing sun and blinked.

"Don't just stand there, Brian!" his mom said irritably. "You're letting out all the cold air!" The van's air conditioner was on full blast.

"Sorry," he said, and hopped out. He felt the heat rising from the black asphalt even through his sneakers.

"Don't forget your water." His mom handed him a bottle. "Stay hydrated! And don't work too hard today! You don't want to get heat stroke!"

As his mom drove away, Brian looked around. There was a crowd of boys gathered near Mr. Simonelli's van: J.P., Joey and Athan were there, plus a few boys he didn't recognize. He walked up just as Mr. Simonelli threw open the back doors and turned to face them.

"Okay guys," Mr. Simonelli said. "We're kind of shorthanded today; George couldn't make it. But we got a few new workers too. "Kevin Snyder—" he pointed to a gawky boy with short curly brown hair. "Mitch Wilson—" He pointed to a handsome boy with wavy black hair and a broad grin. "And Chris…sorry son, what's your last name?"

"Man…Manzinni," said a small, scared-looking boy with straight brown hair.

"So…nice to meet you," Brian said to the new boys. "Where'd you go to school before?"

"Eh, public school," Kevin shrugged. "My parents were going to send me to Sparrow Hills, but that shooting freaked them out."

"Same here!" Mitch said. He glanced up the road. "But we're still pretty close to the public school, aren't we?"

"What about you, Chris?" asked Brian to the last boy.

"Me? Oh! I just moved here. From Georgia. My dad's in the military," Chris said with a nervous laugh.

"So you must be used to moving around," Brian said.

"Yeah, eleven times in fourteen years," Chris said.

"Right. So let's get going." Mr. Simonelli opened the van door and started tossing out big rolls of pink fiberglass insulation onto the curb. "Bring this stuff inside and stack it in the hallway."

Brian grabbed a roll and started towards the door with the others. *None of these new guys mentioned whether or not they were Catholic,* he thought to himself. *But I guess if their parents sent them here, they've got to be, right?*

As he passed into the school, the boy in front of him—Kevin Snyder—stopped abruptly and turned around. "Hey!" he whispered, with a grin. "Look what's coming!"

Brian glanced around his roll and saw three pairs of legs.

He blinked. No…three *girls:* Miranda, Vivian and Kristy. But their legs were the first things he saw. Legs…shorts…

"Dang," Kevin said, his eyes on the blond. "I want a piece of *that.*"

Brian suddenly realized that he had been *looking.* Feeling horrified at himself, he fixed his eyes on the ceiling just as Kevin let out a wolf whistle.

"Real mature," Brian heard Miranda say, but he didn't dare look in their direction until he heard the door close and the girls' voices stop.

"Wow!" Mitch Wilson said, walking in with his roll of insulation. "You see that?"

"Yep." Kevin smirked. "*Totally* want to hit that."

"What?" Brian snapped, suddenly furious. New kids or not, he didn't like this conversation.

But Kevin only laughed again. "Oh, come on, man! Girls who dress that way *want* us to look. You were looking too!"

Brian opened his mouth—and then closed it and turned away. He felt his face growing red.

"So come on!" Kevin said in a prodding voice. "Which one did you like the best?"

"None of them," Brian muttered.

Kevin chortled. "Come on dude. Which one did you like best? The one with glasses? Or maybe the one in the middle? She was *so* hot."

"That would be Miranda," Athan said from the doorway. He tossed his roll of insulation onto the stack. "Miranda Costain. She's the principal's daughter."

"Nice," Kevin smirked. "She totally wanted me—aaaahhh!"

Without warning, Athan had charged forward and hit Kevin square in the chest with his shoulder. Kevin flew backward, tripped over a roll of insulation, and fell to the floor. Brian and the other guys stared in astonishment.

Athan, on the other hand, looked calmly down at Kevin, a slight frown on his face. "Hey man," he said. "Don't talk that way about my lady friend."

"Your...what?" Kevin got to his feet, looking both furious and a little scared. "What's your *problem*, dude? Are you some kind of freak?"

Athan smiled brightly. "An artist, actually. And a football player. Name's Athan. Nice to meet you." He held his hand out to Kevin—and when Kevin's only response was a bewildered look, Athan shrugged, put his hands in his pockets, and walked back outside, whistling.

The other boys roared with laughter at the look on Kevin's face.

"Dude!" Mitch chuckled. "That little guy totally killed you!"

"Yeah, whatever," Kevin muttered, rubbing his shoulder. "What's *his* problem?"

Brian grinned. "I think he made that obvious."

A few minutes later, they were all in the classroom. The old newspaper insulation was gone now, exposing studs and shiny new wiring.

Mr. Simonelli divided them into teams and handed out box cutters and staple guns. "Measure the space between the studs," he said. "And then cut the insulation to fit."

Brian found himself paired up with Mitch. *I don't know what I'm going to say to him,* he thought.

"Hey, you're Brian, aren't you?" Mitch offered him his hand and shook it enthusiastically. "I heard about you! You put out the fire!"

Brian sighed. "Yes, that's me, the fireman." He knelt beside the insulation. At least they were talking about something else.

Over the next hour they made good progress. Brian, Mitch, Kevin and J.P. managed to cover half of the wall they were working on. But the third team—Athan, Joey and Chris—didn't move as fast. Chris seemed kind of lost, and Joey and Athan kept jostling each other, tossing the tape measure back and forth, and pretending to tackle each other. The last time this happened, Joey almost knocked over Brian. "Careful!" he snapped. "I got a box cutter here!"

"Sorry dude!" Joey laughed. "We're just stoked about football tryouts! I can't believe we all got in!"

"Football tryouts?" Brian gave him a puzzled look. "Where? At Sparrow Hills?"

"Yep! We all went together on Monday! And we all got in!"

"Really." *So this is what Hank was talking about.*

Joey turned to Athan. "You were the fastest there. I bet they'll make you wide receiver. You totally smoked everyone, even that varsity guy!"

"Fat chance." Athan grinned. "But I won't play without you and George."

"George went too?" Brian blurted out.

"Yep. Got onto defensive line."

Brian turned back to his work, frowning. *Why would George try out? He's a wrestler.*

He felt someone tap him on the head. "Fellow Conspirator!" someone said in a frenetic whisper.

"Yes, J.P.?" he replied without turning around.

"That's it, just keep on working. Look normal. F.C., we have Top Seeclet Meeting with Masta Planna E.S. in Rloom One One Two at twelve hundred hours..."

"Noon?"

"That's rlight! Rloom One One Two. Lememba! Now keep your eyes on your work. Look normal while I ease away...that's it..."

Shaking his head, Brian continued cutting insulation while J.P. made a show of moving to the other side of the room.

"Hey guys!" Jacinta Summers stuck her head in the room. "Can we come in?"

She walked in, followed by Isabel Reyes and—his heart started beating faster—Mary.

She looked...cute. Very, very cute. She was wearing a light green blouse with tiny sleeves, and jean shorts that ended just above her knees. Her light brown hair was tied back, and her big brown eyes were scanning the room...until they looked right at him.

And then they sparkled playfully. She was *smiling* at him! Brian felt his heart beating faster. He smiled back, barely registering the other two girls—Jacinta in her short-sleeved cotton top and white skirt, Isabel in her usual overlarge shirt and baggy pants.

"Well hello there, ladies." Mitch walked up to Jacinta, who happened to be the closest. "You're looking very nice today."

Jacinta giggled. "Why, thank you, sir!" she said playfully. "I'm so sorry, I didn't catch your name."

"Mitchell. But you can call me Mitch. And you are...?"

"Jacinta," Jacinta said loftily, making a little curtsy. "But you can call me Jace. Or just 'J.' And this is my sister Mary (or 'M' for short) and this is Isabel, otherwise known as 'Bell'—"

"Where's Athan?" Isabel said eagerly.

Everyone looked at Athan, who, oddly enough, looked intensely interested in the piece of insulation he was holding. He looked up, saw Isabel and sighed heavily. "Yes?"

"Hello again Athan!" Jacinta said brightly. "We were just wondering if you'd reconsidered..."

"No," Athan said flatly.

"Oh, come on!" Isabel whined. "I'm painting St. Clare in the girl's bathroom. So you *have* to paint a matching St. Francis in the boy's bathroom!"

"Come on, Athan," Jacinta said appealingly. "It's just one little religious painting—"

"Icon."

"Um..." Jacinta looked confused. "What?"

"I'm Byzantine. We only do icons, which are *not* religious paintings."

"Oh!" Jacinta laughed. "Sorry. So could you paint us an *icon* on the bathroom wall?"

Athan shook his head. "Icons aren't painted. They're written. It's difficult. It takes weeks. You need special training. I explained this to Isabel already," he added, giving Isabel an annoyed look. "So stop asking me, okay?"

Isabel scowled. "Byzantine Shmizantine!" she said. "You could 'write' an icon of St. Francis if you really wanted to!"

"But I don't want to," Athan said. "Not the way you want him drawn. It's not manly enough."

"Manly?" Isabel fired back. "You think it's *manly* to be a big, hulking football player? Yeah, I heard you guys going on about your silly tryouts! All you want to do is drawn comics! But if you're really a Catholic, you wouldn't mind painting St. Francis!"

"Look, if you like St. Francis so much, *you* paint him!" Athan retorted.

Jacinta and Mary exchanged alarmed looks. "Okay, okay," Jacinta said anxiously. "It's no big deal. No one's forcing you, Athan."

"Yeah, Athan!" Isabel said sarcastically. "It's okay if you can't *handle* painting a saint!" She stomped out.

"Isabel!" Jacinta ran after her. Mary followed, looking embarrassed. Athan turned away, muttering under his breath.

"Dude, what's the big deal?" Joey said.

"Yeah!" Kevin said. "Why don't you just paint St. Francis? If some cute girls asked *me* to—"

"You think *she's* cute?" Athan snapped.

"Not the crazy Mexican one! Jacinta! Come on, she's *blonde!*"

J.P. chuckled. "You came to the right place," he said. "We got a lot of blondes here. Jacinta, and Kristy, and Liz, and Allie—"

"Allie? Allie Weaver?" Kevin's face lit up in recognition. "I saw her on TV! She got interviewed about that shooting thing! She was *hot*. Is she here?"

"I don't think so," J.P. said. "Not today anyway. She hasn't been coming to work camp very much."

Kevin shrugged. "Too bad. Well, plenty more where that came from."

"Um...yes," Brian said. "But remember, they're all daughters of God."

The room fell silent. Kevin stared at him like he was nuts.

"By the way, St. Francis used to roll in the snow to purge himself of temptation," Brian said, addressing himself partly to Athan. "Isn't that kind of manly?"

"Yeah, but that's not how Isabel wants him painted," Athan said. "She wants him to be patting a bunny on the head or something."

"Yeah, that would make a great painting on the bathroom wall," Kevin said. "St. Francis, buff, leaping in the snow to avoid looking at a couple of hot chicks..."

Mitch snorted and both boys convulsed in laughter.

"Excuse me?"

They all looked up. Brian blinked. Mary had come back.

"Sorry to, uh, interrupt," she said. "But we need a couple guys to help us move tables in the gym. Any volunteers?"

Kevin and Mitch stepped forward simultaneously. Mary's eyes narrowed. "No thanks," she said disdainfully. "How about...Brian? Can you help?"

Brian stared up at her, hardly believing his luck. "Sure!" he blurted out, standing up.

J.P. raised his hand. "Me too. Seniority, dudes."

The rest of the boys looked disappointed. Only Athan looked as though he were now perfectly happy working on insulation.

We're done one side of the gym," Mary said, leading them down the hallway. "But before we can start the other side, someone's got to move the tables. They're too heavy for us."

They entered the gym. One side was painted sky blue; the other side was still faded green, and a bunch of lunch tables were stacked against the wall, along with a mass of folding chairs. The floor was strewn with abandoned rollers, brushes and paint cans. The kitchen was full of chattering girls. None of them spared a glance for Mary and the two boys.

"Dude," J.P. muttered. "Those are a lot of tables."

Mary looked troubled. "You're right," she said. "Looks like I'll have to ask those other boys after all. I'll go back and—"

"No!" Brian said hastily. "We can handle it!"

"Are you sure!"

"Of course!" he said jauntily. "No problem!"

"Really? Okay." Mary smiled. "Oh, and Brian: can you meet me in the school office at noon? I need to talk to you about something."

Brian gaped at her. "Sure!" he said, his voice cracking.

As she walked away, Brian turned to J.P. "You hear that?" he said eagerly. "She wants to meet me!"

"Yeah," J.P. said unenthusiastically. "But—" he dropped his voice to a whisper, "We have Seeclet Meeting, leememba? Top Seeclet. Loom One One Two…"

"I know. I'll be there, just a bit late." Brian waved a hand impatiently. "And now let's get started on these tables!"

"All light," J.P. said, "so long as you lememba Top Seeclet meeting. If Masta Planna mad, you in Beeeg Beeg Tlouble…"

"Okay, okay, okay."

It didn't take long for Brian to regret his decision. Each table needed to be folded upright and wheeled about fifty feet. A lot of the wheels were rusty and stuck, so they ended up *carrying* half the tables; and they were heavier than they looked. Before long they were both worn out. Brian's arms burned and his back ached—and they were barely halfway done.

They were trying to lift an especially heavy table when J.P.'s grip slipped. The table crashed to the floor, narrowly missing his toes.

J.P. groaned. "Ah! Nearly wounded! Not able to attend Top Secleet Meeting...*must ask* for help!"

"No," Brian panted. "It's not that bad..."

"All right, that's it!" J.P. pointed at Brian accusingly. "Stop it!"

"Stop what?"

"Stop acting crazy! There's only one crazy guy in this school: me! Not you, not that Athan kid—me! Stop stealing my thunder!"

"I'm not...crazy," Brian stammered.

"I know crazy, and you're it! Trying to move all these tables by ourselves—that's crazy! And blowing off Liz—that's even crazier!"

"Who's blowing me off?" Liz walked up to them, along with her brother Joey.

"Ahaa! Masta Planna! You in Beeg Beeg Tlouble now!" J.P. hissed to Brian.

Liz glanced curiously at Brian. "We came to help," she said. "Joey, get going."

"Come on, J.P.," Joey said with a grin. "Let's have another go at that table."

Brian stepped forward to help, but Liz stopped him. "What's up?" she said, frowning. "Didn't J.P. tell you about the meeting?"

"Well..." Brian hesitated. "Mary wants to meet me at twelve."

Liz arched an eyebrow. "Really?"

"Yes!" he said defiantly.

"Wow. Good for you, Burke." Liz shrugged. "Go ahead. It's almost twelve now. We'll start without you."

"Oh," Brian said blankly. "Okay. Thank you." *Didn't expect that,* he thought as he walked away. He frowned. *Or is she up to something? Maybe a big revenge plan?*

The school office was just outside the cafeteria, and the door was open. *She must be inside.* He took a deep breath and stepped forward.

"Tomorrow? He's coming *tomorrow?*"

Brian froze. It was Mr. Simonelli's voice; and he sounded angry. He edged forward cautiously and looked into the office.

There was Liz's dad, pacing back forth and talking angrily into his cell phone. "No, we should be fine, thank God!" Mr. Simonelli's said. "But it's cutting it really close! We can't test the new boiler till tomorrow...and of course you won't be there to deal with him!"

After a short pause, Mr. Simonelli snorted. "Is *that* what he said? He wants to watch us turn the new boiler on? Does he think we can't handle it on our own? He just wants to come while you're out of town."

Mr. Simonelli stopped pacing suddenly. "What? He's being investigated, huh?" He grinned. "Well, maybe he'll lay off of us, then. He's got bigger things to worry about. I'll see you Friday."

He flipped the cell phone closed and spun around before Brian could duck out of sight.

"Brian?" Mr. Simonelli said gruffly. "What do you want?"

"I'm...sorry, sir," Brian stammered. "I was looking for Mary Summers—"

"Mary Summers...oh, right. I kicked her out of here to take this call." Mr. Simonelli grinned. "She mentioned you might come by. She's out in the front."

"Thanks!" Brian said, and ran down the hallway. *Wonder what that was all about.*

He rushed outside and saw Mary standing alone beneath the shade of an oak tree. Pushing down the jolt of panic in his stomach, he walked up to her.

"Hey," she said. "Thanks for meeting me."

"No problem. Is something wrong?"

"Um...yes," she said. "I'm worried about my sister."

"Jacinta? Why? What's wrong?"

"Well..." Mary looked anxious. "You see, Celia's out today, and she sort of left Jacinta in charge. And Jacinta's *really* anxious to do a good job."

"Oh. Okay," Brian said blankly, wondering what this had to do with him.

"That's why Jacinta's so upset over this fight between Isabel and Athan. You were there; you saw it. Isn't Athan being unreasonable?"

"Well..." Brian shrugged. "Maybe. But I don't want to get involved."

Mary's face fell. "Really? You can't get involved?"

"What?"

"Can't you talk to Athan? Persuade him to paint that silly picture or 'icon' or whatever it is? It would just make things so much easier; and you'd be helping my sister." She looked pleadingly at him. "Please?"

Brian stared back at her. "Of course," he heard himself say. "No problem."

"Oh, thank you!" Mary sighed. "I didn't know who else to ask. I *know* you can do it. You're so calm and reasonable...you got me to calm down, remember?"

Brian laughed awkwardly. "You didn't *seem* very calm..." He took off his glasses and wiped them on his t-shirt.

"No," Mary said softly. "No, I didn't."

She took a step closer. He looked up and froze. She had a tender look in her brown eyes.

"I was angry. And you stood up to me. And you were right." She took his hand. "That's why I picked you for this. You're the right man for the job."

Brian blinked rapidly. "Okay," he managed to say. "I'll do my best."

She squeezed his hand. "I know you will. By the way—" She smiled slightly. "You look good without the glasses."

Brian blinked. "Really?"

"Yeah. You got really nice eyes."

She walked away. Brian slapped his glasses back on and watched her go.

He looked down at his hand, still warm from her touch. "Wow," he whispered.

J.P. and Liz looked up as he entered Classroom 112. "Hey, look who's here." Liz said testily. "What took you so long? What did Mary want?"

Brian shrugged. "Nothing much," he said casually. "No big deal. So what's up? Did you find anything out?"

"Sure did." Liz handed him a color photo. "See anything suspicious here?"

Brian glanced at the photo, which seemed to be nothing more than a bewildering mess of pipes and wires. "Um...should I?"

"Dude!" J.P. placed one finger on the picture. "Right here!"

Brian looked again. J.P. was pointing at a black, squarish plastic box mounted to the side of the boiler.

"Look at the back of it," Liz said. "You see those wires coming out?"

"Yes?"

"Well, they're supposed to be attached to something. And they're not."

"Oh." Brian felt a bit underwhelmed. "That's it?"

"What did you expect, Burke?" Liz said impatiently. "A big sign saying DEATH TO THIS BOILER or something? The point is: *that* thing is unplugged."

"But what *is* that thing?"

"That's what we got to find out."

Brian's brow furrowed in thought. "It could be nothing."

"Just like the penny?" Liz snapped. "What will it take for you to believe—"

"I *do* believe it's serious, okay?" Brian retorted. "Look, if this is for real...what do we do then?"

"We catch him in the act!" J.P. grinned. "And kick his keester!"

"Or *hers*. And then tell my dad." Liz smiled smugly. "I can't wait to see his face when he finds out it *wasn't* me!"

"No! You don't get it!" Brian snapped. "This isn't a game!"

The smiles vanished from both their faces. "We know that," Liz protested.

"Do you?" Brian said harshly. "Because if you're right, Liz, then this—" he pointed to the photo. "—isn't just some prank! Allie wouldn't do this! It's too...evil! Whoever this guy is, he's *serious*. And apparently he doesn't care about hurting people! You realize what would have happened if I hadn't put out that fire?"

His words seemed to finally sink in. J.P. turned pale. Liz looked abashed. "I guess you're right," she muttered. "Sorry. I still think it could be Allie, though."

"Well, let's do some research first," he snapped. "Liz, could you email me this photo?"

"Sure," Liz said. "Why?"

"I want to post it online. On an HVAC forum."

"What's that?" J.P. said.

"Heating, Ventilation and Air Conditioning," Liz nodded. "Good idea, Burke."

"But what about us?" J.P. said. "What should we do?"

Brian glanced from Liz to J.P. They were both looking at him expectantly. A subtle change seemed to have occurred; they were looking to *him* now for instructions; like he was the leader of their group. It felt good. But it also felt scary.

"Well..." he hesitated. "There's one thing I can't figure out. Why would anyone *want* to hurt our school?"

"Well, Allie's always hated it here," Liz muttered.

Brian gritted his teeth. "Suppose it's *not* Allie," he said. "Suppose your original theory's correct, Liz. That it's the poltergeist—the same guy behind all that stuff last year. Why? What's he doing it for?"

J.P. and Liz glanced at each other.

"He hates...schools?" J.P. said.

"Or Catholics?" Liz offered.

191

"He must hate them a *lot* to want to burn down a building," Brian said. "No. There's got to be another reason. Something important. So think about it. Try to figure it out."

"What does that matter?" J.P. said

"Because it'll help us figure out who it *really* is," Brian said impatiently. "So...work on that. Both of you."

The classroom door opened, and Mr. Simonelli stuck his head in. "Lunch is over, guys," he grunted. "Back to work."

As Brian turned to leave, he felt Liz's hand on his arm. "Can I talk to you?" she whispered.

He sighed. "Okay." *Here it comes...she's gonna let me have it.* He waited until J.P. had left and then turned around.

Liz was eyeing him, an unreadable expression on her face. "I won't do it again," she said.

"Do what?"

"Wear the ditz outfit."

"Oh," he said, relieved. "Thank you. Why?"

"Because I know it bothers you. I don't know what the big deal is—"

"You don't?" he said incredulously.

"No, Burke, I don't! Hello? I wore gym shorts every time we played tennis, and you never even noticed!"

"Actually, I *did* notice," he said. "A little. But this was different. You were acting like...well..." He shoved his hands into his pockets. "Like you did with Rich."

Liz paused. "You didn't like him, did you?"

"No. I thought he was bad news from the start."

She frowned. "Why didn't you warn me then?"

"You wouldn't have listened to me anyway."

"ctually, I would." Liz's frown deepened. "Believe it or not, I really *do* care what you think. Especially about me." She 1. "How did you know Rich was bad? What tipped you

'ust...the way he looked at you. Like you were a piece of

Liz blinked. "Oh…well…" She laughed harshly. "Maybe I was asking for it. I bet *you* snuck some glances my way too. Admit it!"

Brian smiled slightly. "As long as you promise not to mace me."

Liz scowled. "That's not funny, Burke."

"Sorry. But I don't *want* to look at you like that, Liz. You're my friend. Can't you dress decently when I'm around?"

Liz sighed heavily. "Well, all right. If it means that much to you. From now on I'll wear a burka. Can I at least put some eye holes in it?"

"What? No! That's not—"

"Aw, come on, Burke? No eye holes in the burka?"

"I never said anything about a—"

She punched him in the arm. "Kidding again. Geez, you're fun to be around. Too bad we fight so much."

"Yes…" He rubbed his arm. "Too bad."

"Heck, we keep this up, we'll end up married!"

"What?" Brian stared at her…then jumped away as she pulled back her fist. "I know! You're kidding!"

She snickered. "So how'd it go with Mary?"

"Fine. You're really okay with me talking to her?"

She shrugged. "You told me to back off, so I'm backing off. Just be careful, okay?"

He waved a hand impatiently. "Don't worry, I'm not like Rich."

Liz looked skeptical. "We'll see."

18

TWO OR THREE

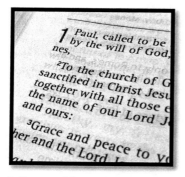

1 Paul, called to be ...nes,

²To the church of G... sanctified in Christ Jesu... together with all those ... the name of our Lord J... and ours:

³Grace and peace to y... her and the Lord ...

Allie pulled into the Cross Bridge parking lot and took a deep breath. *Okay, here we go.*

She grabbed her new Student Bible, got out and walked up to the sleek, brightly lit building. On the way she scanned the parking lot, looking for the battered green Volvo that she knew Celia would be driving. *I should call Celia,* she thought as she entered the crowded lobby, full of noisy teenagers. *I hope she's still coming...*

"Allie! Over here!" There was Ginger, waving to her. Simone was with her, and Tara, and a few other people.

"I'm so glad you could make it!" Ginger gave her a hug. "Everybody, this is my friend Allie; she's new here."

"Hi Allie!" An older girl with long brown hair and a kind face waved at her. "You're the one who just got saved, right?"

"Um, yeah," Allie said with a grin. "How did you find out?"

"Tara told me," the girl said. "I'm her older sister, Jenn."

"Really?" Allie said. Now that she looked again, she could see the resemblance; except that Jenn looked older and a little heavier.

"Yeah," Tara said playfully. "Jenn's the less thin version of me. She's home from college."

"I prefer 'less thin, more fun,' actually," Jenn said, punching her sister in the arm. "But yeah, I'm a sophomore at Hodgeson Bible College; and this is my boyfriend Derek."

"Howya doing, Allie?" Derek shook her hand energetically. He was short—only a few inches taller than her—had spiky black hair, and was dressed in ripped jeans, sandals, and a black t-shirt with the words *Sola Fides* on it in Gothic letters. "Congrats! I hope you stay here!"

"So do I," said another voice. "Especially since you just got rescued." The speaker was a tall, thin boy with lank brown hair, a grumpy look on his pale face. Oddly enough, he wore a black t-shirt exactly like Derek's, except that it said *Sola Scriptura*.

"Um…hi," Allie said, turning to the other boy. "Rescued from what, exactly?"

"From the Catholic Church," the boy said solemnly. "Otherwise known as the Abomination of Desolation, the Whore of Babylon, the—"

"Oh, shut up, Martin!" Tara said indignantly. "Allie, this is my cousin Martin Layman, and you can feel free to ignore him; he was born with no tact."

Martin's face darkened. "That's what they said about Luther," he muttered.

Allie glanced from Martin's shirt to Derek's shirt. They looked exactly the same. She grinned. *They're like Tweedle-Dee and Tweedle-Dum.*

"Jenn and I are meeting with Pastor Holtz," Derek said. "About Bible Camp. Martin's coming too. We're all volunteering as counselors."

"Oh yeah, Keenan mentioned something about that," Allie said. "So what's this Bible Camp like?"

"It's basically a summer camp," Jenn said. "But it's focused all on God. There's gonna be prayer meetings, Bible Studies…"

"And campfires and sports and all that good camp stuff," Simone said. "We're all going. It'll be a blast."

"That *does* sound kind of cool" Allie mused. "Can I get a brochure or something?"

"Sure!" Derek passed her a glossy brochure. "But you better hurry up! Registration deadline's this Friday."

"Cool. Thanks." Allie slipped the brochure into her bible.

Ginger checked her watch. "We're gonna be late. Come on, guys. Bible Study's downstairs in the basement."

As the crowd started to move away, Allie overheard Derek saying to Martin, "Hey, man, I really like your shirt. Where did you get it?" She stifled a laugh as she lingered, looking back into the parking lot. *Where are you, Celia?*

"Allie!" Ginger called back to her. "Come on!"

Reluctantly, Allie turned away. *I hope she makes it...I really should call her...*

"How does this Bible Study work, anyway?" she said, jogging up to the other girls.

"It's simple," Ginger pulled open the stairwell door. "About ten people get together and pray. Then we read a chapter of the Bible we're assigned and discuss it."

"The really neat thing," Tara said. "Is that you get really tight with the people in your group. It's like family."

"Celia would like that," Allie murmured.

They had come to the bottom of the stairs. As the other girls started down a hallway, Allie hung back and pulled out her cell phone.

Darn it. No reception.. Must be because we're in the basement. Maybe I can go back upstairs and...

"Come *on*, Allie!" Simone called back to her, and she hastily ran up to join the others.

They entered a large, crowded, low-ceiling room, filled with teenagers. "Hey girls!" A tall guy with curly brown hair walked up to them.

"Hey Roger!" Ginger said. "This is Allie, and—"

"All right, everyone! Settle down!"

Pastor Holtz was in the center of the room in front of a microphone. Next to him was Keenan with his guitar.

"A few announcements before we start," Pastor Holtz said. "Next week's group is going to be rescheduled..."

"Hey," Allie whispered to Ginger. "Keenan invited me to the beach this weekend. Are you coming too?"

"Of course," Ginger said. "Everyone is. It's part of the Bible Camp thing. I can give you a ride if you want—"

"And finally," Pastor Holtz said. "Just a reminder to sign up for Bible Camp! We've got a great staff assembled, including Keenan here, who will be leading music."

Allie turned to Ginger. "Oh that's right, he told me that too!" she whispered excitedly.

Ginger snickered. "Bet you're coming *now*, huh?"

Allie grinned. "Shut up."

Keenan stepped up to the microphone. "Hey guys!" he said. "Let's give God an offering of praise." He started strumming and singing, and everyone joined in.

Your word is a lamp to my feet
And a light to my path...

The words and the song were simple and sweet. The crowd of teenagers raised their hands to the ceiling, eyes closed. Some even swayed. Allie had never seen teenagers pray like this before: so spontaneous, so heartfelt. She closed her eyes and tried to pray too. *Jesus, please help me. Be a light for MY path. Because I don't know where it's going.*

She followed the others into a small, nicely furnished room filled with armchairs, couches...even a coffee bar. It felt relaxed.

"Okay, let's get started," Roger said, and they sat down with their Bibles. He opened a study guide. "Today we're beginning a new letter: First Corinthians. It's a really powerful book that resonates with a lot of people. Usually I'd start by giving you some background, but I think that tonight we're just going to dive right in. First, I want you to just read the chapter and think about what it means to you. Then we'll go back and find out what it meant to the early church." The group fell silent as Roger started reading:

"Paul, called to be an apostle of Christ Jesus by the will of God, and our brother Sosthenes, to the church of God in Corinth. To those sanctified in Christ Jesus and called to be holy, together with all those everywhere who call on the name of our Lord Jesus Christ—their Lord and ours: Grace and peace to you from God our Father and the Lord Jesus Christ."

Roger handed the bible over to Simone. She continued:

"I always thank God for you because of his grace given you in Christ Jesus. For in him you have been enriched in every way..."

And so it continued, each person reading a few verses and then passing it on. Allie sat and listened, trying to catch every word. She got the feeling that every verse was packed with important things.

Then Ginger handed the bible to her. Allie took a deep breath and read her passage.

"...For the foolishness of God is wiser than man's wisdom, and the weakness of God is stronger than man's strength."

She handed the Bible to Tara and sat quietly through the rest of the reading, musing over the words.

"Lord God," Roger said, "please help us to understand your words...and...accept your mercy, Lord, 'cause we need it...and help us to stay close to you."

"Amen."

"Okay, let me throw out some questions." Roger flipped to the next page of his guide. "The first one is...How is the foolishness of God wiser than the wisdom of man?"

Allie raised her hand before she could stop herself.

Roger looked pleased. "Allie, what do you think?"

"Um..." Allie hesitated. "Well...I just think...I always felt stupid talking about God and religion and stuff, you know?"

Several people nodded and grinned. "Me too!" said a dark-haired girl next to Roger.

Allie grinned. "Yeah! But what the Bible says here...it sounds to me that all the theology and rules and stuff...it's not as important as believing in Jesus and loving Him."

There were several murmurs of assent from the others. "Great insight, Allie," Roger said thoughtfully. "You're right, that's what's the most important."

Wow, Allie thought. *They actually agree with me.* It was the first time she hadn't felt stupid talking about religion.

19

WOW!

"**Wow!" Allie said as** they walked out the front doors of Cross Bridge.

Ginger chuckled. "Wow what?"

"I love the Bible! I never read it so much before—"

"Why not?" Tara said. "Don't Catholics read the Bible?"

"Um..." Allie hesitated. "Well, sometimes...at Mass..."

"Hey, Allie!" Keenan ran up to them, carrying his guitar case. "Glad I caught you! How did you like the Bible Study?"

"She loved it, dear brother," Simone said. "But I bet you didn't come over here to discuss *that*." She rolled her eyes. Tara giggled.

Keenan looked a little sheepish, which made him look even cuter than usual. "Er...Allie, do you want to hang out with me a little? We can...discuss Scripture."

Ginger chuckled. "See you later, Allie."

"Yeah, don't stay up too late," Simone said. "Those Scripture discussions can be *so* involving."

Allie smirked. "See you later, guys."

So long a time had been, that in her presence
Trembling with awe it had not stood abashed...

Brian's eyes followed the lines, re-reading them over and over again. *Trembling with awe...* He rubbed his eyes. *These contacts are scratchy.*

His father's laptop chimed on the coffee table. He closed the Divine Comedy book and leaned closer. *New mail. Did I get an answer already?*

> BrianBurke3,
> that box in your photo is a low water cutoff device. The fact that its disconnected is suspicious. the easiest way to break a boiler is to drain the water out, jump out a water level safety device, start the boiler up while its dry and let it run for a while. it will crack, once thats done, let the boiler cool down, fill it up with water again and turn it on, it will leak and flood the area if its a large boiler. Unfortunately there's no way to prove it but i think you should get some security in the building.

"No way," he murmured. "Well, that settles it."

The poltergeist was officially back. It definitely wasn't Allie; it sounded like this sort of thing would take hours and require expert knowledge. This was the real deal.

Now what should they do? He had to think...

He groaned and stretched on the leather couch in his dad's study. *I'm too tired to think. It was so hot today. What a day...what a week. Things are moving too fast...*He closed his eyes.

Random images danced before his eyes...rolls of insulation...Athan and Joey tossing a tape measure back and forth...Kevin and Mitch high-fiving...

Miranda and her two friends walking past...shorts, legs...

Liz winking at him, hands behind her back...*She's using you, Brian...*

And then he was back at the formal, watching Liz and Rich kissing...

And then he was at the Flynns, sneaking glances at J.P. and Courtney on the couch...

I've never kissed a girl...

And then he saw Mary, her cheeks flushed, her lips parted...

His eyes snapped open. He stood up, breathing hard.

This is getting bad. I got to stop this.

The door opened with a creak. "Brian?"

His father stood there, the light from the hallway glistening on his bald, brown head. "What's going on?" He walked up. "What are you doing here alone?"

"Nothing!" Brian said. He glanced down at the laptop on the coffee table. "I was...just looking something up online—"

"Really? What?" His dad reached out to take the laptop.

"No!" Brian closed it quickly. "Please, Dad, it's private."

His dad looked at him for a long moment. "All right, Son." He squeezed Brian's shoulder. "But don't be afraid to ask my advice, okay? If you need help with something, just let me know."

Brian glanced up at his dad. "Really? Anything?"

"Anything," his dad said solemnly. "Don't stay up too late." He walked away.

"Dad!"

His dad paused, his hand on the doorknob "Yes?"

Brian took a deep breath. "I need your help," he said. "I've been looking at girls. Looking a lot."

For a moment his father stood with his back to him.

Then he walked up to an armchair and sat down. "I see," he said quietly. "How long has this been going on?"

"Not long," Brian mumbled, his eyes on the floor. "It just started this summer."

"Not too long, then. That's good. Look at me, son."

Unwillingly, Brian looked up. His father's brown eyes were full of disappointment. "I'm glad you told me this," he said. "But you'll still have to be punished."

"But...but...I couldn't help it!" Brian stammered.

"Yes, you could," his dad said sternly. He sighed and shook his head. "I know you couldn't help the urge...but you shouldn't have acted on it. You shouldn't have deceived me." He picked up the laptop.

"Dad!" Brian protested. "Please, don't look—"

"Don't worry. I won't." His dad held the closed laptop in his hands for a moment; then he flipped it over and took out the battery. "All right, Brian," he said. "How did you do it?"

"Do what?" Brian stared at the laptop, baffled. "Look at girls?"

"Yes. Did you find the password?"

"Um...I didn't know you needed one—"

"Don't make jokes. Maybe you found it somewhere? Your mom has such a poor memory...I keep telling her not to write passwords down..."

"Um..." Brian blinked. "I don't understand, sir."

His father's eyes narrowed. "Have you been looking at girls or not?"

"Yes!"

"Then you know I have Gateway software on all our computers. Your mother has the password. So how did you get past it?"

Brian stared at his dad—and then at the laptop—and then he figured it out. "No, no, no, Dad!" he said, aghast. "I wouldn't...no!"

"What?" his dad said doubtfully.

"Dad, I've been looking at girls at *school!* It's been so hot lately, and the way they dress..." he faltered. "I'm sorry," he mumbled.

His dad's mouth dropped open. For a full ten seconds he stared at Brian—then he threw back his head and burst into laughter.

"At school?" he gasped, wiping his eyes. "Is that all?"

"Um...yes," Brian said. "So you're not mad?"

"Mad? No! I'm relieved."

"Really?"

"Yes! It could have been much worse." His dad chuckled. "Well, it's the summer. Just try not to look too much, okay?"

Brian stared at the floor, not feeling the least bit relieved. If anything, he felt worse.

"Look, son," his father said after a moment. "You're almost sixteen. Frankly, I'd be worried if you *didn't* notice the ladies."

"Of course I notice them!" Brian scowled. "They *want* me to notice them! Why else would they dress like that?"

"Now, Brian," his dad said. "Don't judge them too harshly."

"But don't they realize what they're doing?"

"Actually, no. They may not." His dad shrugged. "Women don't think that way—especially young women. Sometimes they don't understand how their dress affects men. "

Brian snorted. "What, are they idiots?"

"Nooo," his dad said patiently. "They're just not men. Men are visual, son. We're attracted to what we *see*. Women are attracted to...other things."

"Huh?"

His dad smiled slightly. "First things first. You have to understand, Brian, that this urge to look at girls—it's not going to stop. Not until you're dead."

"Great," Brian mumbled. "So I can't help all these impure thoughts from popping into my head."

"I wouldn't quite put it that way."

"*But* it *feels* impure! And I can't stop, Dad! I can't stop thinking about her!"

"Her?" His dad cocked an eyebrow. "Who's her?"

Brian gulped. "Uhhh..." he muttered.

His dad sighed and rubbed his eyes. "This is harder than I thought. Let's see..." He glanced at Brian thoughtfully. "When you see a pretty girl, how do you feel?"

Brian stammered. "Um...I..." He flushed. "I don't know. I can't describe it."

"Try. Close your eyes, and think about the prettiest girl you've ever seen. Then tell me how you feel."

Half-afraid of what would happen, Brian shut his eyes...

*S*he *walks in beauty, like the night,*" Keenan sang softly, his fingers dancing over the guitar strings.

Of cloudless climes and starry skies,
And all that's best of dark and bright
Meets in her aspect and her eyes..."

203

Allie listened with her eyes closed, her heart aching a little. The music and words seemed to tear at her, shaking something deep inside of her. It moved her. Moved her a little too much. *It's so beautiful...majestic...dangerous...*

Abruptly, Keenan stopped. Her eyes snapped open. "Keep going!" she pleaded.

"I can't," Keenan admitted. "That's all I have so far."

"You wrote that? Wow! A man of many talents!"

Keenan hesitated. "Not exactly. The words are from a poem by Byron—"

Allie chuckled. "Yeah, I took Mr. Foster's English class too. But why haven't you finished it?"

He laughed self-consciously. "I only started it today. I was looking up some stuff for you, about your rosary question, and I just got...inspired..." He flushed. "Sorry. I barely know you...you're probably weirded out."

"No," she said quietly. "I'm not."

She looked into his brown eyes. *I could get lost in those eyes...*

"Okay!" she said suddenly. "What did you find, anyway? About the rosary?"

He chuckled as he put the guitar back in its case and sat down next to her on the bench outside of Cross Bridge. "You got your bible?"

"Right here." She handed it over.

"Okay. Look, before I start, Allie...don't get mad at me."

"Why?" she said. "What did you find out?"

"Well..." He hesitated. "I found a lot of stuff out. About Mary, and the Catholic Church. But it might get you mad."

Allie glanced down at the bible in his hands, and a little shudder went through her.

"That's okay," she said. "Just tell me the truth."

So?" his dad asked. "What do you feel?"

Brian didn't reply at once. He was imagining Mary; her face, her soft voice, her golden brown hair...but it was different, somehow. Maybe because his dad was there. He didn't feel overwhelmed, gripped with passion, out of control. He just felt...felt...

"Wow," he whispered.

"Wow?"

"Yeah!" Brian opened his eyes and grinned "That's how I feel! Just...wow!"

"That's good, son." His dad tapped Brian's shoulder. "A woman's beauty is God's handiwork. It's natural and good to marvel at it, to praise God and thank Him for it."

"But dad..." Brian hesitated. "All this stuff...it's still dangerous, isn't it?"

"Oh yes. Very dangerous. Because of our fallen and weakened nature, we need to guard our eyes so that our marveling looks don't turn into mighty lusts."

"What's the difference?"

"Lust is when you treat a girl like a *thing*—not as a daughter of God. Lust kills the *wow*."

"Kills the wow," Brian repeated to himself. "Okay. Got it. I have one more question." He hesitated. "Remember how you said that girls are attracted to different things than men?"

"Yes..."

"What *are* they attracted to?"

His dad smiled knowingly. "Well, for starters...duty."

Brian blinked. "Duty?"

"Yes." His dad nodded slowly. "As in 'do your duty.' Women like a man who does his duty, no matter how hard it is."

Brian's brow wrinkled. "Are you sure?" he said doubtfully.

"Brian, I've been married for seventeen years. Trust me on this." He tapped the coffee table. "Girls may fall for the flashy guy, but they'll *stay* for a guy who'll take out the garbage every night. Women want stability. They want dependability."

"They want boring?"

His dad chuckled. "Duty's not always boring. Just remember...duty."

"Duty," Brian repeated to himself. "Okay. I can do that." He stood up, rubbing his eyes.

"Contacts still bothering you?"

"Yes," he muttered.

"So…what convinced you to give up the glasses?"

"Um…just thought I'd give them a try," Brian muttered, and headed for the door.

20
ACCUSER

"The truth will set you free." Keenan said
and nodded. "So first of all: you know what the Catholic Church
says about Mary?"

"Well..." She thought for a moment—she wanted to make
sure she got it right. "The Church says that Mary is immaculate;
that she never sinned. And she was a virgin her whole life."

He nodded. "That's what I read too. But, Allie...that's not
what the Bible says. In fact, it says just the opposite."

"What?" she gave him a shocked look. "No, it doesn't!"

"See for yourself." He flipped through her bible, found a
page, and showed it to her. "Romans, Chapter three. Right
here."

She looked down, and read aloud: *"There is no one righteous, not
even one."*

"And that's not all," Keenan turned the page and pointed
again. "Look here, a few verses later."

"For all have sinned and fall short of the glory of God."

"*All* have sinned, Allie. All. It doesn't say 'All, except Mary. It says 'all'."

She rolled her eyes. "So what? Maybe they just forgot to mention her! It's just a mistake!"

He frowned. "Allie, this is the Bible. The Word of God. There *can't* be any mistakes in it."

"Yeah, but—"

"Look," he said, flipping to another passage. "If you don't believe Paul, will you believe Mary herself? Check this out. First chapter of Luke."

She read aloud: "*And Mary said: My soul glorifies the Lord and my spirit rejoices in God my Savior.* So?" she said, snapping the bible closed. "What's your point?"

"Think about it," he said. "She calls God *my savior.* Why would she need a savior if she hasn't sinned? Only sinners need a savior!"

"But...um..." She faltered. "I never thought of that. But what about the second thing? Mary being a virgin forever?"

Keenan sighed. "Actually, this is kind of embarrassing. It's so obviously wrong. Did you know Jesus had brothers and sisters?"

"What are you talking about?" she said, shocked again.

He took her bible, flipped through it and handed it back to her for the third time. "Right here. Matthew 13, verses 54-56. Look what the crowds say about Jesus."

With her heart sinking, she read aloud: "*Where did this man get this wisdom and these miraculous powers?' they asked. 'Isn't this the carpenter's son? Isn't his mother's name Mary, and aren't his brothers James, Joseph, Simon and Judas? Aren't all his sisters with us?*"

"And that's just one passage," he said. "There's a bunch of others. It's really, *really* obvious that Mary was only a virgin in the beginning. Later on she had more kids."

Allie looked down at the bible, her head spinning. Part of her wanted to go back to Celia or Brian or somebody and get their opinion. *But what could they say? It's not like this is...unclear or anything! It's right there!*

And then another slew of thoughts rushed in: *The Catholic Church is just wrong on this. And if that's true...how can I trust it? On anything?*

"I can't *believe* this!" She stood up and paced back and forth, wringing her hands.

"Allie?" Keenan looked alarmed. "What's wrong?"

"What's wrong? What's wrong?" she said franticly. "Don't you get it? If this is true, then it means that everything I've been taught at school...I can't trust any of it!"

"I never said that," Keenan protested. "Allie, why are you so upset?"

"Because..." She couldn't finish. She felt like the whole world was spinning—as if something strong and firm had been knocked out from under her feet.

And that was when Keenan walked over and hugged her. She sank into his arms gratefully; she needed a hug right now. She needed something solid to hold on to. She looked up into his eyes, and kissed him gently on the lips. "Thank you," she whispered.

"Allie?"

She turned around. There was Celia.

Allie pulled away from Keenan, feeling herself blush. "Celia!" she said, laughing nervously. "You finally got here!"

"Um...yeah," Celia said. She looked a little shaken. But she smiled, though it looked a little forced. "Sorry I'm...walking in on this. I was busy going over the work schedule and lost track of time and...then I realized you never...I mean, I never got the directions you said you were going to send..." She trailed off, blushing.

"Oh!" Allie suddenly felt sheepish. She had forgotten all about sending Celia directions to the church. "I—"

"Well at least you got here!" Keenan said easily. "My name's Keenan. Welcome to Cross Bridge." He took a step forward and offered his hand. Are you a friend of Allie's?"

"Um...yeah." Celia shook hands with Keenan, frowning slightly. "I am."

"Keenan," Allie said. "Could you give us a moment?"

Keenan shrugged. "No problem. I need to go anyway. I'll see you later, Allie. Give me a call—let me know if you're coming to the beach this weekend." With another laid-back smile, he sauntered away.

Allie sat down heavily on the bench, filled with conflicting emotions. Part of her was afraid of what Celia might have seen—and heard. Part of her was furious at Celia for being late because of stupid work schedules for the stupid work camp. And part of her was desperate for Celia to tell her everything would be okay...to explain everything, to answer all the questions about Catholicism. She always had before.

Celia sat down next to her. "So...sorry I missed the Bible Study. How was it? I was really looking forward to it." She smiled, but there was still an anxious look in her eyes.

"It was great," Allie said faintly. "Really great. But Seal—I never realized—all these things I learned in John Paul 2 High—they're not in the Bible. "

"What do you mean?" Celia looked perplexed. "Is that what they told you in the Bible Study?"

"No!" Allie said hastily. "No, this came from Keenan. He's a small group leader...not that I'm in his group though..."

"You mean the guy who just left?" Celia gave her a funny look. "The guy you were kissing?"

Allie closed her eyes. "Yeah."

"So..." Celia hesitated. "Are you two dating now?"

"I guess so," Allie mumbled.

"But I thought you barely knew him."

"Yeah. No. I don't know!" Allie covered her face in her hands, overwhelmed with emotions. "I'm sorry I didn't tell you, it just happened so fast...he's such a good guy...he's just trying to tell me the truth..." Tears were coming now. "Seal, I just need to talk to you. I feel so betrayed...and confused..."

"Hey, then let's talk." Celia patted her shoulder. "So calm down." She sighed. "Not that it isn't hard to keep up with you sometimes. I mean, you've been so hard to get a hold of...it seems I can barely find time to talk to you...So who betrayed you?"

"Never mind..." Allie sniffled. "I didn't mean...stupid thing to say. I always do stupid things when I'm angry...like with the boiler—"

"Boiler?"

"Um...the boiler at school," Allie mumbled. She glanced up at Celia, half-afraid.

Celia looked utterly baffled. "What about it?"

"Um...well..." Allie took a deep breath. "After Mrs. Summers yelled at me, I ran away. And I was passing by the furnace room, and I heard some noises. I looked inside. The boiler was shaking. It was making a clanging noise. Something was wrong with it. And I started to go back and tell you, but...I didn't. I just walked away." She looked at her shoes, feeling ashamed of herself. "But it doesn't matter, right?"

"I guess not," Celia said after a moment. "The boiler would have broken down anyway, I suppose." She looked at her hands, frowning. "But...still, you should have told someone. I mean, that was dangerous. I know you were mad at *me*, but—"

"Just forget about it, okay?" Allie mumbled. "Maybe I just wanted to...get your attention. I mean, you're so busy these days, you're never here for me anymore."

She wiped her eyes, laughed shakily, and reached for her bible. "Now I want to ask you about this stuff Keenan said—" She froze. "Seal?" she stammered.

Celia's face had turned red. Her eyes were squinted into slits and her mouth was open. She looked angry. More than angry—*furious*.

"What did you just say?" Celia said in a low, dangerous voice. "I'm never *here for you?*"

"Uh..." Allie suddenly felt cold. She had never seen Celia look this way before. At *anyone*. "I mean..." She laughed nervously. "You're just so busy all the time! It just seems that all you can think about now is work camp, and worrying about the new freshmen, and Miranda, and—"

"*I'm never here for you??*" Celia stood up, her fists clenched. "*You*, Allie? Why do you think I'm doing this? Why do you think I'm here sitting on this bench instead of home getting some dinner and going to bed early? Because I'm HERE! Being *HERE FOR YOU...RIGHT NOW!*" She threw up her hands. "Omigosh, I can't *believe* you, Allie! I really can't! Could anyone be so *selfish*, so self-centered...argh!" She stomped around in circles on the pavement. "Don't you remember why we came up with the work camp idea in the first place?"

"Um..." Allie stammered, trying to recall what Celia had said at that first meeting. "To...um...get to know the new students, and to keep in touch over the sum—"

"Because *you* were feeling lonely!" Celia cut her off. "And *you* wanted friends! You told me this on the phone! Don't you remember? So that's how we came up with the idea for doing this work camp. Don't you remember? I started this whole program just for you. How's that for 'being there for you'? Huh? And then, what do you do? You come to the program just to hang out with my bratty sister and laugh at everything we're doing!"

She glared at Allie. Allie just stared back. She couldn't speak; she could hardly breathe, as if she had been punched in the gut.

Celia started pacing back and forth, spitting out words. "See, I'm just not that important to you! Yeah, I'm dependable, I'm loyal, so you think you don't have to pay attention to me. You just write me off. Well, you know what? The world doesn't revolve around you, Allie Weaver! And it's about time someone told you that!" She wiped her eyes furiously. "I've certainly wasted enough time and energy and emotion...for someone who barely cares about anything outside of her own...personal space!"

"Seal! Look, I'm sorry!"

"*NO!*" Celia turned on her furiously. "No more sorries!"

She resumed her pacing, her voice getting shriller with every word. "You're always saying you're sorry, but you're not! If you were really sorry you'd change—but you *never* change! You're just so full of yourself, so selfish, so me-me-me-me-me, it's all about Allie, and I just sit back and *take* it, because I *care* too much, but *you* couldn't care less! And why should you? Because you can write me off, good old Celia, always takes it, never dishes it out because she's so nice...well, by golly, this is the last straw! I'm through with it!

212

I'm done with all you whiny selfish high-maintenance brats—you, Miranda...But you're *worse* than Miranda! At least Miranda doesn't pretend to be my friend!"

"But I never pretended!" Allie said desperately. "I *am* your friend!"

"Oh yeah?" Celia gave her an incredulous look, and then laughed bitterly. "What kind of friend promises to send directions and then forgets? What kind of friend promises to do all sorts of stuff—and then forgets? Or lies and says she's not *up to it*? You know what kind of friend does that? A *fake* friend. And I guess it's taken me this long to see that's what you are!" Celia stomped over to her and pointed a finger in her face. "It's not gonna work on me anymore! I'm not gonna feel sorry for you anymore—you know who I *do* feel sorry for? Your new boyfriend!" She let out an angry laugh. "You go through the boyfriends pretty quick, don't you? First Tyler, then George, now this Keenan guy. So what's the story this time? Oh, don't tell me. *He's* the one who led you to Jesus, isn't he? That's what your—" She made sarcastic quote marks with her hands. "'spiritual experience' was really all about, wasn't it? I was just too clueless to see it!"

Allie's mouth dropped open.

Celia clenched her fists. "Well, I'm not clueless anymore! Your 'spiritual experience' was really just the latest cute guy in your life who helped you 'get saved.' Well, I'm sick of it! I'm sick of nursing you along and trying to believe it's really for real this time, because *you don't change!* You're still the same self-centered snobby brat who walked into John Paul 2 High last year! Nothing that's happened has done a *thing* to make you change! Nothing! Well that's it! You hear me? I am *DONE!*"

Celia stomped away and vanished into the darkness.

A tiny moan escaped Allie's lips. She sank to her knees, her eyes squeezed shut.

She was alone.

Alone...except for the cold laughter in her head, and the cold voice: *She's right, you know. She's just wrong about the details. Just ask Nikki. It's all a lie...even Jesus...*

She swayed a little. It was back again: the old, familiar darkness, like black churning water.

She was drowning.

And then a thought was flung into her mind, and she seized on it. *No. Jesus isn't fake. Maybe I am, but He's not.*

"Jesus..." she whimpered, and then said the word again, and again. "Jesus...Jesus...Jesus..."

She didn't know how long she knelt there, saying Jesus's name, but eventually she heard footsteps coming back.

"Allie?"

It was Celia again. She must have come back. She must have heard her.

"What are you doing?" Celia asked. She sounded scared.

Allie stood up. "I'm done with all this Catholic stuff," she said flatly. "Here." She pulled the rosary out of her pocket and tossed it to Celia.

Celia caught it, looking startled. "What's that?"

"Your rosary," Allie said. "Yeah, the same one that you gave me the first day at John Paul 2 High. I kept it all this time, but I guess I don't need it any more. Since I was a *fake* friend. Actually, I'm tired of faking it. Faking being a Catholic."

She yanked off the chain around her neck. "And here. Take this. George's Mary medal. Tell him no offense, but I guess I don't need it either. Since I haven't *really changed*."

Celia's eyes were round with shock as she took the medal. She had stopped talking, as though it were slowly dawning on her what was happening.

"Okay, so now this is real," Allie said brutally. "I'm really leaving the Catholic Church. You're done with me. Just like you said. No more faking it. I won't be bothering you anymore. You can walk out of here free. Free from me. Congratulations, Celia. You're done. And so am I."

Allie turned around and, spotting something lying on the bench, grabbed it and shoved it into Celia's hands. "And take this too. It's a bible. Try reading it sometime."

She turned away and strode to her car, but not before she saw, with a savage pleasure, Celia's face crumple in horror. She knew exactly how Celia would feel later. And she was happy.

"Allie, wait, please, stop, I shouldn't have said—" Celia's voice was faint.

"Goodbye, Celia."

A minute later she was driving out of the parking lot. Just before she exited, she braked and looked back, trying to catch a last glimpse of Celia, but she couldn't find her. Maybe she had already left…

She stepped on the gas, and the car shot forward into the darkness. Something like pain stabbed her. But not regret. *It's over.*

21

BEAUTIFUL LETDOWN

"No."

Athanasius Courchraine crossed his arms. "No way. No how. Not gonna do it."

"You know, as a Catholic artist you should jump at the chance to do a religious painting—" Brian said.

"A *Roman* Catholic artist, maybe," Athan said dryly. "I'm a Byzantine Catholic. Like I said, we don't do *religious paintings.* We do *icons.*"

"Fine! So why can't you just do an *icon* of St. Francis then?"

Athan started counting on his fingers. "Number one: I don't want to. Number two: I don't know how to write icons—"

"Write?"

"Yeah. Like I said, you don't paint icons; you write them. Which brings us to number three: I'm not going to learn how to write an icon just to please some control-freak hippie girl. Number four, I don't have the time anyway, not with football practice. And number five: I don't freaking like St. Francis! Okay?"

"All right!" Brian closed his eyes for a moment, thinking hard. "Couldn't you...paint St. Francis in a *non-religious* way?"

"He's a saint!"

"Come on, use your imagination," Brian said earnestly. "Think of it as a challenge. Don't do an icon. Paint him *your* way."

"My way?" Athan snapped…and then, slowly, a gleam came into his eye. "Paint him…*my* way, huh? Hmm." An amused smile came to his lips. "Hey, Brian, you ever see my work?"

"Well, no," Brian admitted. "But I heard you're really good."

"Oh, I'm *awesome!*" Athan said brightly. "And I think you're right; I should share my talent with the world."

"Er…yes," Brian said, slightly puzzled. "So…you *will* do it?"

"I'll do it, brother!" Athan said, slapping Brian on the back. "This'll be the best St. Francis picture *ever!* I'm gonna go get my sketchbook! See ya!" He sprinted away.

"Um…thank you," Brian said to the now-empty hallway. *What just happened?*

Then he realized…he had done it! He had convinced Athan! He chuckled, hardly believing his luck. *You know what? I'm going to go find Mary and tell her.*

He had only taken a few steps when Liz ran up to him, wearing her white coveralls. "Hey," he said. "Have you seen—"

"Hide!" she said frantically. "Now!" She grabbed his arm and tugged him into the nearest classroom.

"Ow!" he said. "Why are you always pulling me into—"

"Hey! Occupied!"

Brian spun around to see Miranda slouching on the windowsill, looking sulky in a black spaghetti-strap top. The only other person in the room was a little boy with black curly hair, playing happily at Miranda's feet.

"Don't barge in here!" Miranda snapped.

"Liz, what's going on?" Brian said.

"Everybody shut up!" Liz snarled. "They're coming!"

At that moment they all heard footsteps in the hallway outside. "Well, the boiler's on," a familiar gravelly voice said. "Happy? Any other hoops we got to jump through?"

"Take it easy, Simonelli," another voice said, sounding dry and amused. "I'm just doing my job."

Mr. Simonelli grunted. "Yeah, well, come to the office and I'll sign the forms."

The footsteps receded. "Whew!" Liz turned to Brian, shaking her head. "Sorry about that."

"Who was that?"

"Bickerstaff," Liz muttered. "The county inspector. I hate that guy—he's got it in for me." She glanced at Brian and frowned. "Hey, where are your glasses?"

"I'm wearing contacts," Brian muttered, rubbing his eyes. "I got them for wrestling a long time ago, but I never used—"

Something tugged on his jeans. He turned around to see the toddler grinning up at him. "Hewwo," he said, and waved a stubby blue pencil in one chubby hand.

"Hey John Mark!" Liz knelt down next to the toddler. "Whatcha doing here? Tired of hanging out with the girls?"

"So he'd rather be with *you*, then." Miranda smirked from across the room.

Liz looked up. "Oh, hey, Miranda," she said coolly. "I forgot you were there. So you found a new place to hide from work?"

"No," Miranda retorted. "I'm babysitting the rug rat."

"And you're doing a heck of a job." Liz snatched the pencil from John Mark and waved it. "He could poke his eye out with this thing. What genius left you in charge of babysitting?"

"My parents," Miranda muttered, walking over and scooping up John Mark. As she did so, Brian looked away. Miranda noticed. "What's *your* problem?" she snapped.

"Lay off him, okay?" Liz said irritably.

"What, does he have a problem with how I'm dressed?" Miranda snapped.

Liz rolled her eyes. "Sure, if you're going to ignore the dress code when your parents are gone."

Miranda's lip curled. "Funny. He never looks at *you*."

Liz's face turned pale. "Shut up," she said. "Okay?"

Miranda smiled coldly. "So," she said, glancing at Liz's paint-smeared white coveralls. "What do you call this outfit? The dumpster dive? What, did you lose all your *girl* clothes, Liz?"

Liz clenched her fists and gave Miranda a look of pure hatred. "Come on Burke," she growled. "Let's go."

"Bye, boys!" Miranda said as they ducked out of the classroom.

Liz stalked down the hallway, muttering darkly to herself. Brian followed her. "Hey," he said hesitantly. "Are you okay?"

"I'm peachy, Burke. What a brat..." Liz shook her head. "Pretending she's the fashion queen...I'll dress how I like. *You* don't mind my overalls, do you?"

"No," Brian said. "Not at all. No tempt—"

"Right," Liz mumbled. "No temptation. That's me." She looked unhappy. "So...I got your email. So somebody *did* mess with the boiler, huh?"

"Um...yeah. You want to talk about it?" Brian said, hoping to get her mind off Miranda.

"Sure. Let's go to my mom's classroom."

But when they got there, the classroom door was closed. "Oh, great!" Liz groaned. "Who's in there?" She sidled up to the door.

"You shouldn't eavesdrop—"

"Quiet, Poindexter. Hmm. Sounds like someone's crying."

"What?" Without thinking, Brian drew closer. He could just barely hear somebody sobbing quietly. It sounded like a girl.

Liz turned the knob slowly and opened the door. They both peeked into the classroom. There was Celia, slumped on the desk, her face buried in her hands.

"Celia?" Liz said hesitantly.

Celia looked up. "Oh...hey Liz. Brian." She made an attempt to smile, but couldn't keep it up.

"Seal, what happened?" Liz ran up to Celia, and Brian followed hesitantly. He had seen Celia upset before, but never *this* upset. Her eyes were red and puffy, and her face was pale and almost haggard, as though she had been crying for a long time.

"What happened?" Liz said again.

"Nothing," Celia said hoarsely. She stood up, snatched a bible off the desk, and turned to go. Something fluttered from the bible and landed at Brian's feet.

"Hang on! You dropped something!"

219

Celia turned around. "What?" she said dully.

He picked the thing up. It was a brochure with the words **Cross Bridge Bible Camp** blazoned on the front.

"It came out of your bible," he said, handing it to her.

She stared down at it. "This isn't *my* bible," she whispered. "It's..."

She sat down heavily on the desk, covered her face in her hands, and started sobbing again.

Liz patted her awkwardly on the back. "Hey," she said. "It's okay..." She looked at Brian and mouthed *do something!*

Brian shrugged helplessly. If girls confused him, crying girls confused him even more.

"Why did I say that?" Celia mumbled. "She's grieving, and I said *that*...and now she's gone, and she'll never come back..."

Brian and Liz exchanged baffled looks.

"No!" Celia stood up, wiping her eyes furiously. "This isn't right," she said. "I shouldn't feel sorry for myself...this is *my* fault." She glanced down at the brochure clutched in her hand. "I got to make it right," she whispered fervently, and ran out of the room.

"Okaaay," Liz said after a moment. "Are you as confused as I am?"

Brian sighed and shook his head. *One mystery at a time.*

So, Allie..." Her mom frowned as she sipped her coffee. "You call me at work and ask me out to lunch. You say it's urgent. And it's all because you want to go to this Bible Camp for the next two weeks?"

"That's right." Allie fingered her own coffee cup nervously.

"But what about the thing at JP2 High? The work camp?"

"I'm not going back there," Allie said. "We're done. I'm done."

Her mom put her fork down. "All right. You can go to this Bible Camp."

Allie breathed a sigh of relief. "Thank you," she said fervently. "Thank you so much, Mom."

Her mom smiled faintly. "You're welcome. But there's something else." She hesitated. "Your dad called me this morning. He's coming into town next Friday, and he'll be staying for a couple weeks."

"Dad?" Allie blinked. "Why?"

"There's a conference in the city. I'll have to check again, but I think...well, it's pretty much the same time as this camp."

Allie's heart sank. She missed her dad so much. Even though he only lived an hour or two away, he traveled constantly for his job and never seemed to have time for her.

"It's not as bad as all that," her mom said. "This camp's two weeks long, right? Your dad can visit you on the weekends, and then he can give you a ride home at the end."

"Oh..." Allie murmured. "Okay. That works for me. Any other objections?"

"Just one." Her mom sighed. "Allie, a month ago you were so excited about seeing your friends at school. You begged me to let you go to that work camp."

"Yeah..." Allie muttered.

"Now you say you're 'done' with JP2 High. Why?"

Allie gritted her teeth. "It's...complicated, Mom. Just trust me, I *have* to do this, okay?"

"Are you sure? I picked John Paul 2 High for a reason, you know. I've known the Costains for years. I trust them. And I thought you liked it there too—even though it took you a while to warm up to it."

Allie stared down at her plate.

"Allie," her mom said gently. "Did something happen? Is this about George, or—"

"I don't think Catholics follow the Bible, okay?" Allie blurted out. "All they do at school is follow all these rules, and rituals, and...that's all the Catholic Church *is!* A bunch of legalistic stuff, all these *rules* about divorce and annulments and mortal sin and...it's all junk!" She bit her lip. "I'm sorry," she muttered. "But you just don't understand."

Brian was eating lunch with the other boys when George tapped his shoulder. "Hey," he said in a low voice. "We're going to have a meeting at 3 p.m."

"We?"

"You, me, Celia and Liz. It's really important."

"What about J.P.?"

They both glanced down to where J.P. was sitting, stretching a rubber band between his fingers. Then his face seemed to light up with a sudden idea. He dug a paper clip out of his pocket, hooked it on the rubber band, aimed, and launched it.

"Hey!" someone shrieked from the girls table, twenty feet away. Looking delighted, J.P. dug another paper clip out of his pocket.

"I don't think so," George said. "Like I said, this is serious."

He walked away, and the table lapsed into silence again. The only sound came from Athan's pencil as he hunched over his sketchbook, scribbling away.

Brian glanced at Athan hopefully. *He must be working on his painting. I still need to tell Mary.*

He looked around and noticed Jacinta walking by, holding a lunch tray. "Hey! Jacinta!" He jumped up and ran over to her. "Seen Mary around? I need to tell her something."

"I'll tell her for you! What is it?"

"Um…" he hesitated. "I'd rather tell her myself. In private."

A knowing smile stole onto Jacinta's face. "Well…" she said. "Mary just went to the bathroom. Maybe you can catch her on the way back."

"Thanks!" He turned away, his heart beating a little faster, and walked quickly to the wooden double doors. The only usable bathroom in the place was the boys' bathroom, just beyond the school office. *So all I got to do is hang out by the school office and wait…*

He pushed through the doors and stopped short. There was Liz, sitting on the bench next to the school office door. She looked up and nodded curtly. "Hey."

"Hey." He looked around nervously. "Look, can you go away? I'm meeting someone here."

"Someone, huh?" Liz gave him an odd, twisted smile. "Let me guess: someone pretty?"

"Yes!" He said impatiently. "I mean..." He faltered. "Not that you aren't...pretty..."

"Real smooth, Romeo." Liz rolled her eyes. "Come on." She patted the bench. "Sit down. We'll wait for Miss Summers together."

He sighed. "Okay, okay." He sat down on the bench next to Liz. *Of all the places she could be hanging out...*

"So, I've been thinking," Liz said. "About what you said. How this is serious. And I made a decision." She took a deep breath. "I showed those pictures to my dad, and your email too. And the burnt penny."

"Oh." He shrugged. "Okay."

Liz gave him a annoyed look, but didn't say anything.

"So what did he think?" Brian glanced down the hallway. *Were those footsteps?*

"He thought...well, he didn't say what he thought." Liz ran both hands through her hair. "But at least he didn't just make fun of me. Maybe he'll take it seriously, I don't know."

"Hang on a sec!" An unpleasant thought struck him. "You didn't tell him how you *got* the pictures, did you?"

"Yeah, Burke, like I'm a total idiot." Liz scowled. She tapped her foot against the wall fretfully. "I wish my dad respected me," she mumbled. "No one else does. But then again, he's got a lot on his mind...what with those stupid Bickerstaff inspections..."

"Bickerstaff again?" Brian glanced at the school office door. "Hmm...you know, I heard your dad talking about Bickerstaff yesterday."

"You did?" Liz glanced up. "What did he say?"

"He said—hey! Mary!"

He leapt to his feet just as Mary turned the corner. She was dressed in a pink blouse and a light blue denim skirt. Her hair was held back by a smooth pink band. "Hey Brian!" she said with a surprised smile. "What's up?"

"He'll do it!" Brian blurted out. "Athan's gonna paint that St. Francis picture! I convinced him!"

"Oh, really?" Mary looked impressed. "I forgot about that. Thank you!" She shook her head. "Isabel was being *so* annoying. Well...I'll go tell Jacinta. See ya!"

Brian watched her walk away. "Thank you?" he mumbled, turning back to Liz. "Thank you?" he repeated glumly. "That's it?"

"Well, what did you expect?" Liz said waspishly. "A 'world's biggest tool' medal?"

"What?"

Liz gave him a 'duh' look. "She's an Eight, remember? She wanted something done, so she batted her eyelashes at you, and you did it."

"She did *not* bat her eyelashes at me!" he snapped. "She just asked me for a favor, and I did it!"

"Really?" Liz arched an eyebrow. "What if I asked *you* a favor?"

"Like what?"

"Sit down. Finish telling me what you overheard."

"Fine. Whatever." He slumped down on the bench. "Your dad was talking to Mr. Costain; he was, um...complaining because Bickerstaff changed the inspection date."

"Is that all?"

"Yeah..." Brian sighed, trying to remember anything else. "Oh, and he said something about Bickerstaff being...under investigation."

"Really? Hmmm..." Liz closed her eyes.

"Is my favor done now?" Brian got up. "Because I'd like to get back to lunch."

Liz's hand closed on his wrist. "Hang on!" she cried, her eyes snapping open. "Bickerstaff! He's it!"

"He's what?"

"He's the guy! The poltergeist!"

Brian blinked. "The county inspector? Why?"

"It doesn't matter! I'm telling you, I *know.*"

"Well I *don't*," he said testily. "A few days ago you *knew* it was Allie."

"I didn't *know*. I was just suspicious. Allie was always a long shot. But Bickerstaff...he's an *adult*, Burke! And he was *here* the day of the fire! And then the boiler broke down right before his inspection!"

"That's just coincidence—"

"And guess what? Bickerstaff came by today."

"Exactly! And nothing happened!

"Just...*wait*," Liz said dramatically.

Brian rolled his eyes. "What, do you think he planted a bomb or something?"

"He tried to burn down the school."

Brian clenched his fists in his pockets. "Look," he said slowly. "That's an interesting theory, but why would the county inspector want to—"

"It's no theory, Burke!" Liz stood up and rubbed her hands together gleefully. "It totally makes sense! From the moment I saw that guy, I sensed something funny about him. You should have seen the way he treated my dad."

"Oh, that explains it," Brian said dryly. "This guy doesn't like your dad, so therefore he's out to kill us all."

"That's not the only reason!"

"Then what? Where's the motive? Where's your proof?" He shook his head. "Sorry. I think you're just mad at this guy. You're getting distracted by your feelings."

"What?" Liz spun around and pointed at him accusingly. "Who's been distracted by his feelings lately? Maybe I ought to bat my eyelashes too, then you'd listen!"

"Look, I'm sorry!" Brian threw up his hands. "She's *pretty*, okay?"

"Pretty?" Liz glared at him...and then, suddenly, her expression turned blank. "Hold on..." she whispered. She poked her finger again, as if she was poking an invisible person in the chest.

Brian gave her a bewildered look. "Liz?"

"Hang on." Liz started looking in the many pockets of her coveralls. "Where'd I put that thing..."

"Put what?"

225

She glanced back at Brian, and her eyes narrowed. "You want proof, Burke? I'll get it." She took off, running down the hallway.

Brian shook his head and slumped on the bench. "Weirdo," he muttered.

22

PERFECT

"Allie."

Her mom spoke quietly. "Have you talked to Mr. Costain about this?"

"No," Allie muttered.

"What about Celia?"

Allie gave a short, bitter laugh.

"Okay...then what about George?"

"You don't understand!" Allie said fervently. "It doesn't *matter* what they say. I've been learning a lot at Cross Bridge, about the Bible, and so much of the Catholic stuff isn't *in* there! All the rosaries, and praying to Mary, and the *stupid* rules about divorce; none of it's in the Bible!"

"Yes it is," her mom said softly.

"The Bible's a lot simpler than...what?" Allie said, startled.

"*Anyone who divorces his wife and marries another woman commits adultery,*" her mom said, and took another sip of coffee.

"That's...in the Bible?"

"Definitely. Jesus said it. You can look it up."

"But..." Allie stared at her mom. "Are you sure?"

"Of course I'm sure!" Her mom slammed down her coffee. "You think I wouldn't know the..." She pursed her lips.

Allie stared at her mom. They had never talked about why her mom didn't go to church anymore; it was just one of those things that was simple and established, a fact of life.

"Mom," she said. "I don't understand. What do you care which church I go to? You don't even *go* to church."

Her mom threw up her hands. "Oh, I don't know, Allie! Maybe I wanted something better for you, all right? Do you think I *like* how my life turned out?"

Allie didn't know what to think. *Jesus said that about divorce?* she thought. *Why? There must be a reason…but what is it?*

She glanced at her mom, and a horrible thought came into her mind: *Would Jesus be mad at my mom? Would He hate her?*

"Allie," her mom said heavily. "I'm not going to tell you what to do. You're old enough now to choose what to believe. But don't tell me it's simple. Nothing's simple."

Allie stared at her, and found that she didn't have an answer. *But that's why I have to go to Bible Camp*, she thought fervently. *I'll get my answers there.*

And that's it," Celia finished sadly. She looked at the others gathered in the classroom—George, Liz and Brian. "Allie's not coming back. She told me so."

Liz frowned. "She's leaving the school?"

"Worse. She's leaving the *Catholic Church*," Celia said. "And it's my fault."

"Don't blame yourself, Seal." George muttered. "It's *our* fault. All of us."

"No, it's not," Brian said. "Allie made her own decision."

"Exactly." Liz nodded. "So what do we care?"

"Liz!" Celia said, outraged. "How can you say that, after everything we've been through—"

"Oh, come *on*, Celia," Liz retorted. "It's not like she ever liked it here."

"You might never see her again!"

"And yet, somehow," Liz said dryly. "I will survive."

"Allie's our friend!"

"Um, no," Liz said. "She's *your* friend. Let's be honest, Celia. You said it yourself: it's your fault. You're the one who went off on her. And now you want us to fix *your* mistake."

Celia gave Liz a disbelieving look. "Don't you care about anybody but yourself?"

"Of course I do," Liz said coolly. "My friends. My family. I just don't care about *everybody*."

"Jesus did," Celia murmured.

"Well, I ain't Him. And neither are you."

"Can I say something?" George looked up. "Remember that poem Mr. Costain showed us at that first meeting? *Christ has no body but yours...*

"The St. Therese poem," Celia said quietly. "Yeah."

"We should have been Christ to Allie," George said heavily. "And we weren't. None of us were."

Brian shifted uncomfortably in his chair, and glanced at the classroom wall. *It took us forever to get this drywall up,* he thought distractedly.

"I think we have to be like Christ now," George murmured. "I think we have to get Allie back."

"And *I* say," Liz said mulishly, "that Allie dumped *us*. Why should *we* care?"

"We didn't care, Liz!" George said. "None of us did! We were all distracted by other stuff, and we all ignored Allie—even though she was the one who needed our help the most! Don't you see that?"

A memory floated up in Brian's mind: Allie standing outside the school building, looking pale and sad.

You two should be kind to her, his mom had said. *Ask her how she's doing.*

But had he? Had he ever even thought of how she was doing?

Well, I had other things on my mind, he thought defensively. *First there was Mary Summers, and then the fire, and then all this poltergeist business...and I don't even know Allie that well!*

Liz scowled. "Fine, Peterson," she snapped, "Have it your way. So what are we supposed to do about it?"

Celia held up a brochure. "Allie's going here," she said. "This Bible Camp. It starts next Friday and runs for two weeks."

"Okay," Liz said. "So we convince her not to go. We hold a big party for her, we tell her we're sorry and give her lots of hugs. Does that work?"

"No, it doesn't," Celia said testily. "Allie's been going to this church for a week now, and she's picked up some...ideas. She told me that the Catholic Church doesn't follow Scripture, and that the Bible says you shouldn't pray to Mary."

"That's not true!" Brian said indignantly. "Nothing about Marian devotion contradicts—"

"I *know*, Brian," Celia said wearily. "But Allie doesn't. She's got no one to watch out for her now; no one to tell her the truth."

"All right, all right," Liz said. "But we can't go to this Bible Camp with her!"

"Actually, we can," Celia said. "The registration deadline's not till tomorrow."

Liz laughed. "You're serious? You think that one of us—"

"Who else?" George looked up. "We're the only ones who can help her. We're the only Catholics she knows."

"Yeah, and she's not exactly happy with us, right now, is she?" Liz sighed. "Okay, suppose I take this seriously. Which of us should go?"

"Not me," Celia mumbled. "She'll never listen to me now and...and I don't blame her."

"I can't either," George said. He glanced at Celia. "It would just be...awkward."

"Great. Just great," Liz groaned, leaning back in her chair. "Well, don't even think about asking *me*. I don't know all this religious stuff. And besides I don't have the people skills. I could knock her out, tie her up, and drag her back here if you want, but persuade her? No."

"So what we need..." Brian frowned as he puzzled it out. "...is someone who knows Scripture and apologetics...and someone who can approach Allie...and someone who's not abrasive. Someone with reasonably good personal skills."

He looked up. The others were all staring at him.

"What?" he said, puzzled.

"Oh," Celia said.

"Yeah!" George grinned. "That's it!"

230

"No way." Liz looked alarmed. "You can't ask...No!"

"Wait a second." Brian broke into laughter. "You don't think *I* should go. Do you?"

"You're *perfect*." Celia, her eyes still puffy, actually smiled.

"No!" Brian shook his head vigorously. "I'm not!"

"You said it yourself," George said. "You're smart, you're a nice guy—"

"Yes, but...come one, you want *me* to go after *Allie?*" Brian laughed again, incredulous. "How am *I* supposed to convince her to come back?"

"You got a better idea?" Liz said glumly. She sat back and glared at him, as if this was all *his* fault.

He took a deep breath. "Look," he said. "Let's think about this. Let's be reasonable."

"We are, I think," Celia said.

"But Allie's a *girl!*" Brian said desperately. "I don't know how girls think!"

To his dismay, Celia and George broke into laughter. Even Liz cracked a grin.

"Welcome to the club, dude," George said. "Look, you got to admit—"

"She's not my type!" Brian said. "I don't talk to people like her! I wouldn't know where to start!"

"We're not asking you to *date* her!" George said, grinning. "Just convince her to come back."

"I can't do it, okay?" Brian said hotly, springing to his feet. "You don't understand! I've got things to do *here*...I've got responsibilities!"

He walked quickly out of the room, ignoring George and Celia's calls for him to stop.

As he walked down the hallway, J.P. ran up to him. "Brian!" he said. "Where is everybody? I heard there was some kinda meeting. Why wasn't I—"

"Not *now*, J.P.!" Brian snapped, and walked right by him. "I need to think!"

He came into the darkened, empty cafeteria and sat down heavily on a chair. *Why can't they just leave me alone? Why do I have to be the one to solve everyone else's problems?*

"Brian?"

Mary Summers was sitting on the next table over, looking right at him.

He blinked, wondering if he was just imagining her. "Mary?" he said finally. "Why are you here? I thought you and Jacinta had gone home..."

"Jacinta did." Mary closed the book. "I wanted to stay later. I told my mom to pick me up later, so I was waiting for this meeting thing to be over." She glanced at Brian. "Is it?"

"I don't know. Maybe." He looked away and laughed bitterly. "A decision's been made...so why are you staying late?"

"Because of you."

He looked up. A moment before, his heart had been pounding wildly—now it seemed to have stopped.

Mary stood up, walked over and sat down next to him. "Is something wrong?" she said softly, a concerned look in her brown eyes. "You look upset."

"No," he said blankly. "I mean yes. I mean...what did you say? You wanted to see me?"

She nodded. "I wanted to thank you. When I saw you before, you were with that Simonelli girl. I was hoping to catch you alone, so I could say..." she trailed off, and some color flushed into her cheeks. "Well...thank you. You came through for me."

"Um...no problem," he said awkwardly. "It's no big deal. You could have told me in front of Liz."

"Liz doesn't like me." Mary scowled. "Sometimes I think that *no*body likes me here. Everyone likes Jacinta. But me..." She sighed and ran her finger along the pink ribbon in her hair. "I'm shy. I feel out of place. Kind of like Allie. You remember what you told me? How she really didn't fit in, but now she's like family?"

He grimaced. "Yes. I remember." *Should have kept my mouth shut.*

"Well, I want to fit in too," she said shyly. "Sorry. I shouldn't be telling you this. I know I make you nervous."

"No!" Brian shook his head. "You don't make me nervous! I *like* you!"

Mary's eyes widened. "Really?"

Brian nodded again. "Yes!"

"Oh…" She looked away, shaking her head. "Oh dear. This isn't good."

His insides seemed to turn to ice. "It's not?"

"No." She looked up. "Because I like you too."

For a few moments he stared at her playful smile. His brain seemed to be working slowly again. Finally something deep inside him screamed *wake up! Say something!*

"My parents won't let me date!"

She blinked. "What?"

"My parents…won't let me date," he said awkwardly. "I just…thought I'd make that clear." *Not that! Idiot! Why'd you say*—

"Oh." She looked away. "My mom won't let me date either. So we're even."

Brian watched her apprehensively.

"How about holding hands?"

"Huh?"

"Do your parents have rules about holding hands?" Her playful smile was back.

"I…um…well, the subject hasn't come up…"

"Well, then," she whispered. "Nothing to worry about." She held out her hand.

Brian took it. It felt soft. Soft and warm…

Wow…

"Brian!" George and reality crashed into the room, making them let go and jump back from each other.

George started. "Sorry to interrupt," he said. "Uh—"

"We were just talking," Brian said hastily. Mary's cheeks were bright red.

George walked up to Brian. "Look," he said. "I'm sorry how that played out in there. We didn't plan it or anything."

"Don't be sorry," Brain said tightly. "You guys were right."

"So you'll do it?"

Brian didn't reply for a moment. Then he said, "You remember what you told me before? How I got steel in me?"

"Yeah."

"Did you mean it?"

"Yeah."

Brian shook his head. "You guys are jerks, you know that?" He looked up. "Well, I guess I can try."

George punched him in the arm. "I *knew* you would do it!" he crowed.

"Do what?" Mary asked.

"Oh...well..." Brian shook his head. "I got to do something. Something I don't want to do." He ran his fingers through his hair. "And it'll take a long time."

"How long?"

"Two weeks. Starting next Friday. It's probably pointless, but..."

"So why did you agree to do it?"

"Because I'm the only one who *can* do it." He sighed, and stood up.

Mary looked up at him, an unreadable expression on her face. "So...you're leaving."

He looked down at her, and a sudden, fierce longing seized him...to do something crazy...to take her in his arms and kiss her...to ignore all the stupid problems people kept pushing on him...

"Yes," he said. "I have to." He looked at George. "But I'll have to ask my parents. They'll need to approve. And pay for it." Brian scowled and rubbed his arm. "And I need to get some things done before I go." *Like talk to Liz and J.P. in private.*

"Sure! Let's go tell the others!" George said.

As they walked back down the hallway with Mary following them, George turned to Brian. "So *will* your mom and dad be okay with this?"

"Probably," Brian muttered. "They'll say the same thing as you, that I'm *perfect*—"

Splash. He looked down.

His foot had landed in a puddle. A puddle that was getting bigger. Quickly. A few feet away, an electric drill lay on the floor, still plugged in.

"Watch out!" Brian turned around in what felt like slow motion with his arms spread wide, knocking George back from the puddle as he jumped away from the electrified water, catching Mary with his other arm.

A split second later, there was a spark, a loud, angry *pop*, and the hallway lights flickered and went out.

Brian landed on the floor away from the puddle, holding Mary in his arms.

"What was that?" Mary's voice was a high, scared whisper.

There was another enormous pop at their feet. Brian pulled her up. "Keep away from the water," he said. Sparks snapped over its surface. George got up shakily.

"We've got to go back," Brian said.

"Too late," George said grimly. Brian glanced back towards the cafeteria and saw more water seeping across the floor behind them.

"Surrounded by dangerous puddles," George said. "Right. Back to the cafeteria. We have to jump—" He glanced at Mary's denim skirt.

"Let's do it," Brian said, grabbing Mary's hand. "I'll help you. George, you go first."

George took a running leap and cleared the puddle.

"Okay, George, I'm going to help Mary over—catch her when she jumps, okay?"

He glanced at Mary. "Jump with me, okay?"

Her face was white but she nodded. "Okay."

"All right, one...two...three!"

They jumped and cleared the puddle, George grabbing Mary's arms and pulling her to safety. He released Mary's arms, and the three of them took a deep breath.

They heard pounding footsteps, and then Mr. Simonelli's bulky outline loomed up in the dark hallway. "What happened?"

He saw the puddle of water, and cursed. "Are you all right?" They nodded. "Good. Get out of the building!" he snarled. "And tell everyone else to clear out too!"

The three of them ran back down the hallway, through the cafeteria and out the back doors. They stopped, breathing heavily and blinking in the bright daylight.

Brian realized he was still holding Mary's hand. He glanced at her and saw her large brown eyes staring admiringly into his.

"Still being a hero, Brian Burke," she said softly.

He swallowed, and wondered what on earth to do with her hand. In the end, he squeezed it and then reluctantly let it go.

A few seconds later, Celia and Liz ran up to them, followed by J.P., his face pale under his shock of red hair.

"What happened?" Celia asked anxiously. "The lights went out, and then—"

"There's some kind of leak," George panted. "The hallway was flooded."

Liz glanced at Brian, and mouthed the word *Bickerstaff.*

THE STORY CONTINUES...

"So," Ginger said. "What cabin did you get?"

Allie looked down at her slip of paper. "Twenty-four."

"Awesome! Me too!" Ginger leaned over and whispered, "Tara got Jenn to assign all of us to the same cabin. Jenn's our counselor. It's a good thing, too, 'cause..."

Allie wasn't listening; she was distracted by a voice she heard behind her. It sounded vaguely familiar.

"Excuse me. Is this where you register?"

"Yes. Name, please?"

"Brian Burke."

Allie spun around. *No way.*

Standing in front of the registration table was a short, thin, black teenager with glasses, two big duffel bags piled at his feet and an uncomfortable look on his face.

"I can't believe it," Allie whispered.

"Allie?" Ginger looked curiously at Brian. "You know that kid?"

"Hold on." Allie marched up to Brian. "Hey! Brian!"

Brian looked up. "Allie!" he said. "Um...hello."

"Hi. Can we talk? Alone?" Without waiting for a reply she walked away. She heard Brian walking after her, still fumbling with his bags.

She stopped by the front doors of the church and turned around. "What are you *doing* here, Brian? Are you coming to Bible Camp?"

"Yes. Yes, I am."

"Why?"

Brian shrugged his shoulders resignedly. "Well…I'm here to convince you to come back to the Catholic Church."

READ MORE IN
John Paul 2 High
Book Four

SEE MORE AT
WWW.JOHNPAUL2HIGH.COM

ABOUT THE AUTHOR

Christian M. Frank is the pen name for a group of writers known as the John Paul 2 High Team. They developed the series and created the characters, and several of them take turns writing the books.

Book Three was written by John Doman. The sixth of ten children, it took John years to find out what he wanted to do with his life. After his graduation from Franciscan University of Steubenville in 2000, he embarked on several different career paths—sports writer, barista, singer-songwriter, pizza guy—before he found his true calling: fixing computers. John lives with his wife Katie near Philadelphia, PA. In his spare time, he posts videos on YouTube of himself playing crazy songs on the guitar for his young son, and writes books for Catholic teens. If you run into him, give him three dollars. Because he's written you another book.

CHESTERTON PRESS
is the publisher of quality fiction that evangelizes the imagination through telling a good story. Find us on the web at www.chestertonpress.com.

CPSIA information can be obtained at www.ICGtesting.com
Printed in the USA
BVOW010743290212

284083BV00005B/4/P